Praise for the authors of

A NASCAR Holiday 2

Pamela Britton
Gina Wilkins
Ken Casper
Abby Gaines

A
NASCAR 2
Holiday

HQN™

ISBN-13: 978-0-373-77332-9
ISBN-10:   0-373-77332-3

A NASCAR HOLIDAY 2

Copyright © 2007 by Harlequin Books S.A.

NASCAR® and the NASCAR Library Collection are registered trademarks of the NATIONAL ASSOCIATION FOR STOCK CAR AUTO RACING INC.

The publisher acknowledges the copyright holders of the individual works as follows:

MIRACLE SEASON
Copyright © 2007 by Pamela Britton

SEASON OF DREAMS
Copyright © 2007 by Gina Wilkins

TAKING CONTROL
Copyright © 2007 by Kenneth Casper

THE NATURAL
Copyright © 2007 by Abby Gaines

CONTENTS

MIRACLE SEASON
Pamela Britton

To Rae Monet, the best friend
a gal could ever ask for and the sister of my heart.
I love you.

Spammy

CHAPTER ONE

"Oh, my gosh, Mom. He is so hot!"

Maggie Taylor rested her fingertips on the steering wheel of her Ford Tempo, trying to ignore her daughter as she stared at the man who was, well, *hot.*

Mike Morgan, famous race car driver—actually, *former* famous race car driver—stood on the porch of her condo, far enough away that he'd merely turned when she'd pulled in, yet not so close that he'd recognized it was her in the dark gray car. But she knew it was *him* in the dark brown slacks and buff-colored shirt.

"I mean, Mom," her daughter said, green eyes wide with excitement, "you never told me he looked even better in person than on TV. How can you stand to work with him and not hyperventilate?"

Maggie glanced over at Brooke, realizing there was something vaguely disturbing about her thirteen-year-old daughter gawking at the same man Maggie had thought was gorgeous, too.

I'm getting old.

Or *Brooke* was getting old.

"Brooke, enough," Maggie said sternly. "He's just someone helping me coordinate the Christmas Miracle fund-raiser. That's all." And he was early, Maggie thought, glancing at her watch. She'd told him to come by at noon to pick up the sample giveaway items for the fund-raiser that he needed to bring back to North Carolina for approval, but that wasn't for another twenty minutes or so.

"Oh, yeah, right," Brooke said. "Admit it, Mom. You hit the jackpot when you found out he's the Helping Hands representative assigned to help you plan your party."

All right, Maggie admitted. Maybe she had hit the jackpot. She worked for Miracles—a charity organization that granted wishes to terminally ill children—but she'd never expected to meet the man she'd gawked at on TV for years. Granted, he wasn't a driver anymore, but that didn't mean she hadn't stopped breathing for a second when she'd walked into a conference room and been introduced to the man who'd be responsible for getting NASCAR drivers to the event. Helping Hands was a North Carolina–based charity organization that acted as a liaison between drivers and other nonprofit foundations around the country. Mike volunteered his time to them.

"He's just a man," Maggie said, her gaze skating over his salt-and-pepper dark hair and tan skin. "Despite the fact that he used to drive cars for a living." She gazed at Brooke sternly. "And my days of having a crush on him are over."

"Oh, you are *so* not telling the truth," Brooke said, her green eyes full of mischief.

Maggie debated with herself whether or not to argue, deciding instead to say, "You know, you're awfully full of yourself for someone wanting to go to a movie with Patty later on in the day."

"Maybe we should *both* go to a movie. You could ask Mike to go along."

"Hah. Right," Maggie said, opening her car door before

her daughter could say another word. As if someone like Mike Morgan would want to spend time with a plain-looking, slightly plump mother of a thirteen-year-old.

"Hey, Mike," she called, her car door slamming and echoing off the front of her condo. She lived at the end of a U-shaped complex, one with a parking area in the middle. Only as she climbed out did she notice that the brown paint on the two-story structure made the place look older than it actually was, and for some reason she felt embarrassed.

What? Were you hoping to impress the famous race car driver or something?

Maybe she was. "I'll be there in a second," she called out, disgruntled with herself.

"Take your time," he called back, his smooth Southern drawl so familiar—thanks to all the hours she'd spent in front of a TV watching NASCAR races—that she would have recognized his voice with her eyes closed.

Brooke gave her a knowing grin. *Stop it,* Maggie silently reprimanded before popping the trunk on her Ford. Inside were a multitude of bags, most of them filled with Christmas decorations. Brooke wanted to get an early start. By next weekend their condo would probably look like the electric light parade at Disneyland.

"Invite him out," her daughter whispered as she leaned in to grab a white bag.

"I will not," Maggie said, grabbing a bag laden with gold garland, the shiny tinsel sparkling in the sunlight. It seemed wrong to be thinking of Christmas when the California sun beat down on their heads so pleasantly.

"Mom. You only get a shot at a man like that once in a lifetime."

"And a man like that wouldn't be interested in little old me."

"How do you know?" Brooke asked as Maggie closed the trunk.

"Shh," Maggie scolded. "He might hear."

"You haven't been out in what, eight months? A year?"

Nine months, six days and twelve hours. But who was counting?

"Go for it, Mom. He's a hottie."

"And you're starting to worry me," Maggie said. "Or at least your fascination with my love life is."

"Clock's ticking, Mom," Brooke said with a lift of her eyebrows.

"Shh," Maggie scolded again. The last—the *very* last—thing she wanted was to jump into a relationship with a man, especially a man like Mike. Someone who lived a few thousand miles away, and who'd probably had a string of lovers at least twenty miles long. He might not drive anymore, but he was still one of NASCAR's most recognized personalities.

But despite the fact that Mike Morgan was out of her league, her heart still pounded as she walked up to him. The truth was, she was attracted to him. What red-blooded female in America hadn't thought him handsome? It had been part of his appeal back when he'd raced cars.

Their gazes met.

And it hit her again. That same fluttery sensation that always seemed to happen whenever he was near.

"Sorry I'm early," he said, his mouth lifting into a smile.

"No, no. That's okay. Glad you could make it by." She stopped in front of him, his tall form looming over her, Maggie thinking that he seemed shorter on TV.

But every bit as handsome.

It was hard not to blush like a freshman in front of the high school football captain. He had the build of a marathon runner. Long and lanky with just the right amount of muscle tone. And those eyes. Female hearts all across the land had succumbed to the brilliant green of his eyes. She was no different.

"Um, Brooke," she said, having to clear her throat. "This is Mike Morgan."

"Nice to meet you," Brooke said with a knowing grin. "I've heard *all* about you."

Maggie wanted to jerk her daughter to her and cover her mouth with her hand—probably would have, too, if she hadn't been carrying shopping bags.

"Can I help you with those?" he asked. He had a slight five-o'clock shadow, something Maggie found highly attractive on a man. Oh, hell, everything about the man attracted her. The first time she'd met him, her cheeks had lit up as if he'd somehow gleaned every erotic fantasy she'd ever had about him.

"No, no. We've got it. Come on in. Don't mind the mess," she said, even though she'd scrubbed the apartment the day before.

"You should see my place," he said.

Oh, yeah right. She'd seen his place on one of those NASCAR shows. Ten bedrooms. A pool the size of a lake. Acres and acres of green lawn. She had a two-bedroom, one-bath condo that had the same beige walls and brown carpet it'd had for years. She might own it, but she had little money to make improvements. Raising a child in the Bay Area, a community that had one of the highest costs of living in the nation, made for tough times.

"Thanks," she said, setting her bags down on a small table to the left of the front door. Unfortunately, she was so discombobulated by his presence that she miscalculated, and one of the bags slid off the edge. They both reached for it at the same time. Maggie caught the bag. Mike caught her hand.

"Oh," she said, all but jerking her hand back. "That was silly of me."

Brooke came up behind him, glancing at her oddly as she set her bags down next to Maggie's.

"Getting ready for Christmas?" he asked, obviously spying the contents of the bags.

"We always set up for Christmas early," Brooke said, smiling a Cheshire cat grin as she stared between the two of them.

Brooke, behave, Maggie silently warned, because she recognized the look of crafty machination on her daughter's face.

"It smells good in here," he said.

They'd bought their tree already, and the sharp tang of pine needles filled the air. In the window overlooking the spot where they'd parked, Brooke had already hooked up lights, and even though it was the middle of the afternoon, they twinkled merrily. In the corner opposite the window and a beige couch stood a Douglas fir. The thing looked like a Snoopy tree without any decorations on it.

"Here," Maggie said, picking up the bag of sample giveaway items from the table. "Sorry I forgot these yesterday." She all but thrust the bag at him.

"Thanks," he said.

"Let me know if NASCAR likes any of them. It'll only take a couple weeks to get them in, so you have a couple weeks to decide. The fund-raiser's not until the twentieth

of December." Which he probably knew. Which meant
she was babbling.

"I'll give you a call once I hear something."

She nodded, headed for the door pointedly.

"You're not flying back until tomorrow," Brooke said,
her freckled face wreathed in a friendly smile as she stared
up at Mike.

"That's right," Mike said.

"That's what my mom told me," Brooke said. "So I told
her that she should ask you to a movie today. You know,
maybe even show you around a bit. Show you some of our
California charm."

"Brooke," Maggie cried.

Mike stared between the two of them, a slight smile on
his face. "Actually," he said, the word sounding slow and
very Southern with its rich drawl, "I was planning on doing
some sightseeing today. I have to leave early in the
morning, so this is my last chance to do it."

"Oh, that's too bad," Maggie said in a tone that indicated
she wasn't really disappointed. The last thing she needed
was Mike thinking she'd orchestrated this whole deal.
"Well, have a great time."

"Why don't you take my mom with you," Brooke said.

"Brooke," Maggie said again. "Mr. Morgan obviously
wants to do his own thing today." She glanced up at him.
"Sorry. I know you're probably in a hurry to get going."
She moved toward the door.

"Actually, it might be kind of nice to have some
company today."

Maggie almost stumbled. For a split second she was
almost certain she'd misheard. But when she turned back
to Mike, there was a smile on his face.

"Awesome," Brooke said. "You can drop me off at Patty's while you two go drive around."

"Brooke, don't be silly," Maggie said. "Mr. Morgan is merely being polite."

"Not at all," he said. "It'd be great to bring along someone who knows her way around."

Ah. Just as she thought. Not interested in her. He just wanted a human navigational system.

"Well, I appreciate the invitation, Mr. Morgan."

"Call me Mike," he said with another smile, the same polite grin she'd seen him use on network reporters.

"Mike, I appreciate the offer, but I have way too much to do here this weekend. We need to decorate the tree—"

"We can do that later," Brooke said.

"I need to make lunch," Maggie said.

"I'll make myself a sandwich."

"Do chores—"

"I'll help with those tomorrow," Brooke said.

"Brooke!"

"I'll go call Patty," Brooke said. "Tell her to ask her mom to take us to the movies later—"

"Brooke," Maggie said again, grabbing her daughter's hand. She smiled up at Mike. "Will you excuse us for a second?"

"Sure." As Mike watched them walk away, a smile slid onto his face. To be honest, he really *did* like the idea of taking Maggie along for the ride. Not because he was interested in her or anything. No, no. He had a long-standing policy about dating single moms. It was difficult enough for two people to work through a relationship. Add a child into the mix and things became even more complicated. Worse, if the couple ended up calling it quits, the child suffered, too. No way he wanted to do that to a kid.

But he doubted she'd read anything into his invitation, anyway. Maggie Taylor seemed all business.

He heard a raised voice, although he could tell Maggie tried to keep her voice down. When the door opened a few moments later, sans Brooke, he knew Maggie had gotten her daughter under control and that she was about to decline his invitation.

"Look, before you say anything," he said, "I don't want you to think I'm coming on to you or anything."

He saw something flash in her pretty blue eyes. Was it disappointment?

"No, of course not," she said. "I never thought that. And I'm sorry about my daughter's outspokenness. I just explained how rude it was for her to invite me along. You don't have to feel obligated or anything."

"I don't. Look, honestly, it'd be nice to have some company." He spent far too much time on the road. And now with the team he was hoping to form up, and his work for Helping Hands, not to mention various other obligations, it seemed as if he had less and less time for himself. It would be nice to spend some time with a woman— purely platonic, of course—and not by himself.

"Well, thank you for the invite," she said, "but I really do have a lot to do today."

"We can do it tomorrow," came a voice from the bedroom.

Mike laughed. Maggie shook her head and glared in the bedroom's direction, and Mike had to admit she really was cute in a Suzy Homemaker kind of way. Definitely not his type with her kinky brown hair and bright blue eyes, but cute.

"Sounds like your daughter has other ideas."

"My daughter is about to be grounded."

"Don't do that. Honestly, she's done me a favor. I didn't realize how good the idea sounded of spending some time with someone other than myself until she mentioned bringing you along. But if it'll make you feel better, we can talk about the fund-raiser on our way."

"Where are you going?"

"I want to see the coast. And then I thought I'd pop by Watsonville."

"What's in Watsonville?"

"Just something I want to see. You can help me get there."

But he could tell she wanted to refuse, and it struck him as odd that he fought so hard to change her mind. He must truly be desperate for company. "I promise to get you back before dark," he added.

"I don't know…."

"Please," he added.

He saw her look toward the bedroom door, watched as she frowned. But the frown was quickly replaced by a smirk. "All right," she said. "Because I have a feeling if I don't agree, I'll be hearing about it for the rest of my life."

CHAPTER TWO

MIKE MORGAN SAT next to her. And they were going to the beach.

He sat next to her.

Yes, he'd sat next to her before, but that had been in a professional environment. This was different. For one thing, she could *smell* him. He smelled like cinnamon and cedar. She *loved* cinnamon.

She glanced over at Mike, and when she did, she caught him looking at her, the expression on his face one of thoughtful consideration.

"How long have you worked for Miracles?"

"About eight years," she answered. Okay, *this* she could handle. As long as they kept things impersonal, she could keep her mind off things that were distinctly personal—like how long his fingers were. And how rock hard his thighs looked—

Maggie.

"Do you like it?" he asked.

"I love it." It was the best job in the world…and the worst. The kids they worked with were so sick, more than a few of them didn't make it. When that happened it was like losing a close friend. Frankly, it sucked.

"Indi tells me it's a tough job."

Indi was her best friend and fellow Miracles worker. Although that was due to change, too, Maggie thought with a pang of sadness. Indi would be moving to North Carolina right after she got married. In the next few weeks Maggie would have to find someone to take her place, although to be honest, Indi could never be replaced.

"It is," she said. "Sometimes I wonder why I do it."

Cripes. Had she said that aloud?

"You do it because you're special," he said. "And all I can say is thank you for doing a job not many people want to do."

She *had* spoken the words aloud. "Thanks," she said, the edginess returning.

Darn it. Why did he make her feel this way? She'd met plenty of other good-looking celebrities before. Why was Mike Morgan different?

"Um, when'd you meet Indi?" Maggie asked to help cover her discomfort.

"At the awards banquet last year."

She looked away, felt her tummy flutter, knew that her face burned. *Why* was he having this effect on her?

But she knew why he affected her this way.

He might not drive stock cars anymore, he might not be as famous as he once was, but the sheen of his successes clung to him in a way that turned Maggie on. She'd reasoned out long ago that that was why she—and millions of other women—lusted after him. He'd been one of the biggest names of the NASCAR NEXTEL Cup Series before the accident off the track that had stolen part of the vision in his left eye.

"How long have you been with Helping Hands?" she asked.

"Since May."

"Do you like it?"

"It's a job."

She could tell it wasn't a job he wanted. Oh, she didn't doubt he enjoyed working for a charity organization just as she did, but she could tell he wanted to do something else.

Drive.

So the rumors that he was talking to people about racing again were true. Interesting.

"Don't get me wrong," he added. "I love helping people, but I miss being at the track."

And in that, they were vastly different. Maggie loved her job. She could never see herself doing something different. Yeah, the pay wasn't all that great, but each time she helped grant the wish of a terminally ill child, she was reminded of what was important in life. She had her health and happiness. So did her daughter. She couldn't ask for more.

"Do you think you'll find another ride?"

Another ride. NASCAR lingo for being hired to drive another car. Amazing how much she'd learned in her few short years as a fan.

"I don't know," he said with a shrug. "After the accident, my team owner promised I'd have a job when I got better. I even went and had surgery that is supposed to restore my vision, although we won't know the results of that for a few weeks yet. My owner doesn't want to put me back in a car with my vision being the way it is. I've done some testing for other owners, but they all say the same thing—wait until we get the test results back. They're too afraid of me wrecking and so I guess we'll just have to wait and see."

Before his accident he'd been one of the best. A legend. She'd had no idea he'd been more or less forced into retirement.

"I heard you might be forming your own race team."

He nodded, glancing at her again. She'd started to breathe normally, the hands she'd placed in her lap relaxing atop her jeans. He was just a man, she reminded herself. Someone who'd had ups and downs, like her. It made him seem real. That, she realized, was part of her attraction to him. When she'd first met him she'd been surprised at how down-to-earth he was. The second time she'd met him, just this past Friday, she'd admitted to herself that she could get herself into some serious trouble obsessing over him at night. How ironic that she'd end up sitting next to him the very next day.

"Well, whatever you end up doing, Mike, I wish you luck."

Try to remember, Maggie, that he comes from a different world than your own. One day, he might be back in the limelight. He might once again make it to the top of his field. She hoped that he did, but she knew that life would never include her. She almost laughed at herself. As if she had a chance at catching his interest.

"Where is it you wanted to go?" she asked, because talking about what he did for a living depressed her. "You know, after we drive by the beach."

"I promised a friend of mine I'd look in on someone while I was here."

"Oh."

"You don't mind tagging along with me, do you?"

She supposed at this point she really didn't have a choice. "No."

"Good. I hear the speedway in Watsonville is a nice track. You'll be able to sit in some nice grandstands if you want."

"What did you say?"

He smiled. "*Speedway.* We're going to a race."

CHAPTER THREE

MIKE EXPLAINED on the way to the track that from time to time he did some scouting for NASCAR team owners. When one of his friends, Blain Sanders, had heard Mike was going to be in California, he'd asked him to stop in on a local driver to see if he was any good. Mike had agreed and so that was that.

The speedway in Watsonville was nestled near the base of a tall mountain range, one colored dark green by redwoods and California pines. Maggie knew this because they were at the track well before the sun set, the stop at the beach along the way so brief Maggie wondered if Mike's main goal for the day had always been to get to the track as soon as possible.

Sightseeing. Hah.

Brooke would be sorely disappointed when she learned that instead of her and Mike strolling along sandy shores, they'd pulled to a stop at an overlook, peered out the front window at the gently rolling waves, then drove off. Mike's only comment was that it looked different than the beaches of North Carolina. Well, okay then, Maggie had thought.

So now she found herself at the track, Mike piloting his car down a side road that lead to the pits. The speedway doubled as fairgrounds for a few weeks during the year, so sheep and cattle pens were part of the landscape, as was a massive grandstand along the front stretch of the track.

"You'll have to go up to the office with me to get your pit permit," Mike said.

He parked in front of a minioffice set up by a chain-link fence that kept spectators out of the racetrack area. In front of them, near the backstretch, were rows and rows of race rigs. Even though they were some distance away, Maggie could still hear the sound of revving motors. People buzzed around the rigs and colorful cars, some team members wearing color-coordinated outfits, others in jeans and T-shirts.

"Lead the way," she said.

They walked by a couple of guys who'd obviously just gotten their own permits because they were in the midst of tucking them into the back of their pants. One of them did a double take when he saw Mike. Maggie watched as he nudged his friend. The guy turned, followed his friend's gaze, then stopped dead in his tracks. Maggie knew how he felt. Nobody had told her she'd be working with Mike until their first meeting at an off-site conference room. When she'd walked in the room, she'd just about dropped the file she'd been carrying.

"Hey, there," Mike said, his tone just as friendly as it'd been when he'd met her for the first time.

"Wow," one of the guys said. "You're Mike Morgan."

Mike smiled but kept on walking.

Those two weren't the only ones to do a double take. One of the women working the booth did the same thing. She was an older woman, but her eyes were as giddy as a schoolgirl's when she asked Mike to sign in.

"I've always been a big fan," she said as she pointed to a blank line.

"Really?" he asked, his name nothing more than a scribble. "Thanks."

"You here to look someone over?" the woman asked.

"Yup."

"Who?"

"Jerry Talbot."

"Oh, yeah…he's good." The woman's gaze moved past him to settle on Maggie. "You'll need to sign here, too," she said, pointing to a spot right below Mike's name.

Maggie did as asked, but she suffered through a moment of embarrassment when the lady said, "That'll be twenty-five dollars." She hadn't brought that much cash.

"Here," Mike said, coming to her rescue.

She looked up and caught Mike staring at her. He tucked the change in his pocket. "Ready?" he asked.

"Ready," she echoed.

"Don't forget to put on your wristbands," the woman behind the counter said, handing them two pink plastic strips.

"Here," Mike said, "I'll put it on for you." He fastened the wristband on her, then took her hand.

Every muscle in Maggie's body froze. She glanced up at him, surprised to find him staring into her own eyes intently.

"If you don't get it right the first time, you can't remove them," he said.

"Oh," she muttered, unable to pull her eyes away from him.

Settle down, Maggie. You're acting like a teenager.

"There you go," he said, releasing her.

It took every ounce of self-control she possessed not to rub the spot where he'd touched her. "Thanks," she said, forcing herself to look away. There was a man standing behind Mike, a look of barely contained excitement on his face.

"Mike Morgan," said the man, who looked about twenty years older than Mike, at least judging by his sun-wrinkled face and gray hair. "It really is you, isn't it," he said, holding out his hand when Mike turned around.

"Hi, there," Mike said, taking the guy's hand and shaking it.

Maggie was no stranger to celebrities being recognized. Just about every time she fulfilled a sick child's wish involving a famous personality someone came up to them and shook their hand, or asked for an autograph or a picture. What she wasn't prepared for was the warm way Mike appeared to greet everybody. He appeared genuinely pleased to meet anyone who knew his name.

"I've been watching you race since you were a kid. The speedway in Dartmouth was spitting distance from my house."

"No kidding. Imagine that," Mike said with a wide smile.

"How's the eye?" the guy asked.

"Better," Mike replied. "Thanks for asking."

"You getting behind the wheel again?"

"Just as soon as I can," Mike said.

"Well, good. I look forward to it," the man said, patting Mike on the back as if he'd known him forever. "Good luck when you do. I'll be watching."

"Your fans love you," Maggie noted as they walked away.

"Yeah. I've always considered myself fortunate to have their support," Mike said. He slid behind the wheel of his car again. They would be parking inside, along the perimeter of the track which, fortunately, had a retaining wall around it that would keep cars from sliding off the oval.

"Do you miss it?" she asked.

He stared out at the track. His hand was on the ignition key, but he didn't turn on the motor. Instead he looked at her.

"Yeah," he said, his hand sliding back to his lap. "I miss it. A lot. Maybe one day I'll go back to it...."

When he looked into her eyes, Maggie felt something inside her still for a moment. "I'm sure you will," she said.

There it came again, that funny feeling in the pit of Maggie's stomach. She told herself to look away, worried that if she didn't, he might see something in her eyes, something that might cause him to think she had the hots for him.

You do, Mags.

Yeah, but she'd never let him see that. No way. She'd sworn off men when Brooke's father had walked away. She'd done a pretty good job of avoiding entanglements ever since. The last thing she needed was to become embroiled with a man, especially when that man was a celebrity.

Suddenly Mike Morgan was leaning toward her. He was drawing so near that she could smell cinnamon and cedar again. His mouth was getting closer, ever closer.

He kissed her cheek. "I appreciate your support."

She had to bite back a sigh of disappointment, especially when his lips rested against her heated flesh for about 1.9 seconds—which wasn't long enough! When his hand lifted to pat the top of her head, she bit back a groan of dismay.

"You're a good listener," he said.

She wanted to do a heck of a lot more than listen. She wanted to rip his shirt off and have her wicked way with him. She wanted to run her hands through his hair and see if it felt as soft as it looked.

"Oh, ah…" She struggled with what to say. "Thanks."

Obviously, she'd been without sex for far too long.

Take heart, Mags. At least you have some new fodder for your fantasies.

Yes. There *was* that.

When he started the car she drooped against the seat, her heart beating hard. When he put the car in gear and the side of his hand accidentally brushed her leg, she just about gasped. But when he shot her an impersonal smile that clearly said, "Oops. Sorry," she just about groaned.

He wasn't the sorry one. *She* was.

CHAPTER FOUR

HE'D JUST ABOUT kissed her, and *not* on the cheek.

Damn, Mike thought, steering the car toward the row of cars lined up near the pits, that'd been the first time in a long time he'd felt the urge to do something completely impulsive. Usually he liked to do things in small steps. And usually he liked his women a little more—he glanced at Maggie, at her unkempt, nearly wild curly hair, makeup-free face and casual clothes—polished. And yet the urge to lean in and try to kiss her again had him gripping the wheel as though he were about to start a race.

"You can stay in here if you want," he said, shutting off the motor.

"That's okay," she said. "I, um, think I'll take a look around. I've never been on this side of the wall before."

"Be careful," he said. "When they start to hot lap cars will be buzzing in and out of here. If you're not on your toes, you might get run over."

"On second thought," she said, seeming to sink down in her seat. "I'll stay here."

He had to bite back a smile. "No, no," he said. "Why don't you come with me?" And then he winced because there he went again. It was just like at her house. One moment he was telling himself to take her giveaway items and run, the next he was inviting her along.

"That's okay," she said. "It's probably better if I let you conduct your business on your own."

Walk away, Mike.

But instead he traveled to her side of the car, held out his hand and said, "Come on."

"Oh, no. Really."

He reached in. She reluctantly placed her hand in his. He was almost sorry to have to let her go.

"Come on," he said, having to almost physically restrain himself. People did double takes as he walked by, but he was used to that. It happened in the garage all the time.

He glanced down at her, taking in her wide-eyed look of wonder when they emerged from between two of the race rigs.

"Have you seen Jerry Talbot?" he asked some guy in the midst of tuning a revving motor.

"Over there," the guy said, not even lifting his head, his gaze intent upon the timing marks on the front of the engine.

Mike finally gave up and grabbed Maggie's hand again. He felt her try to pull away, but it wasn't a hard pull, more like a you-can-let-go-if-you-want-to tug.

He didn't want to. That shocked him to the point that he almost let go. Almost.

"There he is," Mike said, recognizing the paint scheme from the résumé the kid had sent Blain Sanders, one of racing's best-known NASCAR owners and Mike's would-be silent partner if this kid looked good. The plan was to run a partial schedule, Jerry trading seat time with another driver—maybe even Mike himself—in one of the NASCAR Craftsman Truck Series cars, but that was only if the kid raced half as well as his résumé made him sound. Word on the street was that he did.

"Is Jerry around?" Mike asked a big guy with dark hair and a neatly trimmed goatee. He wore a yellow team shirt already stained by dark oil.

"Damn," the guy said, just about dropping the part he held. A rear-end gear by the looks of it. "You're Mike Morgan."

"And you're Brian," Mike said, glancing down at the name of the shirt.

"You made it," Brian said, still sounding incredulous. "You're really here."

"I'm really here." Mike glanced down at Maggie and gave her a smile. "This is Maggie," he said.

"Hi, Maggie," Brian said, and Mike noticed this time he wiped his hands on the front of his black pants before he clutched Maggie's fingers.

"When Jerry said you might come by, we all couldn't believe it. I think even Jerry thought it might be a joke. I mean, you're Mike Morgan. What are the odds that you'd come to a race all the way out in California to see our driver race."

"Pretty good considering I'm here."

"Yes," Brian said with a grin that strung itself from ear to ear. "You are. Come on," he said. "I'll introduce you to Jerry. Man, is he ever going to freak."

"This is kind of neat," Maggie whispered to Mike as Brian led the way. "I mean, you might have the power to change this kid's life."

"Maybe," Mike said, giving her hand a squeeze.

And then she smiled.

Mike just about tripped and fell. It was the first genuine

smile he'd had from her and it transformed her face. She went from cute to gorgeous in a split second, her blue eyes seeming to light up the space around them.

"I hope he's as good as your friend thinks he'll be," Maggie said.

"Me, too."

He was. It didn't take Mike long to realize that the kid had the goods. Watsonville was a short track, but Jerry outclassed the competition by a mile. He had nearly four car lengths on his nearest competitor after only a single lap, and when it came time for his heat race, he won it handily.

"I've seen enough," Mike said a short while later, pulling the headset Jerry's team had lent him off his head. Maggie did the same.

"That's it?" Maggie asked. "You watch him circle around a few times and you can tell if he's good or not?"

"No," Mike said. "There's more to it than that. I wanted to hear him on the radio. See how he communicates with his team. How much knowledge he has about his car's setup. If he's calm and cool or loud and obnoxious. The last thing we need to do is to hire ourselves a headache driver."

"But don't you want to see him win a race?"

"No. Jerry already has solid wins under his belt. He was last year's NASCAR Whelen All-American Series champion. Blain just wanted me to see him in person, judge for myself what he might be like to work with."

"And do you like him?"

"He'll be getting a call from Blain by the end of the week."

"Neat," Maggie said, smiling at him again. "Are you going to tell him?"

"Of course."

"Can I watch?"

She was really excited for the kid. Obviously, she thrived on other people's happiness—why else would she do what she did for a living? What a unique way to live a life. And how amazing that she'd rather do that—bring people joy—than earn a six-figure salary. Indi had mentioned that working for Miracles was an incredible job, but that it was one that didn't pay well.

"Let's go," he said, resisting the urge to grab Maggie's hand again. The truth was that he needed to watch himself. He was starting to like Maggie, something that wasn't good given the fact that her type was strictly taboo. But there was more to it than that. Three, four months he'd be back in NASCAR again, and one of the main reasons why he'd never gotten deeply involved with a woman in the past was because life on the road was no place to raise a family.

Maggie was the type of woman a guy would want to have kids with.

That realization had him drawing up short, had him running a hand through his hair and darting her a glance.

Not his type, he reminded himself.

But it dawned on him then that she was not his type for a reason. The flashy ones weren't the ones you settled down with. Those women had no depth. More than likely, Maggie had layers of depth he'd probably never seen before, and it scared him.

"We'll head home right after I talk to Jerry," he said, more to himself than her.

"Okay."

"Did you need to call your daughter?"

"No, no. I spoke to her while you were inside the rig talking to Jerry. She's heading off to her movie."

He nodded. Maggie fiddled with the headset she'd worn while Jerry had practiced.

Mike Morgan had held her hand.

Maggie stared straight ahead, trying to pretend that walking next to him was no big deal. It was still light out, although sunset was less than an hour away. People kept staring at them as they headed back to the pits. Out on the pavement she could hear a new set of cars circling the track, the sound of their engines pitched high and then low depending on whether they were leaving or entering the corner.

It was obvious that word had spread that Mike Morgan was around. Teams stopped working as they passed by, a few cameras flashing along the way. Maggie had been around celebrities before, but this was the first time one had actually taken time to chat with the people who stopped him. She really liked that. Really liked *him.* It was ridiculous. Foolish. She barely knew him.

Yet she felt as smitten as the time she'd fallen head over heels for Brooke's father.

And look where that *got you.*

She'd been pregnant at seventeen, delivering Brooke two months after high school graduation. Alone. Brooke's father had left town, ostensibly to go to college, but he'd never been back. Brooke was lucky to get a birthday card from him. And child support? *Hah.*

She struggled to make ends meet. But she did it. *I'm not going to sleep with the man,* she told herself. *I just want to stare at him so that when our time together is over, I can remember what it was like to feel young and carefree and maybe just a little bit special for the first time in a long, long time.*

They reached Jerry's rig at last and Maggie's admiration for Mike reached new heights as he broke the news. Jerry just about jumped into Mike's arms, but Mike didn't look perturbed. Oh, no. He shared Jerry's excitement, his grin as big as the one he wore in Winner's Circle.

"Is this how it feels when you grant the wish of a Miracles child?" he asked her, the two of them watching as Jerry's team laughed and cried along with the driver.

"It is," she said, getting teary-eyed herself. Jerry's father had just been told the good news and the man was holding on to his son and bawling.

"I see now why you do it."

"Yup," she said, grinning from ear to ear. "There's no better job in the world."

CHAPTER FIVE

LATER, QUITE A BIT LATER actually, because Jerry's dad insisted they raise a glass of sports drink in Jerry's honor, they set off for home. Maggie fought back a surge of disappointment as they pulled away from the track. Her time with Mike was nearly at an end. Less than an hour from now she'd be back at home in the Bay Area.

"Looks like the fog's staying away from the coast," Mike observed.

She'd explained on their way to the beach that late fall was the best time of year to visit the coast. Although Christmas was right around the corner, you wouldn't know it by the California weather. For whatever reason, the fog tended to stay away from the shoreline, whereas any other time of year, they'd have been socked in by now.

"Yeah, it'll probably be a beautiful sunset."

"You want to head back to the beach?" he asked.

"Oh! No. I didn't mean to sound—" Like a silly fool with fantasies of romantic strolls on the beach. "Like I wanted to do that."

"No, of course not," he said, shooting her a smile.

He had a *great* smile.

"We could have spent more time there earlier, but I

wanted to meet Jerry before he went out on the track. Come on," he said. "Let's go back."

"No. I really shouldn't. Brooke—"

"Call her."

"I'm not sure I can get hold of her," Maggie said. "She might be at her movie…."

"Call her," he said again.

She pretended not to hear him.

He handed her his cell phone. "What's the number?"

She knew that if she kept arguing it might look strange so she shook her head at his cell phone and pulled out her own instead. Of course Brooke squealed with delight when Maggie told her that her mom might stay out later than expected.

"Cool. I'll just spend the night at Patty's, then," Brooke said.

"No, you're not."

"It'll make it easier, Mom."

Easier to do *what?* "We won't be back *that* late," Maggie insisted.

"So, call me if it's an early night. Otherwise, I'm spending the night."

Just who was parenting whom?

"I'll call you on my way home," Maggie said.

"Have fun, Mom. Don't blow it."

Don't blow *what?* Surely her daughter wasn't inferring…

Maggie glanced at Mike. No way could she clarify the matter with Mike sitting right next to her. "I'll call you later," Maggie insisted.

"Have fun."

They were just going to the beach.

But you're hoping that'll lead to more.

All right. Fine. Maybe she was. But that was just a fantasy because it'd been so long—so very, *very* long—since she'd had any action in that department. But what was she thinking? Mike wasn't even interested in her that way. She'd been around enough professional athletes to know they preferred their women on the showy side. Cripes. When most men found out she had a kid, they ran for the hills. If Mike was interested, it would have to be because he was desperate.

She then had a moment of panic strike because what if he *was* desperate enough to make a play for her? What if she couldn't resist him? What if he saw her naked?

She had cellulite.

And a baby belly.

And legs she might have forgotten to shave last night.

Nope. No way. She couldn't allow him to see her naked.

In your dreams would he see you naked.

She glanced over at him. It was a face that was at once familiar and yet strange. On television she'd never noticed how squared off the back of his jaw was. Or that he had a bit of a bump in the middle of his nose. Was that from his recent accident or had it always been there? His chin was square, too. And his eyes. She'd always been enamored of his eyes, and looking at him from the side they appeared almost translucent, as clear as the curve of a marble.

"What did Brooke say?" Mike asked.

"She said to call her on our way home."

He nodded.

Maggie squirmed. This was bad. The guy had her just about hyperventilating. But if she were honest with herself, it had less to do with his good looks than the way his smile reached his eyes. Or the way he'd taken her hand earlier.

Or the look on his face when he'd told Jerry he wanted him to drive his race truck.

They seemed to reach the beach in record time, Maggie's shallow breath growing even more shallow as Mike pulled into a public parking spot. This time of day the lot was nearly deserted, the beachgoers having left along with the light. But it wasn't completely dark yet. The sun hung low on the horizon, the fog that hovered far offshore turned the color of mercury, and above that a sky so blue it seemed almost purple.

"Now *this*," Mike said as he came around her side of the car. "*This* is what *I* call a sunset."

He took her hand.

Maggie's whole body seemed to freeze, and then melt, the sensation so surprising and bizarre it was all she could do to think. "Yeah, it is beautiful, isn't it?"

He held her hand again. *Held her hand.*

He glanced down at her, and everything seemed to fade away—the beach, the roar of the ocean, the breeze that kicked up off the sand and brought the smell of brine to her nose.

She blushed, had to look away.

"Let's go down to the water," he said, tugging on her hand.

He hadn't let her go.

It took a second or two for her feet to move when she ordered them to. Mike glanced back, as if worried she might not follow. She almost didn't because something told her that if she went where he led, she might end up in a place she had no business going. Not with Mike Morgan, famous race car driver.

How about Mike Morgan, the man?

Yes, she admitted to herself. She liked Mike Morgan the man. More than liked him.

She took a first, tentative step forward.

"Cold?" he asked.

She shook her head. How could she be cold when every nerve in her body seemed to be on fire?

He guided her to the edge of the parking lot. Beach grass framed the parking area. In between tall tufts, narrow pathways wound down to the ocean. Overhead, a gull cried out; Maggie started at the sound.

She was nervous. On edge. Maybe a little scared.

He's not going to make a pass at you, Maggie. What have you got to be worried about?

"Let's take our shoes off," he said.

He let go of her hand. The whole time she took off her shoes, she was conscious of him doing the same. When she glanced up to see where he was in the process, his rear end was facing her.

Oh, my. That was definitely something the TV didn't show.

"Ready?" he asked a moment later.

"Yes," she said, squishing her toes into the sand. It felt good. Like a cold pumice scrub.

"What did you do before you worked for Miracles?"

"I was an administrative assistant. That's how I got in with Miracles. I was hired to help out, but then there were some personnel changes and before I knew it, I was in charge."

"Do you travel a lot?"

He hadn't taken her hand again, and even though Maggie told herself that was good, she couldn't help but feel disappointed. Maybe that look she'd seen earlier had just been wishful thinking.

"I travel some, but it's hard with Brooke."

She glanced up at him, trying to gauge why he wanted to

know. Was he curious if she ever made it to North Carolina? Did the thought of her having a daughter put him off?

She could tell nothing by his face.

"What about you?" she asked. "Do you travel a lot?"

"I do," was all he said.

They'd made it to the shore, the foamy outline of a long-gone wave zigzagging across the sand.

He stopped suddenly. Maggie did likewise, but she was frozen solid—unable to look him in the eye or even turn to him.

"This is crazy," she thought she heard him mumble.

"What's crazy?" she asked, the roar of the ocean no louder than the booming in her ears.

"You feel it, too, don't you?"

She nearly choked on a gulp of air. "Feel what?" she asked softly.

He took her hand again. She stared down at their entwined fingers, thinking that this was surely a dream.

"We're attracted to each other, aren't we?"

And there it was, how she felt for him out in the open. The shock was that he felt the same way.

"Mike," she said, though his name came out sounding like a moan of distress.

At last she mustered the courage to look him in the eye.

"Would it help to know that I'm dying to kiss you?"

She gasped, searching his eyes, because he had to be kidding. He couldn't seriously want to kiss her. Plain Jane Maggie. Mother of one.

He lowered his head.

"I've been dying to do this for at least an hour. Maybe two," he said.

"Do what?" she asked absently, even though she knew.

"Do this," he said softly, his mouth capturing her own. And it was so much better than her fantasies. And, yes, she'd fantasized about this. Women across the country had fantasized about what it might be like to kiss him. That should have given her momentary pause. But it didn't. Oh, no. Because at this moment, during these seconds— however long they lasted—he was hers and hers alone.

Big hands grasped her waist, pulled her to him, up against him.

Yes.

The word echoed in her head. Yes, yes, yes. He tasted sweet—like the grape sports drink they'd drunk earlier. He felt rock hard, the sides she'd suddenly clutched sculpted in a way that made her want to slide her fingers over the breadth of him. So she did.

He pulled her even closer, deepened the kiss.

She fell off the edge of the earth.

"Mike," she murmured. "I don't think... I'm not sure..."

"I am," he answered softly. "I'm very, *very* sure."

She leaned toward him because there was no sense in denying it. She didn't want it to stop. Ever. What she wanted was him. And why shouldn't she have him? Why couldn't she do something impulsive for once? He might leave in the morning, but at least she'd have the memory of tonight to keep her warm.

He pulled her closer, kissed the side of her neck, and the scruffy feel of his chin against her flesh had her leaning her head back and moaning the words, "Let's go back to my place."

CHAPTER SIX

SHE'D SLEPT WITH Mike Morgan.

Maggie lay in bed and replayed every frenetic moment of the previous night. The mad rush home. The near-crazy way he'd driven over Highway 17. The way she'd almost broken the lock on her door because she'd been in such a hurry to get inside.

He stirred. She glanced over at him. It was Sunday morning. Brooke would be at Patty's for most of the morning. If Maggie wanted to, she could wake Mike, perhaps entice him into kissing her again.

Instead, she stared.

He was so good-looking, even in the morning half light. His salt-and-pepper hair looked more silver, his skin more pale than tan. He had a wide forehead, she noticed. And thick, masculine brows. Not bushy, she quickly amended. Just masculine. She marveled that he lay in bed beside her. No longer did she think of him as Mike Morgan, race car driver. Now he was simply Mike.

She lay back in bed. Well, collapsed, really. Although that wasn't really true, either. She sort of wilted because every muscle in her body had been given a workout that made her body ache and her face burn as she recalled every marvelous thing he'd done to her.

"You're smiling."

Her eyes sprang open. "You're awake?" she asked, instantly rolling to face him.

"I am," he said, sleep still clinging to the edge of his smile.

"Do you want some breakfast?" she asked.

"No," he said with a shake of his head, glancing at her digital clock. "I'll get a bite to eat on my way to the airport."

Ah, yes. The airport. He was leaving this morning.

Reality hit her like a cold ocean wave.

Last night had been incredible, marvelous, unbelievable, but now the morning had come and Cinderella's coach had turned back to a pumpkin.

"When do you leave?"

"We're scheduled to take off at ten."

That was two hours from now. "So you're going to need to leave pretty soon?"

"Yup," he said, pulling back the covers and getting out of bed.

She looked away. It was ridiculous. Last night she'd felt every inch of him with her hands, but this morning she couldn't look him in the eye as he walked toward her tiny bathroom.

"Did you, ah… Did you want me to drop you off?" she called after him.

Had that sounded too needy? she wondered.

"No," he said. "No, thanks. I'll have to take my rental car back beforehand."

Right then his watch began to beep, no doubt an alarm he'd set the night before to remind him he had to leave. She scooted across the sheets, picked the thing up.

Rolex.

Of course it was a Rolex. She could feed herself and Brooke for a year just from the money she'd get pawning it. She wasn't quite sure how to turn the alarm off, but pushing in the wind-up dial seemed to do the trick. She set the watch back down, darting off the bed and opening her closet door. Another stupid thing. He'd seen every inch of her the night before and yet here she was, totally self-conscious. She was tugging her robe closed when he returned.

"So, ah…" Damn it. She didn't know what to say. She hadn't been with a man for so long, she'd forgotten the protocol. Was she supposed to offer to call him sometime? Did she ask for his phone number? Did she do anything other than kiss him goodbye and say thanks for the good time?

She sat down on the end of her bed, watching him get dressed.

"You look so sad," he said, coming around in front of her and tipping her face up.

She shrugged, offered a plaintive, "You're leaving."

"We'll see each other again."

When? How? He lived clear across the country. "I know," she said.

"I'll call you when I get back to North Carolina," he said, sitting down next to her.

She nodded, looked away.

"Maggie," he said, turning her chin to him. "Last night was amazing."

Had it been? Or was he just saying that?

"I realize we barely know each other, but this was more than a one-night stand."

"Oh" was all she said, because to be honest, that's exactly what she'd been thinking. He might not be driving race cars anymore, but he was still famous. She had only to recall the look on people's faces last night to be reminded of that.

"I promise. I'll call you."

"You'd better," she said, smiling to take the sting out of the words.

"I will."

And that was that. He bent down, pulled on his shoes, stood up, straightened his shirt, then bent down and kissed her on the cheek.

"See you soon."

A few moments later she heard his car start up, the Mustang coming to life with a distinctive roar. She stood up, too, ran into her tiny little family room and climbed atop the battered sofa bed that sat beneath the window. She parted the curtains, but not so much that he could see her. The last thing she needed was for him to spot her staring after him like some moonstruck child.

He pulled away without a backward glance.

She turned, sinking onto the cushions. So now the waiting began.

But the truth of the matter was, if he didn't call, she'd feel like biggest fool on earth for falling under his spell.

HE REALLY DID CALL, and Maggie felt her insides sting in shame that she'd doubted his sincerity.

"Looks like our next meeting isn't until the week after Thanksgiving," he said. Maggie realized in an instant how much she'd been hoping he wouldn't let her down. Her eyes closed in relief at the sound of his voice.

"I know," she said. She'd checked the schedule first thing after going into work that Monday morning. They'd be meeting on the thirtieth, at the hotel where they'd be having the fund-raiser.

"Doesn't look like I'll be able to hang out there for more than a few hours," he said, and she could hear the disappointment in his voice.

She settled back on her couch. Brooke was in her room, but she peeked her head out, Maggie shooing her away. Maggie could tell by the look on her daughter's face that she knew who it was.

Way to go, Mom, she silently mouthed.

Go away, she motioned again.

"What do you mean?" she asked Mike once Brooke's door had closed.

"Looks like I have a charity event to attend that night. I'll fly in for the meeting, then fly back out."

"That's a lot to go through just for a meeting."

"Happens all the time," she heard him say, his Southern drawl making her think of soft kisses and the prickly feel of his chin against her…

Maggie!

"I feel like I'm constantly flying somewhere," he added.

She felt as if she were flying, too, but for an altogether different reason.

Careful, Mags. It's too soon for you to be thinking the L *word.*

"So what does that mean?" she asked.

"We'll only have three, maybe four hours together."

Plenty of time for a repeat performance of the other night.

Maggie! she yelled at herself, more sternly. Maybe he didn't want to do that. Maybe this was just an excuse he handed her to avoid spending time with her.

And maybe you should stop being such a pessimist.

But she couldn't help herself. Too many times she'd been down this road. It was one of the reasons she'd sworn off men altogether. Once they got what they wanted, they rarely stuck around. And if it wasn't that, it was Brooke. Men were scared of ready-made families, and Maggie was frightened of her and Brooke getting hurt. Again.

"We'll have to do our best to make the most of those hours," he said, the suggestive lilt in his voice hard to miss.

That made her feel better. "I suppose we will," she said back, just as suggestively. She looked up and found Brooke peering out the door again.

"Go back in your room," she whispered.

"I would," Mike said, "if you were here with me."

Maggie blushed, but she was feeling better and better by the moment. "Sorry," she said. "My daughter is making a pest of herself."

"How old is Brooke?"

They spent the rest of their time on the phone filling in background information about each other. She learned that Mike was an only child, and that both his parents had passed on. She told Mike about Brooke, and how—most of the time, anyway—she was proud of her daughter. Brooke was at the top of her class, and never once had Maggie heard her complain about the lack of a father. The lack of any family, really, because like Mike, Maggie didn't have parents to run home to.

When it was time to hang up, Maggie wasn't certain what depressed her more—the fact that she wouldn't see Mike again for two more weeks, or that with him living on another coast the odds of their relationship working out were slim to nil.

Just take it one day at a time.

And that's what she planned to do.

THE DAY OF THE MEETING she was nervous. It was chilly, the warmth of a few weeks ago having faded away thanks to numerous cold fronts streaming down from Alaska. And while it rarely, *very rarely,* snowed in the Bay Area, it sure felt as if it would today. Her black silk suit might look chic and elegant, but it seemed to absorb the cold air rather than repel it.

The meeting was at the Hotel De Anza, where they'd be holding the fund-raiser. On her way over, Maggie noticed that now Thanksgiving was over, all San Jose seemed to be in the Christmas spirit. Lampposts held bright red bows. Giant wreaths hung off the front of the hotel. She even heard Christmas music when she walked inside the Spanish-style interior.

Mike had told her he'd be arriving around eight and, barring any unforeseen delays, he'd get there right at nine; that was ten minutes from now. She'd tried to get him to come early—had felt vague disappointment that he hadn't—but he took his job with the Helping Hands Foundation seriously. Apparently they kept him pretty busy coordinating drivers' appearances on behalf of the foundation, not to mention helping to organize events such as the one they were currently working on.

"Hey, Maggie," called one of her fellow Miracles workers as she walked across the gaily decorated lobby. Terry was a director for one of the other offices and she'd come dressed rather festively—a bright red suit that nearly matched her bright red lipstick.

"Hi, Terry," Maggie said, shifting the briefcase she held to the other hand.

"You ready for the big day?" the brunette asked.

"As ready as I'll ever be," Maggie said, swiping a lock

of her loose hair away from her face and taking a moment to admire the beautifully decorated lobby. The hotel's staff had strung Christmas lights in every available plant, and there were many—the kind of lights that blinked on and off and helped put people into the festive spirit. Christmas was still a few weeks away, their fund-raiser less than three, and if she were honest with herself, she knew she really shouldn't be taking the afternoon off. But that's exactly what she planned to do—spend a few hours with Mike.

They found the conference room that had been reserved for Miracles. Since the fund-raiser was a joint effort, there were representatives from around Northern California sitting along the edge of the massive oak table. The overhead fluorescents reflected on the polished surface, and the window blinds were open so they could see outside. They had a perfect view of city traffic.

Where was Mike?

When the meeting got started and nearly fifteen minutes went by and he still wasn't there, she started to get worried. She was so on edge that she nearly jumped out of her seat when the door opened.

"Sorry I'm late," Mike said, scanning the table until their eyes connected.

"That's okay," someone said.

Maggie would never know who'd spoken. All she knew was that the moment he walked in her heart had leaped like a person startled from sleep.

You've got it bad, kiddo.

In his black suit with a white dress shirt beneath he looked a far cry from the man who'd come knocking at her door. More powerful. More handsome. More masculine.

And she'd slept with him.

It took all her effort to focus her attention on the task at hand, but when it came Mike's turn to talk, her gaze locked on his lips.

The lips that had kissed her.

"We've got five drivers confirmed to attend the event," he was saying, "one of them last year's champion."

And that mouth had nibbled on her ear.

"The media interest is high. A few of the major sports networks will be there, broadcasting live. The night of the event, I'll be answering questions on Helping Hands' behalf.

"We've approved the giveaway items. The foundation wants to go with the luggage tag. We'll want our logo on the front as well as Miracles'."

The rest of what he said faded away. Maggie hoped someone was taking better notes than she was. Somehow she had managed to pull it together before the meeting ended, but every time she caught Mike's gaze her cheeks burned.

This was a man whose interest she hoped to keep? A man whose dark hair and sexy green eyes drew the gaze of every female in the room?

She wanted to dash away, but couldn't. She heard the meeting wrap up. Hung around for a minute or two waiting for him, but he was busy talking to one of Miracles' VIPs. She turned, not wanting to be seen loitering and waiting around for him. People might find that odd, so she made her way toward the front of the hotel. He caught up with her shortly after.

"Hey, wait up," he said, his footsteps echoing on the hotel's marble floor, a briefcase she hadn't even noticed he'd been carrying swinging alongside him. "Where the heck are you going in such a hurry?"

"Nowhere," she said. "I, ah, I just need some fresh air."

"Well, good," he said. "After my long flight here, I do, too. You don't mind if I join you?"

"Of course not." Why would he ask that? Oh, Lord, maybe *he* didn't want to spend time with *her.*

Don't be silly, Maggie.

"It's good to see you," he said, shifting the case to his other hand. He tried to hug her, but she stepped back, mindful of the fact that some of her coworkers might be milling about.

"It's good to see you, too."

He seemed to understand her hesitation, even glanced around as if looking for people from the meeting. "Let's put our stuff in my rental car."

His vehicle was parked outside—another Mustang. The valet kindly opened the door for them.

"Where do you want to walk?" he asked.

She thought quickly. Truthfully, she really didn't know, just needed cool air against her face. It might be gray and overcast, but she needed to breathe.

"There's a Christmas display in a nearby park. We could go there."

"Sounds good."

But she felt just as awkward when, after their short walk, they arrived at what Brooke used to call "winter wonderland." This was no ordinary Christmas display. Behind a knee-high picket fence, people had set up numerous nativity scenes. But it wasn't just Mary and Joseph. There were life-size camels. Numerous giant Christmas boxes painted in bright colors and decorated with shiny bows, and Maggie's favorites—the miniature houses that were like movie sets, the walls cut open so you could see inside the house where fake fires roared and Christmas trees glistened with lights.

"This is stunning," he said.

She nodded. "Brooke and I come here every year."

They walked in silence for a bit, past a giant Christmas tree that would do the one in Rockefeller Plaza proud, through a tiny forest decorated with fake snow, stopping by a life-size toy train, the caboose carrying Christmas presents.

"Maggie," he said. "What's wrong?" He stopped her, took her hand, turned her to him.

"Nothing," she lied.

"Come here," he said gently, pulling her to him.

She didn't want to go, she really didn't. Wasn't it better to let things cool off between them? Sure, they'd had some great conversations on the phone in recent days, but that didn't mean they were anything approaching boyfriend and girlfriend or, Lord help her, *lovers.*

"I've missed you," he said.

You could have come into town earlier, she thought. But she didn't say that. If she'd spoken the words aloud they'd have revealed the Mount Everest of insecurity that was clogging her throat and filling her eyes with…

Tears?

Oh, Lord, she wasn't really crying, was she? That just wouldn't do, she told herself, inhaling deeply.

But he saw them. "You're crying," he said, drawing back to look into her eyes.

"No, I'm not," she lied. "I'm just—" she searched for an appropriate excuse "—cold."

"I know a way to warm you up."

"But you have to leave in a couple hours."

"So? That's a couple hours we could spend together. Warm," he said, pulling her to him again. "In bed."

She closed her eyes, allowed herself to believe for just a moment that they could surmount all the obstacles in their way. His job. Her living in California. Her own damn fears.

"I'd love to do that. I really would."

He drew back again. "But," he prompted, green eyes narrowing.

"I just don't think it's a good idea." She licked suddenly dry lips, her face heating when she watched his eyes follow her tongue's progress. "Last time, it all happened so fast. Maybe we should slow down. Take it a little easier."

She expected to see disappointment on his face, maybe even some anger. Instead all she saw was amusement.

"What?" she asked, taken aback by the glint in his green eyes.

"Usually it's me telling women to slow down."

"Really?" That made her feel better. Or did it? Exactly how many women had there been?

"Really," he echoed. He grabbed her hand, turning her toward the park. "So trust me when I tell you that it's a nice change to meet a woman who just wants to get to know me better."

She almost pointed out that she already knew him. Intimately. But she didn't. Instead she walked.

They talked, and as they did, Maggie forgot her earlier fears. They discussed the women he'd dated in the past—she knew the names of a few of them—but he professed none of them serious. She told him about Brooke's father and how he shirked his parental duty. He told her that he'd always hoped to one day have kids.

And in the end they went back to his hotel room, where they made love in the brief amount of time left to them. When it came time for Mike to leave, Maggie felt like crying all over again. But she didn't. This was the way it would be for them, she realized. A hurried date here, some time spent together there. And where it would lead she had no idea.

"I'll call when I get back to North Carolina."

She nodded, resisting the urge to say she'd heard that before. "Have a safe trip home," she said.

He kissed her on the cheeks. And that was it. He was gone.

CHAPTER SEVEN

MIKE MEANT TO CALL MAGGIE the moment he got back. He really did. But time got away from him and it wasn't until the next day that he phoned her. Maggie would soon realize that life was sometimes crazy for him. Between starting up his own race team and working for the Helping Hands Foundation, his life was hectic.

"Hey, there," she said the moment she recognized his voice.

"Hi," he said softly, his spirits lifting when he heard her voice. "How's it going?"

"Good," she said.

There was a pause on the phone and Mike wondered what to say. She beat him to it.

"I've been meaning to ask you, did that driver we went to see get a call from your friend?"

"Yup," he said. "The kid's going to a speedway in Nashville for a test."

"Wow. That's wonderful. Do you think your friend will hire him?"

"If his test goes all right, which it should."

Another pause. Mike wondered why he was so damn tongue-tied all of a sudden.

Maybe because he hadn't been able to get her out of his mind since their second time together.

"How's Brooke?" he asked, wincing on his end of the phone. What a mundane thing to ask. He should be asking her how she was. If she missed him.

Instead he gazed out his kitchen window, which overlooked his front lawn. It was raining outside and Mike felt as morose and gloomy as the day.

"Brooke's fine," Maggie said.

"Good. Good."

"You coming out to California before the big event?" she asked.

"I'm not sure. I'm supposed to be there for the rehearsal in a couple weeks. But it's been crazy here. Not sure I'm going to make it," he said. Although if he put this development deal together with Blain Sanders, he might not be working for Helping Hands all that much longer. But he didn't want to mention that. She might take it wrong, especially with the awkward silence hanging between them. Was she still worried that things were happening too fast between them? To be honest, he was worried about that, too.

"Do you think you could try to come out early if you do?"

"I'll try," he said softly.

He thought he heard her breathe a sigh a relief. "Well, good. Call me when you know for sure."

"I will."

When he hung up, Mike turned away from the window and brushed a hand through his hair.

If he put together this deal with Blain he'd be driving again, and if that happened, his relationship with Maggie would suffer.

He shook his head, admitting to himself that he'd have to take it one day at a time. If he ended their relationship now he'd look like a jerk. And the truth of the matter was, he didn't want to end it. Not now. Maybe not ever.

"YOU'RE FALLING for this guy."

"Brooke, I hardly know him well enough to be falling for him."

"Then why are you preening in front of the mirror?"

"I'm not preening," Maggie said to her daughter, suddenly deciding that the cotton dress was too casual for a simple rehearsal. Then again, there would be tons of people there, including celebrities and her coworkers. This was their last meeting before the big gala in a couple of weeks.

"Wear the red one," Brooke said.

"Brooke, would you just let me get dressed?" Maggie asked.

"I'm trying to help out," Brooke said. "Mike seems like a nice guy. You need to hook him while he's still interested."

Hook him. Hah. Sure, he'd phoned her a couple times, but he'd never once mentioned coming to California just to visit her. And he hadn't made it into town early, contrary to his earlier promise. Something about putting together a new deal. But the thing that bothered her, that had her fretting all night, was that he hadn't called her in the past few days. That was weird given that they'd talked just about every day for the past month.

Stupid, stupid, stupid.

She yanked a dress out of her closet. The red one. To hell with it, she thought. Why not go all-out?

Still, she was as nervous as a cat near a creek as she headed to her meeting less than an hour later. Brooke had helped her with her hair and makeup. As a result her curly locks were pulled back in a smooth chignon. She'd piled on more mascara than normal, too, but she'd drawn the line at bright red lipstick.

"Wow," Indi said when they met up in the lobby of the Hotel De Azra, the place seeming to be even more decorated than before. Although maybe that was her imagination. "You look…" Words must have failed her friend because all she did was stare her up and down.

"I feel overdressed," Maggie said.

"You look great," Indi enthused. "Just right for Mike."

"Thanks," Maggie said. She'd told Indi all about Mike the other day. Indi had been delighted; so had Maggie at the time. But that was then and this was now and Maggie couldn't shake the feeling something was wrong.

You're just being paranoid. And she probably was. But still…

"You ready?" Indi asked, turning toward the ballroom where their meeting was located.

"Yes," Maggie said reluctantly, scouting around for Mike. Maybe he was there in the lobby, waiting for her. Maybe he was planning to surprise her. But all she saw was a bellboy, one who gave them a second look—or gave *Indi* a second look. Her friend was drop-dead gorgeous with her blond hair, tall form and light hazel eyes. She couldn't look bad on a *bad* day.

"It's going to be a full house today," Indi said.

"Yeah, I know."

This would be the one and only chance to rehearse for the night of the event, not that there was a whole lot expected of people. Still, celebrity publicists, Miracles officials and probably a few actual celebrities would be inside the room where everyone would learn what was expected of them the night of the event.

What if something had happened to Mike? she thought. She'd left him yet another message yesterday. But maybe he hadn't gotten it.

The plush ballroom they entered looked barren without scores of tables set around the floor. Beneath the ornate chandeliers, several groups of people congregated. Maggie recognized some of the Miracles higher-ups—their CEO and their CFO. There were celebrity publicists to the left, their clients' time too valuable to bother with a piddley rehearsal. To the right were the NASCAR personnel.

And Mike.

He stood by a driver she recognized—Lance Cooper—and another even more familiar face—Todd Peters, Indi's fiancé.

"Hey, guys," Maggie said, not able to look at Mike because suddenly she was scared to death.

Why hadn't he called?

Calm down, Mags. Maybe he had a good excuse.

One he couldn't share with her before their meeting? Somehow she doubted it. Because if he were truly glad to see her, *if* he'd wanted to see her alone, he could have asked her to meet with him before their meeting. Instead he hung back.

"Hey, sweetie," Todd said, wrapping Indi in his arms.

"Hey, there, stranger," Indi said. Maggie knew it was the first time in over a week that Indi had seen her fiancé. She'd missed their last meeting because she'd been in North Carolina, the two of them doing a good job of maintaining their bi-coastal relationship.

Unlike her and Mike.

"Hi, Maggie," Todd said, releasing Indi and stepping forward to kiss Maggie on the cheek. "Long time no see."

"Hi, Todd," Maggie said, barely able to speak over the lump of emotion in her throat.

"Hello, everyone," someone said from behind them—Randy Lewis, one of Miracles' CEOs.

"Mike," Randy said with a wide grin on his bearded face. "Good to see you again."

"Same here," Mike said.

"You know Indi and Maggie, right?" Randy asked.

"I do," Mike said with a polite nod. "In fact," he said to Randy, "I was hoping for a moment of Maggie's time."

Indi shot her a look, one that said, "Aww, how sweet."

But Maggie wasn't so certain it'd be "sweet" at all. Something floated in Mike's eyes. A glint of regret. A hint of apprehension, but most of all, deep, deep sorrow.

"Sure," she choked out, deciding she could sound equally professional. "Follow me."

She led him into an adjoining ballroom—this one much smaller—on legs that felt as stable as an old building. Her hands shook so she clenched them.

"Maggie," he said softly, facing her.

It was as if a dam broke. "Why haven't you called me this week?" she asked, panic making her sound shrill.

Calm down, she told herself again.

But he didn't answer.

She unclenched her hands. "We've been talking practically every day, and all of sudden you just stop."

"I've been busy."

"I've been busy, too. But that didn't stop *me* from calling *you*—not that you ever phoned me back."

He didn't meet her gaze for a second and Maggie realized that something between them had changed. There was a tension between them. A wall.

"What's wrong, Mike?" she asked him, clenching her hands to stop them from shaking.

He scrubbed a hand through his hair, shook his head. "Look, I've been searching for a way to tell you this for days."

Oh, God. He was dumping her.

"What?" she asked, her throat tightening for a second.

Still, he wouldn't meet her gaze.

"What?" she asked again.

At last he stared into her eyes. "I'll be going back to driving next year. It's official. The surgery I had fully restored my vision. I can go back to driving after Christmas."

"Good for you," she said, bewildered. "What's that got to do with us?"

He met her gaze and she saw the answer in his eyes.

"You're breaking things off with me, aren't you?"

"Maggie—"

"No," she said, sucking in a breath. "You are, aren't you?"

He took a step toward her. "No. Not really."

Not *really?*

"I'm just letting you know things will be a little different now. I tried to find time to call you, but our phone conversations never last less than an hour and I just didn't have an hour to spare."

"So you didn't call me at all?" she asked. "You couldn't spare two minutes to pick up the phone and tell me you wouldn't be making it out to California a day or two early so we could spend time together?"

He looked away for a second, his head shaking as he fought to find words. Well, good, because she didn't understand. Didn't get it at all.

"Look," he said, meeting her gaze again, his hand reaching for her for a second before falling back to his side. "I know I should have called, but I wanted to tell you my news in person."

"Well, congratulations. Message received." Maggie turned away, knowing that if she stood there a second longer she'd start to cry.

"Maggie," he called out after her. "Wait. Don't go."

"Out of my way, Mike."

"No. Don't leave. Not like this."

"Why not? Isn't that exactly what you want me to do?" she asked, anger finally catching hold of her and helping her to stand her ground. "Leave?"

"No, I—"

"Don't," she said. "Don't even try to excuse your actions because I know what's going on. Let's be honest here, all right? Getting involved with me was fine when you were Mike the charity worker. But now that you're about to become Mike the famous race car driver again, I'm not good enough."

"No," he said firmly, emphatically, a horrified look on his face. "That's not true. I never once thought that. I care for you," he said, his fingers finding hers. She almost wrenched them away. "These past few weeks I've told you stuff that I've never told another person. I've spent more time on the phone with you than I have with my friend Blain Sanders all year. And now, standing here in front of you, I'm reminded of our time together, and how terrific it was—"

"Well, bully for you," she said, stepping back. "You have some fond memories."

"Wait, Maggie. No. We don't have to break up over this."

"Yes, we do."

"I know you're mad. And I'll admit, I messed up. But next time I'll try and do better—"

"Try?" she asked with a flick of her head. "No. Not good enough." Because she would never let a man walk all over her again. *Never.* "I want a promise, Mike. I want you to treat me with the same respect as you do your racing career. I want commitment. With a thirteen-year-old daughter, I can't afford anything less. If you get any closer to Brooke and me, then you'll be hurting us both if you decide your racing career is more important."

"I know," he said, his voice wavering for a moment. "I've struggled with that same thought all week. It's why I wanted to talk to you in person. I wanted you to know how much I want this to work out."

"Then why didn't you call, Mike?" she asked. "Because not calling hurt. And if you're already doing that, then maybe getting involved with you isn't such a good idea."

He almost told her no. Almost told her that she was wrong. But something made him stop.

"Look," he said. "I'm tired. You're upset. Maybe I should call you later on this week and we can talk about it some more."

"Fine," she said, but he could tell it wasn't *fine* at all. "You do that."

"Maggie…" he said when she started to walk away.

But this time she ignored him. And this time he didn't give chase. Obviously, she was furious. Obviously, he'd messed things up. But things would sort themselves out.

He shook his head.

And if they didn't, well, it was better to know that now rather than later. Race schedules were hell on family life. If she thought he was busy now, then wait until the season started.

"Damn it," he cursed.

Because only when she walked out that door did Mike admit how much he'd come to care for her. And that maybe, just maybe, something might have become more important to him than racing. And that wasn't good, especially not right now.

CHAPTER EIGHT

MAGGIE HAD TO FIGHT back tears the whole way home. She called in sick—albeit from the hotel parking lot. A sudden bout of food poisoning she'd told Indi. But she could tell Indi didn't believe her. Well, that couldn't be helped because there was no way Maggie could go back into the ballroom.

How she made it home she'd never know. The trip back was nothing more than a blur. The moment she arrived she climbed into bed, red dress and all. Then, and only then, did she let all her emotions out.

Damn him. Didn't he realize how hard it'd been for her to open up to him over the past few weeks? She purposely kept a wall between herself and Brooke and the men she dated. She didn't want herself and Brooke to get hurt again. But with Mike she'd opened up. Made herself vulnerable. They might not have known each other for more than a few weeks, and most of their conversations might have taken place over the phone, but she *knew* him. Knew him intimately. And he'd known her, too.

Only now he didn't have time for her.

She wiped at her eyes, knowing she'd probably smeared mascara all over her face, but she didn't care. She felt sick, damn it. She got up out of bed, made herself some tea and paced her tiny condo, all the while wondering where she'd gone wrong. Had she let her guard down because she'd always had a crush on the man? Was that it? Had she been enamored of the image of Mike? The man on TV. Is that why she'd slept with him?

But, no, she admitted to herself. There'd been more to it than that. That first day she'd fallen head over heels. Or maybe if it wasn't love, it was something close. That's why his sudden silence wounded her so much and that's why she was so upset to find out he hadn't called her because he'd "been busy."

Indi tried calling her. Maggie heard her voice come through her message machine. She sat in her kitchen for so long her legs started to go numb.

"Mom?"

Maggie jumped and turned. She hadn't even heard Brooke's bus pull up outside.

"Are you okay?" Brooke said, taking the seat opposite her, their tiny kitchen table between them.

"Fine," Maggie said, knowing she didn't sound fine at all. Her nose was red from crying, and no doubt her makeup was all over her face.

"You don't look fine. What happened today? How was Mike?"

The fact that her daughter sounded so concerned had Maggie fighting back tears all over again.

"Nothing happened, sweetie. I just started feeling sick while at work."

"Did something happen?"

Maggie thought about denying it again, but her daughter wasn't stupid. "Yeah," she said. "Mom is officially foot-loose and fancy-free again."

"Oh, Mom," Brooke said, coming around to her side of

the table and hugging her. Her daughter's consolatory touch was nearly Maggie's undoing. "I'm so sorry," Brooke said gently.

"It's all right," Maggie said, even as fresh tears sprouted. "I'll survive."

"Can I make you something? More tea? Coffee?"

"No," Maggie said. "I've drunk enough tea to float to China."

"Then I'll just stand here and hug you."

"Thanks," Maggie said. "I could use a hug."

"I love you, Mom."

"I love you, too, honey." And that love would have to last a lifetime, because from here on she was staying single. Men did things to hurt her, and she was never going there again.

Never.

"WHAT THE HELL did you do to her?"

Mike looked up from the solitary meal he'd been forcing down. Indi Wilcox crossed between a table of diners, a furious look on her face, hazel eyes flashing and blond hair swishing.

"Indi," he said, glancing around at the other guests, most of whom stared over at them curiously. "What are you doing here?"

The restaurant lighting was low, but he could still hear the anger in her voice. "Don't give me that," she said, jerking out a seat and sinking down opposite him. "I know you and Maggie broke up today. What I want to know is why."

"We didn't break up. At least I don't think we did. She's mad at me."

"Why?"

"I'm going back to driving."

"So?"

She sounded just like Maggie, Mike thought. "I don't think she's comfortable with me getting back behind the wheel again."

"There has to be more to it than that."

"Hell if I know," Mike admitted. "All I know is she stormed off on me. I tried calling her again before dinner, but she didn't pick up."

"Go over to her house."

"I thought I'd give her time to cool off."

"That's ridiculous, Mike. If you care for Maggie at all, then you need to go after her."

"I think we need some time to cool off."

"Loser."

He jerked in his seat. "Indi, wait. No," Mike said when she stood up. "I'm not saying I'm *not* going to call her. Or see her again. I'm just saying that maybe a little time away from each other is good."

"That's all you've *had* is time away from each other."

"I know that. And maybe that's a good thing. We can both stop before things get too serious."

Indi sank down again. "Stop? Why the hell would you stop?"

Mike looked away for a moment. "You know better than anyone that this job is hell on family life."

"Maggie's the sort of person who'd give it her all."

"She has a daughter."

"Is that was this is about?" Indi asked, leaning toward him. "The fact that Maggie has a kid? Because if it is, you're not the person I thought you were."

A waiter came up to them and tried to hand Indi a menu.

She waved the menu off, the look she gave the man clearly conveying she wanted privacy.

"This had nothing to do with Brooke," Mike said.

"Then what's the problem?" Indi asked.

"The problem is now's not a good time to be jumping into a relationship."

"Mike," Indi said, placing her elbows on the table, "there's *never* a good time to enter into a relationship."

"That's not the way I see it."

"And that's probably why you're still single after so long. You're waiting for the perfect moment. But here's a news flash, Mike—a woman as good and as wonderful and as loving as Maggie Taylor comes around once in a lifetime. I thought you saw that. I was thrilled that at last someone recognized her worth. Obviously, I was wrong. But what I want you to consider while you both cool off—" she made quotes with her hands "—is if are you willing to risk that you'll never find someone else half as good as Maggie, should you decide to walk away."

"I haven't decided to walk away."

"Think about it," Indi said, standing up. "And while you think about it, enjoy your career. Just remember it's lonely at the top. But you know that, don't you? It's why you got involved with Maggie in the first place. All that fame and glory bought you a lonely life and a lot of lonely years. Congratulations. Looks like you're headed that way again."

CHAPTER NINE

HE NEVER CALLED.

Maggie didn't know what upset her more. That Mike appeared to have chosen his driving career over her, or that she continued to feel the sting of his rejection.

Damn it, she thought, trying to smooth back a stray curl.

"Mom," Brooke said from behind her. "You look great."

It'd been two weeks since she'd seen Mike. Tonight was the Christmas Miracle fund-raiser party. But Maggie dreaded it with all her heart.

At least Mike won't be around.

She'd heard from Indi that he'd quit working for the foundation. He'd chosen driving over charity work. What a disappointment.

"Go on, Mom," Brooke said, her legs crossed as she sat on the bed. "You're going to be late."

They were in a hotel room donated for Miracles' staff to use. Maggie wouldn't need to worry about Brooke getting into trouble. She'd been given strict instructions to stay in the room and watch movies all night. But just to be certain that Brooke was safe, Maggie would be checking in throughout the evening.

"I'm going, I'm going," Maggie said, walking forward

so she could give her daughter a kiss on the cheek. "Remember, I'll be right downstairs if you need me."

"I know."

Maggie drew back and grabbed a gold clutch that matched her gold ballgown, which was on loan from one of the local department stores. The dress had a long, wispy skirt that hugged her ankles and seemed to float behind her, and a tight bodice that actually made Maggie look as if she had cleavage.

"If you get hungry, you can order room service," Maggie said to her daughter.

"Mo-om. I *know.*"

"And if the hotel fire alarm goes off, remember not to use the elevator."

"Mom!"

"All right. All right. I'm leaving."

"Mom," Brooke said, suddenly serious. She darted up from the bed. "Have a good time."

"I will," Maggie promised, even though she knew she more than likely wouldn't. Now that the event was actually taking place, there wasn't a whole lot for her to do. She'd spend the night on a pair of heels that felt two sizes too small, in a gown that might make her look buxom, but that nearly cut off her circulation, all the while trying to make small talk with people she didn't know.

Fun.

She slipped out the door. Brooke would be fine on her own. According to her daughter she was long past the age of needing a babysitter. Still, Maggie worried that maybe she should have hired one.

You're just procrastinating.

And she was. She didn't want to go down to the event. Attending a Christmas party made her feel too depressed.

And lonely.

Her relationship with Mike was obviously over and Maggie ached over the whole thing. Yes, she'd been the one to walk out on him, but a part of her had assumed he really would call her. Why she'd thought that after he'd ignored her for weeks she had no idea. Still, it stung. Only after he wasn't in her life anymore had she come to realize how much she cared for him.

Obviously, he hadn't felt the same way.

The lights in the hotel lobby still twinkled merrily, but Maggie hardly noticed. Giant poinsettia plants decorated every surface. A massive tree dominated the main foyer, its lights reflecting on the polished marble floor.

Maggie handed the ballroom doorman the special pass she'd been given earlier. On the other side of the door she could hear the band. They were playing something festive. It sounded like "Frosty the Snowman."

"Enjoy yourself," the man said, opening the door with a flourish.

Maggie had been in and out of the ballroom at least a hundred times the previous day. Setting the place up had been a major undertaking, and yet nothing had prepared her for the beauty and splendor of the room beyond.

Gold and silver swathes of fabric hung from the walls. Stage lights had been aimed directly at them, illuminating the metallic cloth and setting it aglow. Silver bells hung around the room. Real silver bells. They were worth a fortune, but thankfully had been lent to them for the night. From the crystal chandeliers hung yards and yards of ribbons, and more twinkling lights. And, of course, in the center of the room stood the tree. Placed all around the room were elegantly set tables, two-foot ivy topiaries inlaid with tiny red poinsettias and more silver and gold ribbons sprouting up from the center. Even the plateware was gold, silver chargers set beneath.

"Doesn't it look great?" Indi said.

Maggie turned, gasping at the stunning picture her friend made in her silver gown. "You're the one who looks great."

"Never mind me," Indi said with a dismissive wave. "Isn't this amazing?"

Maggie nodded, starting to move toward the Christmas tree. She could smell its pine scent from across the room. "Makes all our hard work seem worthwhile."

"We've raised nearly a million dollars for Miracles already," Indi said proudly, scooping two glasses of champagne off the tray of a passing waiter. She made a half turn, the gown she wore clinging to every curve, her hair swept up atop her head. "And the silent auction over there—" she pointed to one side of the room with her chin "—is still going strong. I bet we'll hit two million by the time the night's over. That's money we'll use to fulfill the wishes of dozens of children."

And such a worthy cause.

Not that Mike would ever know. Damn it. She still couldn't believe he'd given up working for Helping Hands.

"He's here, you know," Indi said.

"Who's here?"

Her friend handed her the glass of champagne. "Mike."

Maggie's almost dropped the glass. *"What?"*

"I wasn't going to tell you, Maggie. He made me promise not to, but he's here and I thought you should know in case, I don't know, you want to leave or something."

"What's he doing here?"

"Well, he *did* help plan the event."

"Yeah, but I thought he'd be off testing race cars, or hiring people for his new race team or meeting with potential sponsors or something."

"He gave me a check for a hundred thousand dollars."

"Well, good. I hope it makes his conscience feel better."

"No," a masculine voice said. "It doesn't."

Maggie jerked. Indi turned right. "Mike," Indi said coldly. "We were just talking about you."

"So I gathered," Mike said.

Maggie felt his gaze upon her.

"Didn't you say you needed to use the powder room?" Indi asked her friend.

Maggie recognized the escape route Indi provided, but there was no sense in running. This might be a crowded affair, but she was bound to run into Mike sooner or later.

"No. Not right now," Maggie said.

Indi seemed to understand. "I'll talk to you later, then."

"So, Mike," Maggie said once Indi faded away. She steeled herself to look at him. "How's the driving career?"

He looked tired, she noticed. And anxious. Not the least little bit happy.

Good.

"I'm okay," he said, his eyes staring intently into her own.

"Great," she said. "Good to hear." *I'm still feeling like crap.* "Enjoy the party." She tried to turn away.

"Maggie," he called, stepping in front of her.

They were attracting a crowd, although she reasoned that might have something to do with who Mike was. He might not have driven a race car in well over a year, but he was still recognizable.

"Don't go," he quietly said. "Please."

"I've got nothing to say to you."

"But *I* have things to say to you," he said.

"Then say it quickly, Mike, because I'm short on time."

She saw him take a deep breath. "Look, I deserve your censure. I know I do. I've been a jerk. I didn't call. I didn't try and see you. I didn't do anything. I was wrong, but I have an excuse."

"And what's that?"

"I fell in love."

She nearly dropped the glass again.

"I know it sounds crazy," he said. "But something happened when we were together. Something unexpected and amazing. It threw me for a loop."

Maggie had to look away. Music played in the background, around them people chatted, but for Maggie this all felt like a dream.

"I know it sounds hard to believe," he said. "I didn't believe it myself until something happened to help me realize it."

"What was that?" she managed to croak out.

"I have the world at my feet," he said. "Everything a man could ask for—fame, fortune, a great career—but it all means nothing, absolutely nothing without you by my side."

Maggie shook her head. "I don't think I can do this again."

"Please," he said softly. "Maggie, I *need* you. I realize that now."

"Why?"

"You're my grounding rod. I look into your eyes and I see that the world is good. When I'm with you I know I'm with someone real. Someone special."

She shook her head again.

"Maggie," he said, taking her glass from her and setting

it down on a nearby table. He held her hand. It was the same hand that'd held her own all those weeks ago, and as his fingers enveloped her own, she felt the same falling-from-earth sensation.

"You've spent years creating miracles for other people," he said. "It's time to believe in a miracle of your own."

"I thought I'd found one."

"Only I threw it away."

She nodded, pulled her hand away.

He stared at her, and she could see the disappointment in his eyes.

She had to blink back sudden tears.

"I'm not a man who begs, Maggie, but I'm begging you now. Give me a second chance. I'll never blow it again."

He held out his hand. Maggie stared at it, knowing that if she took it she was taking the biggest risk of her life.

Or finding the greatest love of her life.

"Please," he said.

"I'm scared."

"I know," he said. "I am, too. I can drive a car at one hundred eighty miles an hour, but I'm scared to death to lose you."

She closed her eyes.

"Maggie," he said softly, scooting next to her, touching her. "I know it happened fast, but this is *real*."

It was that touch more than anything that made her give in. She still felt it, whatever *it* was. After all these weeks, after all the heartache and tears, she still felt something, and that something was strong and undeniable. She'd be stupid to throw that away.

She felt his arms wrap around her for the first time in

weeks, and it felt just as good as the first time…just as right.

"I promise you, Maggie, this isn't a mistake."

"You say that," she said, wiping at her eyes, "but I hope you're not offended when I ask you to prove it."

"I'm not offended at all," he said, pulling her into his arms again. "And I will prove it."

ONE YEAR LATER, on Christmas Eve, he did prove it…by marrying Maggie in a ceremony every bit as opulent as the party they'd helped to plan. It was, Maggie tearfully confessed to Indi, a minor miracle that it had all worked out.

But that wasn't the only miraculous occurrence.

Eleven months later Maggie gave birth to a baby boy. And as Mike held his newborn son in his arms, he wondered why he'd waited so long to have a child. But then he met the loving gaze of his wife, his newly adopted daughter, Brooke, sitting on the hospital bed next to Maggie, and the answer was simple. He hadn't had kids before because he'd been waiting to find the right woman.

He'd been waiting to find Maggie.

* * * * *

Watch for Pamela Britton's
upcoming NASCAR LIBRARY COLLECTION *title*
ON THE MOVE
coming from HQN in fall 2008.

SEASON OF DREAMS
Gina Wilkins

For my friends Bill and Terry Allen
and their beautiful daughter, Kristin,
all NASCAR fans. Merry Christmas with love.

CHAPTER ONE

TOM WYATT WAS NOT in the mood to celebrate Christmas. Or anything else, for that matter.

The former NASCAR NEXTEL Cup Series Champion had just completed his third lousy season in a row, having failed to make the most recent Chase for the NASCAR NEXTEL Cup for the first time since he'd moved up to NASCAR NEXTEL Cup Series racing six years ago. Hoping to at least end up among the top of those eliminated from the Chase, he had, instead, been hit with a string of bad luck that had resulted in two DNFs—Did Not Finish—to conclude the season.

He'd finished seventeenth in points for the year, his worst finish ever, giving fuel to the numerous detractors who liked to refer to him as a thirty-two-year-old flash in the pan who'd somehow lucked into a championship only three years after moving up to the top echelons of stock car racing. Just because he had little patience for dumb questions from reporters, and even less tolerance for boneheaded moves on the track that took out other drivers who were trying to race clean, he'd gotten the reputation of being a racing "bad boy." And there was nothing the media loved more than building someone up only to tear him down when they decided his head had gotten too big for his helmet.

He would rather eat a big bowl of bugs than sit through another taped segment in which some powdered and polished interviewer asked him how he felt about his recent three seasons. How the heck did they think he felt? He was angry, disappointed, frustrated, embarrassed. But he'd spent the past few weeks doing those interviews, dashing from one public appearance to another, filming silly TV ads, signing autographs until his hands cramped, shaking hands until his fingers went numb. Smiling until his teeth ached. All to improve his public "image." Anything to keep the owner, the sponsors and the fans happy.

As for himself—well, *happy* wasn't a word he would have used to describe his mood lately. And his girlfriend of almost two years wasn't making things any better.

"Would you make a decision already?" he all but snapped at her. "I can't stand on this stepladder all day."

Seemingly unfazed by his curtness, Melissa Hampton tilted her head to study the big, fragrant wreath he held in his hands. "Move it just an inch more to the left," she decided finally. "And turn it so the bow is just left of center at the top."

Grumbling, he moved the wreath he was holding against the red bricks above his massive fireplace. "There?"

"Perfect. Hang it right there."

"You're sure this time? Because I'm not moving it again."

"I'm sure. And stop being so grouchy."

"If you'd wanted me in a good mood, you'd have listened when I said I wanted no part of this ridiculous contest." Pushing a metal clip over a brick, he hung the wreath on it, then climbed down off the ladder without lingering to admire the results. "How much more stuff have you got? My house already looks like a tag sale at the North Pole."

She tucked a strand of auburn hair behind one ear and turned toward a box she hadn't even opened yet. "Just a little more."

Sighing heavily, he dropped onto his big leather couch, then shot back up again to move the plastic reindeer that had just jabbed him painfully in the rear. At least it hadn't torn the couch, he noted in relief, tossing the decoration onto the floor.

"Careful. You almost broke it."

"Yeah, well, it almost broke my—"

"Boy, you are on a tear, aren't you? Well, get it all out of your system. Twenty-four hours from now, when we greet your guests—on camera, I might add—I want you grinning like Saint Nick, himself."

There were a few drawbacks to being involved with the always-organized and highly ambitious vice president of marketing for his primary sponsor. Even stickier when said vice president was also the daughter of the president of the company. He'd known when he started seeing Melissa that they were taking a risk on a professional basis, but he'd let his reservations be overruled by the attraction that had existed between them from the beginning.

"This is a good opportunity for you, Tom," she added more seriously, her dark brown eyes focused intently on his scowling face. "You need this sort of warm and fuzzy thing right now. The PR blitz you've been on since the end of the season has shown some results in increasing your positive name recognition, but this, the 'Spend Christmas with a Champion' contest, has been the most successful promotion we've run yet. That ad photo we ran of you propped in your doorway in your jeans, with your arms crossed over a V-neck, green sweater and that sexy smile on your face? Pure gold. I wouldn't be surprised if it's plastered on walls and computer screens all across the country."

Slightly embarrassed, he pushed a hand through his crisp brown hair, which she had insisted he have trimmed for the holidays. "Now you're just trying to sweet-talk me into a better mood."

She laughed. "True. But I'm also being honest. Heck, I use that photo for my own desktop wallpaper."

He cleared his throat, having no clue how to respond to that.

"Anyway," she continued, taking pity on him, "the contest was a great success for both you and RightTime Realty. You came off looking like a warm, accessible guy willing to open his house to a fan family at Christmas, and it was a great way to kick off RightTime's theme for the new year, 'RightTime Realty welcomes you home.' It's a win-win situation for all of us."

He didn't have the heart to argue further. This contest had, after all, been Melissa's idea from the start. Bypassing his usual public relations team, she had conceived the Christmas contest while he'd been in the midst of trying to salvage what was left of his season.

He had been too distracted to pay a lot of attention to the details, and by the time the season was over, it had been too late to stop her. Ads had already gone out soliciting entries from fans to share a big Christmas dinner with their immediate family and Tom in Tom's beautiful West Virginia mountain home. The winner also received a five-thousand-dollar cash award and several other prizes in the form of Christmas gifts for the family, an appealing prospect that had drawn tens of thousands of entries.

Melissa's mother, Nancy Hampton, the president of RightTime Realty, had been quite pleased with the campaign, as had Tom's owner, Philip Shaw. Both had been aware that his increasingly difficult image wasn't exactly the best face to present to the potential customers of a national home realty company. Showing him in his own home, at Christmas—they'd thought that was a stroke of genius on Melissa's part. Tom had endured some ribbing for that "sexy" photo Melissa had raved about, but he could tell that lots of people thought the contest was a way to salvage the reputation that seemed to be slipping out of his control.

While he was pleased for Melissa's sake that she was getting so much praise for the contest, it wasn't her home that was about to be invaded by strangers. She'd known when she came up with the plan that his privacy was one thing he was almost obsessive about. He had never been what anyone would call a sociable type, and he didn't host dinner parties.

Had she really thought this would be good for his professional image, or was it all about her looking good in *her* job? Or was the truth, perhaps, that she didn't know him as well as she should after dating for almost two years?

"I need you to hold one end of this garland," she said over her shoulder, standing in front of the mantel again. "I'll do the draping and tacking."

He rose reluctantly to his feet, moving closer to take one end of the evergreen garland from her. "There's about an inch of space over in that corner that isn't covered in Christmas decorations."

She gave him a look that told him she knew he was being sarcastic, but she said only, "I'll get to it after we finish here."

"Yeah, I figured," he muttered.

So how well *did* she know him, really? Sure, they'd been dating for a while, but they hadn't shared that much time together, overall. He spent a minimum of thirty-six weekends a year at race tracks all over the country, while she had been concentrating on her own career. Having just celebrated her thirtieth birthday, she planned to take over the presidency of RightTime Realty when her mother retired in ten years, and she was intent on accomplishing as much as she could in her current position before moving up.

When they were together, it was great, but it seemed like those times were getting further and further apart. He'd found himself missing her more during those separations lately, especially toward the end of the season when his luck had been so rotten. There had been many times when he'd wished Melissa had been waiting for him rather than a barrage of reporters hoping for a newsworthy moment from him. Like a flash of temper. An injudicious comment. An unguarded expression.

Sure, he'd had his team waiting to bolster his spirits. His crew chief, his pit crew, the people behind the scenes. All of them good friends, loyal supporters and yet…he had still missed Melissa. Not that he'd ever told her in so many words, of course. He didn't want to come across as too demanding. Too insensitive to her own career obligations.

So, what did they do when they finally had a few hours to spend together? He stood by while she turned his treasured private refuge into a glittering setting for a publicity stunt, preparing to be invaded on Christmas Day by a Midwestern family he'd never met.

Which made him wonder if perhaps Melissa wasn't quite as lonely for him as he'd been for her. If she was beginning to see him as just another part of her job—or had maybe thought of him that way all along.

And then he wondered if he had allowed his third lousy season to sour his attitude about everything in his life, including a great relationship with a beautiful, bright, non-clingy woman who still believed he had a shot at another Championship. If he wasn't careful, he was going to ruin that, too—and then what would he have left in his life?

AFTER ANOTHER HOUR of decorating—and pretty much bullying Tom into helping her—Melissa stepped back to admire her handiwork. The place looked great. Festive. It did *not* look like a "tag sale at the North Pole."

Tom had a lovely home. Unlike the drivers who chose to live in lakeside or golf-course community mansions, Tom had chosen to build on a secluded mountainside. The house was a sprawling two-story with a rustic theme—lots of open beams and wood trim and big windows to make the most of the sweeping vistas outside. He'd had it professionally decorated, more for soothing comfort than for cutting-edge style. His colors were earth tones, with heavy wood furnishings covered in leather and nubby fabrics. Numerous throw pillows looked inviting, rather than fussy, and knick-knacks were kept to a minimum, so that the very nice pieces he had collected in his travels were well showcased.

This was where he recharged on those extremely rare days when he had no professional obligations. He could be himself here, with no microphones shoved in his ruggedly handsome face, no hungry fans clamoring for his autograph, no owner or sponsor or crew chief making

demands on his time. Next to being behind the wheel of a
powerful car screaming around a racetrack, this was where
he was the happiest, the most relaxed. So, even though
she'd known how much he would resist it, she'd thought
this would be an ideal place for the Christmas promotion
to take place.

She wanted the rest of the world to see him as she knew
he could be—warm, pleasant, funny, even charming. He
needed that boost in the public eye, needed to feel popular
and admired again. She had thought this was just the place
for him to chill out enough to handle the event without the
frustration and defensiveness he'd shown during the past
few months.

Now she was beginning to wonder if she'd made a big
mistake. His mood seemed to be getting worse instead of
better, and she worried about how warm and inviting he
was going to be when the guests and camera crew descended on them tomorrow. Couldn't he see that the
success of this project was as important to him as it was to
her?

"You have to admit the house looks beautiful," she said,
turning to face him with a hint of challenge in her voice.

He studied the garlands and ribbons, the wreaths and
candles and baubles that covered so much of his big living
room. A huge, perfectly decorated Christmas tree stood in
the center of the wall of windows, framed by the backdrop
of the winter-blued West Virginia hills.

"It looks good," he admitted. "A little more elaborate
than I would have expected, but not over-the-top."

"I'll take that as a compliment and say thank you," she
answered a bit drily. Tired now, she pushed a strand of hair
out of her face and picked up an empty box to carry to the

storage closet where she had stashed the others. "That's pretty much all we can do today. Everything else, like the food and gifts, should arrive tomorrow morning. The LeMays are due at one tomorrow afternoon."

"What kind of family wants to spend Christmas with strangers?" he asked, not for the first time. "I understand the appeal of the money and the prizes, but giving up Christmas at home—well, that just seems strange even to me. And my family never had particularly great Christmases together."

"Debra LeMay claims to be your biggest fan," Melissa reminded him, returning from the closet. "She's thrilled at the thought of spending Christmas with you. I guess they're doing their family things back in Missouri today, since we're flying them into Charleston early tomorrow morning and then driving them straight here."

"Still just seems weird to me," he muttered, shaking his head.

It always surprised her how bemused Tom could be by the idea that he had fans who were willing to go to almost any lengths to meet him. He'd told her that he couldn't imagine why anyone would stand in line in a cold rain for more than five hours just to get his autograph, and yet he'd had a crowd do just that for an appearance at a Michigan car dealership last year.

He appreciated his fans' support, but he couldn't imagine why they would find him particularly interesting off the track. He did his best to give them exciting races to watch, but he considered his personal life to be private. Irrelevant to his skills as a race car driver. He just couldn't get into the celebrity thing, he'd said.

She looked at him, sitting on the couch with his arms

crossed and wariness in his navy-blue eyes, and she worried again that tomorrow's event was going to be a PR disaster. She had less than twenty-four hours to get Tom into a jolly holiday mood—and that might be the biggest challenge she had faced yet.

CHAPTER TWO

MELISSA WAS STILL obsessing about the decorations when Tom went into the kitchen to make dinner, telling her he would rather cook than look at one more glittery bauble. She had kept her decorating out of the kitchen for the most part, though he noticed immediately that she'd hung a couple of Christmas-themed tea towels on hooks and set a large porcelain Santa Claus cookie jar on the work island.

At least she had filled it with cookies, he thought, pulling out what appeared to be a homemade sugar cookie cut out in the shape of a bell and decorated with green crystals. He munched on the cookie while he assembled the ingredients for a meal, deciding it made a very nice appetizer.

Since Melissa had already set up the dining room for the big Christmas meal tomorrow, he laid plates and flatware on the table in the bow-shaped breakfast nook. It was already dark outside, obscuring the view of the mountains, so he drew the drapes and lit a couple of candles in simple glass holders in the center of the table.

Melissa enjoyed romantic little touches like that, he mused, adding a bud vase with a single red rose to the tableau. He had bought the rose at the same time he'd purchased the ingredients for this meal, and had stashed it in the fridge to keep it fresh. He didn't know if she'd already seen it or not, but he figured she would like the gesture anyway.

She wandered into the kitchen just as he set the last item on the table.

"I was just about to call you," he said. "Dinner's ready."

"Already?" She looked at the table and smiled. "It looks lovely."

"So do you." He reached out to snag a hand in the back of her thick auburn hair and draw her mouth to his for a long, very thorough kiss.

She emerged flushed and laughing, her hair tumbled appealingly around her face. "What was that for?"

"Because you look good in my kitchen."

"Then maybe I should spend more time here."

"Maybe you should." He held her chair for her. "I grilled a couple of steaks. Salad and fresh vegetables on the side. And I picked up a bottle of your favorite merlot."

Her smile made him glad he'd made the effort. "I'm touched that you went to so much trouble for me."

"It wasn't any trouble. I used the electric grill for the steaks and the electric wok for the veggies. The salad came in a bag and the bread from the supermarket bakery. Couldn't be easier."

She laughed. "You're supposed to tell me you slaved for hours over the meal. But it doesn't matter. I appreciate it, anyway."

"It's been a while since we had an evening to ourselves. I thought we should make the most of it."

"Absolutely. And it's Christmas Eve. That makes it special, too."

"Of course." He sliced into his steak, noting with some

pride that he'd managed to cook it exactly the way he liked it. A nice medium rare.

She must have heard something in his voice that he didn't intend to reveal. "You're not a big fan of Christmas, are you? I noticed last year that you never really got into the spirit of the holidays, but I figured it was because you weren't happy with the way your season had just ended. I guess this season was even worse, in your opinion. Is that why you're not feeling festive, or are you still just dreading the media thing tomorrow?"

He swallowed the bite of steak and reached for his wineglass. "Let's just say Christmas is not my favorite holiday."

"No good family memories?"

He and Melissa hadn't talked about his family much. His choice, admittedly, since he didn't like to dwell on the past and usually changed the subject when she tried to get details. Hearing distant echoes of fighting and tears, he shook his head, both as an answer and an attempt to clear the unpleasant memories. "Not many."

Her expression went soft. "I'm sorry."

He shrugged. "I've told you my family wasn't the happiest in the world. My folks divorced when I was twelve, and should have done so years earlier. Holidays seemed to bring out the worst in them—maybe because they were forced to spend too much time together then. Now my dad and stepmother spend Christmas in Utah with her daughter and grandchildren, and my mother likes to take a cruise at Christmas—at my expense—with some of her girlfriends. We send gifts through the mail, and see each other in passing sometime during the holidays. It's all very civil and calm, the best solution for everyone."

He didn't like the pity he saw in her eyes then, so he abruptly changed the subject. "I'm surprised your family didn't object to your spending Christmas working instead of with them. I know they think the contest was good PR for the company, but didn't they want you to leave the supervision to someone else so you could be home for the holiday?"

"I told them I need to be here. This project was my baby, after all, and I want to make sure everything goes the way I planned. Besides," she added, "I want to spend Christmas with you."

"Me and some strange family neither of us have ever met," he muttered.

She gave him a chiding look, but didn't bother to argue about the importance of the contest again. Instead, she said, "Mother and Daddy are so pleased that you're joining us for our belated family Christmas the day after tomorrow. And I am, too."

Melissa had talked him into that, also. When he had suggested he didn't want to intrude on her family's holiday celebration, she had reminded him that they'd been dating long enough that he was almost a member of the family. He'd spent time with her parents before, of course, mostly at business-related events. But there was something very different, and intrinsically uncomfortable, about the idea of sharing a Christmas celebration with them.

So much of his and Melissa's relationship had revolved around business, he mused, eating without speaking for a few minutes. It was how they'd met, how they'd gotten acquainted, what they'd spent most of their time discussing during the past two years.

What would happen if things went sour with the sponsorship? If RightTime Realty decided they couldn't continue to justify the exorbitant expenses of sponsoring a NASCAR NEXTEL Cup Series car? Or if they decided that he was no longer the person they wanted as their representative in NASCAR? After all, they had signed a reigning champion, and that had probably outweighed his weaknesses in the natural charisma area. Now, he was increasingly referred to as a "former" champion.

If his alliance with RightTime Realty ended, would his relationship with Melissa follow suit? And was there any way to ask that question without either insulting her or scaring her away? He hadn't had enough experience with long-term relationships to know how to go on from here.

"Tom?" She was looking at him oddly now, as if something in his expression puzzled her. "You *are* still planning to join my family, aren't you?"

"If you still want me to after tomorrow," he said, and tried to smile to make it a joke.

She smiled in return, but as he turned his attention back to the meal that had lost some of its flavor for him, he noticed that her eyes looked more worried than amused.

THOUGH MELISSA INSISTED she should clean the kitchen since Tom had cooked, he stayed to help. He had a handy habit of cleaning as he went, so there was very little to do. Within a few minutes, they had all evidence of the delicious meal cleared away. They left the kitchen spotless, and ready to be invaded by the caterer who would serve the Christmas meal tomorrow. She didn't mention that, of course, since Tom had made it quite clear that he didn't want to think about tomorrow until he absolutely had to.

She looked around in satisfaction when they entered the

living room. It really did look pretty, she thought, even if she had done it herself. She could have hired a decorator to come in, of course, but she'd had fun doing it herself, despite Tom's grumbling.

She readily admitted to having control issues, having some difficulty delegating instead of attempting to do everything herself. She and Tom had engaged in a couple of near arguments over that very subject. He'd suggested that she might have a bit more time for herself—and at the same time for them—if she would let some other people handle a few responsibilities without her direct supervision.

She had retorted that she hadn't relied on her familial connection to the president of the company to rise to her position; she had earned it with hard work and total dedication. That family connection actually made her feel compelled to work harder than she should have, she supposed. When the time came for her to take over the reins from her mother, she didn't want anyone to imply that she couldn't handle the responsibility.

Tom lit a fire in the fireplace, which made the setting just about perfect, as far as she was concerned. She gave a long, contented sigh as the fragrant warmth spread through the room. "I love your house. It always looks nice, but it's especially beautiful all decorated for the holidays."

He dropped onto the deep couch facing the fireplace and patted the cushion beside him. "I just wish we could spend more time here."

We. She liked hearing that, but she didn't know how seriously he meant it. They had never talked about living together, though during the past year they usually ended up here when they both had a free weekend. She had come to think of this place almost as much her home as her apartment in Charleston, where she did little more than sleep and dress for the next sixteen-hour workday.

What would she say if he did ask her to live with him? She had asked herself that question quite a few times lately, and she still wasn't sure what her answer would be. As much as her first instinct would be to say yes, she still had the feeling that something was missing between them. A few barriers on both parts that should have been let down by now. A few doubts, on her part at least, that they were both equally invested in the relationship. And a secret, deep-seated fear that their careers and their romance were too closely intertwined.

She didn't really think Tom had gotten involved with her because she was vice president of marketing for his primary sponsor, she assured herself, as she had many times before. But she couldn't help wondering how much he'd been subconsciously drawn to her for that reason.

CHAPTER THREE

"ARE YOU GOING TO SIT DOWN or just stand there frowning at me?"

She blinked and forced a bright smile. "I think this is a great time to exchange our own Christmas gifts, don't you? I mean, tomorrow's going to be so hectic."

"What makes you think I got you a Christmas present?" he drawled, but his faint smile told her he was teasing.

She wrinkled her nose at him and turned toward the doorway. "I left yours out in my car. I'll be right back."

"Be careful. There's still a little ice on the sidewalk from that snowfall earlier in the week."

She moved toward the door. "Thanks. I'll watch my step."

Motion lights activated when Melissa stepped outside. Her breath hung in the air as she moved quickly to her car, shivering in the cold night breeze. Maybe she should have put on a coat, she thought, huddling into the thin chocolate-brown turtleneck she wore with dark jeans and brown suede boots that were more decorative than practical for slippery walkways. She really would have to be careful. Hurting herself in a fall would ruin her carefully scripted agenda for tomorrow.

She took a beautifully wrapped package out of the trunk of her car, then looked at it nervously for a moment.

It had been so hard choosing a gift for a man as wealthy and complex as Tom. He wasn't particularly materialistic, not overly sentimental, nor a collector of anything in particular. When he wanted or needed something, he bought it for himself. His biggest indulgences had been his house here and the ultraluxurious motor home he lived in at the racetracks.

Pretty much a man who had everything, except the Championship trophy that had eluded him for the past three years, and she couldn't buy him that.

Though she made a decent income as a vice president of her mother's growing and thriving realty company, Melissa wasn't wealthy, especially when compared to Tom. And while that didn't matter to either of them, she'd still agonized for months about what she could get him for Christmas that would have some meaning for him. She had ended up spending more than she had intended. Staring at that wrapped box now, she hoped she'd made the right choice.

"Melissa?" she heard him call from the house. "You okay out there?"

"I'm coming," she said, slamming the trunk.

It was nice that he worried about her, she decided, picking her way carefully to the front door. He wasn't the type to express his feelings in flowery words or declarations, but the nice dinner he had served her earlier, complete with candles and a rose, and his concern for her safety were his way of telling her she was special to him. At least, that was what she wanted to believe.

"You should have worn a coat," he scolded when she walked back inside. Closing the door behind her, he drew her closer to the fire. "Your teeth are chattering."

"Not quite." But she shivered as she handed him the

eight-inch-square package wrapped in green-and-red plaid paper with a big red bow. "Merry Christmas, Tom."

He took the gift a bit awkwardly. "Thank you."

She smiled. "You haven't opened it yet."

"I'm sure I'll like it."

They moved to the couch and sat side by side on the deep cushions. "I have a gift for you, too," he said.

"Open yours first." She couldn't wait any longer.

He pulled off the bow, tore away the paper, then studied the hinged, dark box he'd uncovered.

"You're supposed to look inside it," she said, wondering why she was suddenly so anxious.

Maybe her tension was affecting him. She would have sworn he looked rather nervous when he lifted the lid of the box. He went very still when he saw what was inside.

"You're always looking at your watch," she said, a bit self-consciously. "Always wondering how much longer you'll have to stay at a publicity event, how long until you're back behind the wheel of your car. I hoped maybe you would think of me when you look at this one."

"It's— Melissa, it's amazing."

"It's vintage," she said, knowing she was babbling. "I couldn't afford a fancy new Rolex or anything like that, but I thought this one was interesting. It's a—"

"It's great," he murmured, lifting the watch almost reverently out of the box. "Stainless steel case and band, 17 jewel Swiss movement. Bidirectional pilot's bezel. Three subregisters. Made in—what? The early seventies?"

"In 1967," she said wonderingly. "How do you—"

"My granddad had one almost exactly like this. He's the one who got me into racing, you know. He worked the pits at a couple of dirt tracks, hung out with some of the early legends of stock car racing. He took me to the track for the first time when I was four years old and my parents were having one of their knock-down, drag-out weekends. He won the watch in a poker game when a race had been rained out one Saturday night. He loved that watch. How did you know?"

"I didn't," she whispered. "I just always picture you looking at your watch, and I thought you might get a kick out of a vintage one. When I saw this, I knew it was the one I wanted to buy."

There had been more expensive vintage watches for sale, a couple that she'd been told were more desirable to collectors—but this one had immediately drawn her attention. It had cost her a few months' rent, but she'd decided it was worth watching her budget for a while. Though she'd hoped he would like it, she'd honestly had no idea it would have any special meaning to him. Another shiver ran down her spine, and this one had nothing to do with the cold. "I really didn't know about your grandfather's watch. What happened to his?"

"My father still has it, I guess. Unless he's sold it. He and granddad were never particularly close."

He took off the watch he'd been wearing—and which had probably cost him twice as much as she'd paid for the vintage one—and clasped her gift around his wrist. "It's really great."

"It's been fully reconditioned to keep accurate time. It has to be wound manually, of course, but—"

"It's perfect," he assured her, leaning down to press a hard kiss on her lips. "Thank you."

Swallowing a lump in her throat, she beamed up at him. It looked as though she had chosen the right gift, after all.

WITH ONE LAST GLANCE at his wrist, Tom turned on the couch to retrieve the small, wrapped package on the table behind him. He looked at it for a moment before offering it to Melissa, who accepted it with a smile of anticipation.

He wasn't good at this sort of thing, he thought glumly. He wasn't the type to come up with the perfect, clever gift. He'd never really given it that much thought.

His family had always shopped, sometimes not until the last minute, because it was expected of them rather than for any real joy in giving to each other. And even though Melissa meant more to him than anyone who shared his gene pool, he hadn't had a clue about what to buy for her. Things didn't mean much to him—at least, not usually, he thought with another glance at the watch he knew he would always treasure. Melissa had never seemed to care that much about fancy stuff, either, though she always dressed well and invested in state-of-the-art technology for her business.

Now he found himself wishing he'd put just a little more thought into his gift for her this year. Instead, he'd walked into a jewelry store, consulted for a few minutes with a saleswoman, and walked out twenty minutes later with a wrapped gift that had seemed fine at the time.

How could he have known that she would have put so much effort into what she got him? Even if it had been an accident that she'd bought him a watch just like the one that had meant so much to his grandfather, she'd still gone to a lot of trouble to find something he didn't have. Something that would make him think of her whenever he looked at it, she'd said.

She peeled away the gold-and-white paper the jewelry store gift wrapper had decorated with gold ribbon, and opened the velvet box she had revealed. "Oh, Tom, this is lovely. Thank you."

She sounded sincere enough, he decided cautiously, studying her expression as she lifted the diamond necklace from the box. Her eyes had lit up when she saw the expensive bauble, and her smile looked genuine when she turned her face toward his.

"I told the salesperson that you've got a thing for starfish," he told her a bit awkwardly. "She showed me this necklace. If there's something else you'd rather have…"

"This is perfect," she assured him, studying the pendant more closely.

The whimsically shaped, diamond-encrusted gold starfish hung from a gold chain. It had been ridiculously expensive, but the saleswoman had assured him it was a quality piece set with fine stones. It had made Tom think of the brass starfish paperweight she kept on her desk, and the little starfish that served as a zipper pull on the soft leather briefcase that was never far from her side.

He'd asked her once about her penchant for starfish, and she'd said with a shrug that they always made her smile. When the saleswoman had asked what sort of thing his girlfriend liked, that comment had popped into his head.

"Thank you," she said again, reaching up to kiss his cheek. "It means even more to me because you went to so much trouble to find something that made you think specifically of me."

He cleared his throat, wishing it had taken him more than one stop to find the necklace, just so he'd feel that he'd worked a bit harder for it.

She handed him the necklace, then scooted around to

turn her back to him, lifting the hair off her nape to expose the back of her neck to him. "Will you put it on me?"

His hands weren't quite steady when he looped the delicate gold chain around her neck and fumbled with the clasp. She turned back around as soon as he'd fastened it, one hand touching the pendant as she asked, "How does it look?"

He didn't even glance at the pendant when he murmured, "Beautiful."

A light flush warmed her cheeks. She moved her hand from the necklace to his face, stroking her fingertips across his mouth. He caught them, kissed them, his gaze locked with hers. Her dark eyes glittered with reflections of the fire, the candles, the colorful Christmas lights. He moved closer until it was his own reflection he saw in them.

Her mouth was soft beneath his, her lips warm and eager. Tom lifted a hand to the back of her head, burying his fingers in her thick, auburn hair holding her still as he changed the angle of the kiss. Not that she seemed in any hurry to move away.

They finally surfaced for air, and after inhaling deeply a few times, Tom stood and held down a hand to her. Smiling tremulously up at him, Melissa placed hers into it and let him draw her onto her feet and into his arms.

CHAPTER FOUR

HIS HAIR STILL DAMP from the shower the next morning, Tom dressed in khaki slacks and a dark green shirt embroidered at the pocket with the RightTime Realty logo. It was what Melissa had asked him to wear, assuring him it would look nice in the still photos and videos that would be taken of him that day. He was really dreading this thing, but he would do his part.

This was work, he told himself. He'd much rather be on a racetrack, but if entertaining a fan family was the way to keep his owner and sponsor happy, then he would be a gracious host.

He could hear sounds coming from the kitchen as he walked downstairs. It was rare that Melissa was up before him. She usually preferred to grab a few extra minutes of sleep when she had the chance.

Wearing a bright red sweater with beautifully tailored black pants, she was just pouring a cup of coffee when he walked into the large, sunny, red-brick-and-stainless-steel kitchen. She turned with a smile and pressed the cup into his hands. The diamond starfish pendant at her throat glittered with the movement.

"Good morning," she said, lifting her face to his. "And Merry Christmas."

Clutching the cup in his left hand, he buried his right hand in her hair and crushed her mouth beneath his for a very thorough kiss. They were both breathless when he lifted his head and glanced at the table she had already set for two. "You made breakfast?"

"I did." Smoothing her hair, she turned to set two steaming bowls on the table. "Steel-cut oatmeal with raisins and brown sugar. Whole wheat toast with fruit spread and fresh-squeezed orange juice."

"How very healthy."

She laughed. "We'll make up for it with the meal I'm having catered for the LeMay family later. Turkey and Southern dressing, sweet potatoes with marshmallows, a half dozen other side dishes and enough desserts to give us all sugar highs until New Year's Day."

The good mood left by their kiss evaporated that quickly. "Oh yeah. Can't wait."

"Now you're scowling again." Melissa sighed and shook her head. "On Christmas."

With a grunt, he picked up his spoon and dipped into his oatmeal. "You say that as if it's an unusual thing."

"Yes, well, whatever your feelings about the holiday, you're going to be Santa's little elf when the LeMay family gets here. Got it?"

Smiling a little at her exaggeratedly stern tone, he said meekly, "Yes, ma'am."

IT WAS BARELY eight o'clock by the time they'd finished breakfast and cleared away the dishes. The food and gifts were scheduled to arrive at eleven, the camera crew shortly afterward, and the LeMay family at one. That gave Melissa a minimum of three more hours to obsess about last-minute details.

"Okay, we'll eat soon after they arrive, and then we'll move to the living room to let the family open their gifts," she said, rearranging a basket of shiny ornaments sitting on a side table. "Jim, the photographer, said he'll stay out of the way, but he'll get plenty of pictures. Oh, and there will be a stack of things for you to autograph before the family gets here. Hats, T-shirts, a couple of jackets. And don't forget—"

"Take a breath, okay?" Tom broke in wryly. "And calm down. Everything's going to be fine."

She wrinkled her nose, acknowledging the wisdom of his advice with a nod. "You're right, of course. I guess I'm just falling back into my 'control freak' habits. I really want this day to go well, for everyone's sake."

"I'm sure it will."

"You'll try to smile a lot and act like you're having fun? I know this isn't your kind of thing, but—"

Maybe she had pushed a little too hard. He was frowning when he interrupted this time. "I'll do my part."

She spoke conciliatorily. "I know you will. Sorry."

He shrugged and turned away.

No one would have called Tom the embodiment of Christmas spirit at that moment. His attractive face was carved into a stern expression, his smoky blue eyes clouded with his frown. He looked good, no doubt about that, but not exactly approachable.

They had spent so little time together lately. Even after the hectic racing season ended, they had both been so busy for the past month, he with his PR blitz, she with her own work obligations. She knew he was unhappy with the way his season had ended, and she'd tried to bolster his spirits, but that hadn't been easy long-distance.

It bothered her greatly that she had seen something fading away in Tom during the past year. He'd lost some of the fire and vibrancy that had drawn her to him from the beginning. His team had noticed, his fans had noticed, and heaven knew the media had noticed. And what worried her was that he was pulling away from her, just as he was from everyone else.

Physically, they still shot off sparks—witness the sizzling kiss in the kitchen earlier—but emotionally, there were obstacles between them that seemed to be getting more troubling all the time. Shouldn't they be drawing closer during this stressful time, rather than pulling apart, if their relationship was truly going to survive for the long term?

"I think I'll take advantage of this time to call my parents and wish them merry Christmas," she said, reaching for her purse, in which she'd stashed her cell phone. "Are you calling your family?"

He nodded without much enthusiasm. "I'll call Dad and Daphne in Ogden, but I'll have to wait until Mom calls me from the cruise ship."

It still seemed odd to her that his family was so disconnected, especially at Christmas, but she had known since the beginning of their relationship that Tom wasn't particularly close to his parents. She had met them only once each, both times at races. While both had seemed fond of Tom, and quite proud to claim kinship to the successful racing champion, his mother had been a bit spacey and his father had paid more attention to his much younger and determinedly pretty second wife than to his son from his unhappy first marriage.

They were nice enough people, she reminded herself quickly, not wanting to be uncharitable, especially at Christmas. She supposed they'd done the best they could within the circumstances of their unsuccessful marriage. After all, Tom had turned out well. Ambitious, hardworking, successful, focused. Also moody, temperamental and too self-critical, she added candidly—but then she had a few flaws herself and she'd had a much more stable background than he had.

Her parents were predictably pleased to hear from her. They shared their Christmas wishes, expressed their regrets that they weren't yet together to celebrate, then wished her success with the promotional event. If there was one thing both her parents understood, it was the importance of business.

The first delivery arrived soon after she'd disconnected the call. She and Tom piled the gaily wrapped presents under the tree, grouping them by size and color to best display in photographs. Or rather, she told him where to place things and he obliged, still with the general lack of enthusiasm he had shown for this entire project.

"What are these things, anyway?" he asked, glancing at the tag on one of the gifts. "Who's Dustin?"

She answered rather absently, having just noted on her watch that they had only about ninety minutes remaining until the family descended. "I've told you, Dustin is the LeMay's eleven-year-old son. Their daughter, Angela, is nine. Debra's the mother and Dan is the dad, both in their midthirties. These gifts have been chosen by your sponsors specifically for each member of the family. It was part of the prize package."

"Right." He set Dustin's gift in place, then stood and

looked at the results. "Very photogenic. Lots of swag to really get everyone into the Christmas spirit."

Maybe it was mounting nerves that made her feel suddenly defensive and snappish. Or maybe she was just getting tired of his surly attitude about the event which she had worked so hard to bring about. "Look, would you please just stop with the snarky comments? Just do what you agreed to do, will you? After all, I put this whole thing together mostly for your benefit. Maybe I should have just left your problems to your PR people to deal with—not that they've been doing such a great job of that lately."

He stiffened. "*My* benefit?" he repeated a bit too softly. "*My* problems? I would have sworn all of this was a promotional stunt for RightTime."

Still annoyed with him, she shrugged. "It certainly looks good for RightTime, but you're the one who's making everyone have to scramble to redeem your nice-guy reputation. All that snarling and scowling you did this season didn't exactly put anyone in mind of a happy home, you know."

"Sorry if I was more concerned with my career going down the drain than trying to help you sell more houses."

She caught her breath. "We haven't been pressuring you to win, but we do expect you to make an effort to promote the company that spends almost all of our annual advertising budget sponsoring your car."

"*We?*" he repeated, planting his hands on his hips, that famous temper glinting in his eyes. "Just who are you right now, Melissa? The RightTime V.P. or the woman who spent last night in my arms?"

"Obviously, I'm both."

Shaking his head, he said, "If you don't know the difference, then we could have a serious problem here."

Something inside her tightened. "Do we?" she asked quietly.

She couldn't read his expression when he said, "I don't know. That depends on how important it is to you that I perform to your satisfaction today."

She lifted her chin defensively. "I'm only trying to make sure everything goes well today."

"Yes, well, as much as you might want to overorganize everything you're involved with, you can't control Christmas, Melissa. And you can't control me."

They stood there staring at each other, both of them almost vibrating with barely suppressed emotions. Things she didn't want to say trembled on her lips, and he looked as though he was also biting back words.

The doorbell rang before either of them let those words spill.

Melissa took a deep breath and ran a hand through her hair. "That will be the caterer, most likely."

Tom nodded, visibly drawing himself together as he turned away. "I'm going out for a walk. I'll be back in a few minutes."

He turned and headed for the back of the house as she moved to answer the front door, plastering a bright, false smile on her face.

CHAPTER FIVE

THE LEMAY FAMILY ARRIVED promptly at one o'clock, just as scheduled. They were delivered by a driver Melissa had employed, who probably wouldn't dare be a minute late, Tom thought as he braced himself for the meeting.

He had been thoroughly drilled on his role for the afternoon. He opened the door with a smile, knowing the photographer would be standing behind the family to record the meeting. "Merry Christmas," he said to the foursome on his doorstep. "Come on in."

"Oh my God, it's really you," the chubby, red-faced blonde he assumed to be Debra LeMay gasped, her hands clasping in front of her. "Tom Wyatt."

"He knows who he is, Deb," her husband, a square-built, suntanned man with thinning reddish hair muttered from behind her. Of all the family, he was the only one who didn't look particularly starstruck.

Closing the door behind them, Tom watched as Melissa hurried forward to take their coats. "This is Melissa Hampton, vice president of marketing for RightTime Realty," he said smoothly, keeping both his voice and his expression as politely bland as possible.

"I'm Debra LeMay, the one who won your contest,"

Debra said to both of them. "This is my husband, Dan, and our kids, Dustin and Angela."

Tom shook the woman's shaking hand, then her husband's, who looked much less excited. "It's nice to meet you."

"Yeah, you, too," Dan replied. "My wife's a big fan of yours."

Tom didn't miss the fact that Dan hadn't claimed to be a fan, himself. "Do you follow racing, Dan?"

"I've been watching most of my life. I was the one who got Debra interested in the sport. Some of my favorite drivers have retired during the past couple of years, but I guess you could say I'm a Ronnie Short fan now."

"Yeah. Great guy," Tom acknowledged about one of his biggest rivals. He liked the guy okay, but had been beaten by him entirely too many times this past season.

He turned then to the kids, who were impatient for their share of attention. The boy was stocky, like his father, blond, freckled and self-conscious when he shook Tom's hand. Like his mother and chubby, red-haired sister, he wore a Tom Wyatt T-shirt with jeans. Dan wore a plaid cotton shirt with khakis.

Angela pumped his hand enthusiastically, no shyness at all evident in her behavior. "You're my mom's very favorite driver. She watches you every week and she's got your car number on the windshield of her minivan. She just about fainted when she heard she won this contest. She told everybody that we were having Christmas at Tom Wyatt's house. And she—"

"That's enough, Angela," her mother broke in hastily, setting a hand on the child's shoulder. "Your house is absolutely beautiful, Mr. Wyatt. The decorations are breathtaking."

"Thank you. Though I can't take credit for the decorating, I'm afraid. And please, call me Tom." He could be sociable when he had to, he thought, resisting an impulse to glance at Melissa.

"Why don't you all stand in front of the tree so I can get some pictures," Jim, the lanky, twentysomething photographer, suggested.

"Hey, cool, my name's on some of these packages," Dustin said as he obligingly moved to the tree.

"There are gifts for everyone," Melissa said. "Courtesy of RightTime Realty and Tom's other sponsors."

Angela whirled toward her mother. "When can we—"

"After lunch," Melissa replied, anticipating the question. "First, everyone line up in front of the tree. Jim, where would you like them to stand?"

Melissa was back in full directorial mode, Tom thought, posing as instructed. He didn't think she had directly met his eyes since their guests had arrived.

The kids were restless during the photo session, eager to get on with the planned events, charged by the sight of all those presents with their names on them.

"I'm hungry," Dustin complained.

"Mama, Dustin's pushing me out of the picture," Angela whined.

"Dustin, stop it," Debra ordered through a frozen smile, her cheeks flaming. "Remember the talk we had on the way over."

"I know your family is hungry," Melissa said, skillfully stepping in. "Let's all go to the dining room, shall we? The chef has our meal ready."

"Hear that, kids?" Debra was beaming again. "A real chef."

"I'm starving!" Angela squealed. "Can I sit by Tom?"

"Mr. Wyatt," Debra hissed.

"He said we could call him Tom."

"He said the adults could call him Tom."

"Everyone can call me Tom," he interrupted hastily. "I really prefer that to Mr. Wyatt, anyway."

The rather smug look Angela gave her mother made him wonder if he'd made a tactical error there, but at least it stopped the argument.

"I want to sit by Tom," Angela sang out again, rushing toward the dining room.

"No, I want to sit by him," Dustin argued, hurrying after her. "Mom—"

"Both of you just wait up." Debra gave Tom an apologetic grimace and moved after her children, with Dan following unenthusiastically behind.

"Yeah, this is going to be great," Tom muttered to Melissa, who was beginning to look harried as her "perfect" party spiraled out of control. She gave him a look that let him know he had just made yet another tactical error.

DEBRA LEMAY COULDN'T SEEM to stop raving about Tom's beautiful home during the meal. "The view is breathtaking," she enthused. Her seat at the dining room table faced a wall of windows which offered a clear view of the mountain scenery on this beautiful winter afternoon. "And everything inside is so nice and decorated so beautifully," she added. "You must love spending time here."

Sitting at the head of the table, with Angela on his right

and Dustin on his left, Tom nodded. "I don't get to spend as much time here as I would like, since we're on the road so much during racing season."

"That must be so exciting, going to all those fascinating places," she said. "We don't get to travel much, ourselves. This was the kids' first time on a plane and only my second time."

"Actually, I spend most of my time at each location in the hauler, the garage or my motor home," Tom said with a wry smile. "Or out on the track, of course."

"You're, like, a hero or something, aren't you?" Dustin asked naively. "People always want your autograph and pictures of you and stuff."

Melissa noticed that Dan's frown deepened at hearing his son refer to Tom as a "hero." Dan had said very little during the meal, though he'd seemed to enjoy the food. She'd wondered if he just hadn't had a chance to get a word in with his garrulous family, but the truth was, he didn't act as though he really wanted to be there. She wondered why.

"I'm no hero, Dustin," Tom replied kindly. "Heroes are the guys who run into burning buildings to save lives or who arrest bad guys or teach school or defend our country overseas. Or the moms and dads who work to raise their kids to be decent citizens. I'm just a guy who's lucky enough to make a living doing what I love to do, race cars."

It was a comment Melissa had heard him make before. He honestly didn't consider himself a hero, though he'd told her once that he was all too aware that some considered him a role model. Even that weighed heavily on him, especially when things were going badly for him, making it difficult for him to control his emotions.

"Would anyone like more sweet potatoes?" Melissa asked, motioning toward the enormous bowl that was still half-filled. "Or anything else?"

"Can I have some more of that red stuff?" Angela asked, pointing toward another bowl at Melissa's left.

"The cranberry sauce? Of course you may." Melissa passed the bowl toward Angela.

"Say thank you, Angela," her mother prodded.

"I was going to," the girl replied indignantly. "Thank you."

"You're welcome."

Deciding he had enough footage and photos of the group dining, Jim set down his cameras and piled a plate for himself. He sat at one side of the big table next to Melissa, who had convinced Dan to sit at the opposite end from Tom. Since Tom was still being pelted with questions from Debra and the kids, Melissa chatted quietly with Jim for a while, confident that Tom was handling the situation well enough without her assistance.

Not that he wanted her assistance, of course, she thought, pretending to concentrate on what was left of her meal as resentment flooded through her again at the things he had said to her earlier. He had accused her of trying to control him. And Christmas, for that matter. He'd been very cutting about why she'd put this event together, even about her feelings for him. Had he really implied that their relationship depended on how well he represented RightTime Realty?

If that was what he believed, then he was right about one thing. They had serious problems, she thought with an ache in her heart that she tried to conceal as she socialized with Tom's guests.

Desserts were served, to the children's delight. Debra

smiled as she watched them dig into pastries filled with chocolate and topped with strawberries and whipped cream. Her gaze met Melissa's.

"Winning this contest has been like a dream come true for me," she said, her eyes misty. "The prize money, the chance to meet Tom, all the nice things you've prepared for my family. It's the best Christmas I've ever had."

"Me, too!" Angela agreed, her round face smeared with chocolate. "Can I have some more dessert?"

"No, Angela, that's enough," her father said.

"Then can we open presents?"

"You will sit quietly until everyone else is finished with dessert," Dan ordered her firmly.

Apparently, there was something in her father's voice that made Angela decide not to test him this time. She subsided into a pout.

Debra made an effort to quickly divert attention away from her daughter. "You must be looking forward to February, and the start of the next racing season," she said to Tom.

He nodded. "I'm always looking forward to the next season."

"Think you'll win the Championship next year, Tom?" Dustin asked, still relishing his permission to use the first name.

Dan made a sound that was a bit like a snort. "Going to have to make some big changes for that to happen," he muttered.

"Dan!" Debra said with a gasp. "You shouldn't talk like that."

"He's absolutely right," Tom assured her, his smile frozen in place. "We're going to be making a lot of changes next season. New crew chief, new strategies, new attitudes. We fully intend to be in the running for the championship come the end of the season."

"You can do it, Tom," Dustin assured him loyally. "You're a champion."

Dan set his coffee cup down on the tabletop with a thump, but he didn't say anything.

Feeling the tension mounting at the base of her neck, Melissa left her own dessert barely touched. She didn't know what was bothering her so badly. Debra was obviously thrilled with the way the day was progressing, the kids were better behaved than some she'd been around and Tom was making a visible effort to be on his best behavior. Sure, Dan was being rather surly and she didn't know quite why, but she could handle that, too. But there was still a heavy weight sitting directly on her chest—right in the vicinity of her heart.

CHAPTER SIX

THEY MOVED to the living room after everyone had finished dessert. Melissa was glad the interminable meal was finally over. Now all they had to do was get through the next couple of hours and they could send the LeMay family on their way—bubbly wife, noisy kids, sullen husband and all.

Which would leave her alone with Tom, she thought with a hard swallow. And then what?

Looking at his unrevealing face as she directed everyone into position for the next round of photos, she wondered if it wouldn't be easier to spend a little more time with the LeMays.

With the camera recording every moment, Tom played Santa, making sure the kids got their gifts first. He watched with obviously, to her at least, feigned indulgence as they ripped into the packages. As part of the grand prize package their mother had won, they received video game systems stocked, of course, with racing games; die-cast cars; autographed green-and-gold driver jackets; caps and T-shirts; mugs and other officially licensed merchandise, all courtesy of Shaw Racing.

There was more licensed merchandise for Debra and Dan, who opened his obligingly and then set it aside. And then Melissa and Tom presented the big gift from Right-

Time Realty for the whole family, a big-screen high-definition TV on which to watch next season's races. Jim dutifully recorded their reactions to the surprise. Melissa thought for a moment that Debra was in danger of fainting. Dustin and Angela didn't look to be far from it, either.

As for Dan—well, she thought the guy was trying to look pleased for his family's sake, but for some reason he was having to struggle. She just couldn't figure Dan out. Was he shy? Bored? So much of a Tom Wyatt "hater" that he couldn't enjoy anything about sharing a day with him? And why did she get the odd feeling that there was a hint of sadness behind his antipathy? What on earth did he have to feel sad about?

Overstimulated by the events of the day, Dustin and Angela became even rowdier, squealing and demanding attention, comparing gifts and eventually getting into pushing and fussing. Their mother tried to settle them down, but she was still so flustered herself that she wasn't particularly successful.

"How about we get one more picture for a keepsake?" Jim suggested loudly. "This one can go in your family album. Tell you what, why don't you all put on your Tom Wyatt jackets and pose with Tom in front of the fireplace?"

Everyone but Dan reached obligingly for their jackets.

"Put yours on, too, Daddy," Angela insisted, shoving her arms into her slightly too large green-and-gold garment.

"It's a little warm in here, especially in front of the fire," he said. "I'll just stand in the back behind the rest of you guys, okay?"

"No, Dad, wear the jacket," Dustin chimed in. "You won't be wearing it long enough to get too hot."

"Let's just get the pictures taken," his father said,

leaving the jacket behind as he moved toward the fire-place.

"Dan, put on the jacket," Debra said, her voice tight.

"I don't want to put it on. Now, do you want me in this picture or not?"

"Not if you're just going to keep scowling and ruining everybody's day."

"Fine." He threw his hands in the air and turned away. "Y'all just go ahead without me."

Melissa was horrified by the way her meticulously planned day was falling apart. The kids seemed to be on the verge of tears now. Tom cleared his throat, and she remembered with a slight grimace that he'd told her his own family had always fought at Christmas. This must be bringing back painful memories for him. "There's really no need for Dan to wear the jacket. It's no big deal."

Everyone whirled on Tom then—even the man he'd been trying to defend. "I can speak for myself," Dan muttered.

Tom looked as though he'd had just about enough of the other man's attitude. His own ready temper was beginning to simmer. "Hey, I was just trying to help. There's no need to be a jerk about it."

"Yeah, well, my family doesn't need help from a big shot driver who didn't even make the Chase last season."

Debra's gasp sounded very loud in the shocked silence that followed the outburst. And then she burst into tears and turned to rush out of the room, heading toward the kitchen. Wailing, Angela bolted after her. Dustin seemed uncertain about what to do, but then he gave his father an angry look and followed his sister.

Tom had definitely had enough. He moved toward the

door, looking fully prepared to leave and let Melissa deal with the fallout from this great idea he'd protested from the start.

"Do not take another step toward that door," she ordered, loudly enough to make him look around at her in surprise. Tom wasn't the only one who'd reached his limit. She didn't lose her temper very often, but she was on the verge of blowing her stack now.

She glanced at Jim, who hovered with his camera ready, as if uncertain whether this was part of what he was supposed to be recording for posterity. "Why don't you take a break, Jim. There's a TV in the sitting room upstairs. I'm sure Tom would be happy for you to relax up there for a while."

She shot Tom a look, daring him to argue. He didn't, though he scowled when he crossed his arms over his chest.

"Now," she said when the photographer had climbed the stairs, "I don't know what's gotten into the two of you, but this is ridiculous. It's Christmas, for crying out loud! I have worked my fingers to the bone for this thing and I'm not going to let you two boneheads ruin it. I'm going to go try to calm down Debra and the kids. You two," she added, pointing furiously at each of them in turn, "sit in here and be nice to each other or I'm going to…I'm going to do something very unpleasant to both of you."

On that admittedly lame threat, she spun on one heel and left the room.

LONG, TENSELY SILENT moments after Melissa stormed out of the room, Dan cleared his throat, the sound unnaturally loud. "She's, uh, got a temper, hasn't she?"

Remembering the way she had looked with heat in her eyes and a flush of outrage on her cheeks, Tom swallowed. "Apparently."

"You've never seen it before?"

"Not like that, no."

Dan shoved his hands in his pockets. "Guess she's seen your temper often enough."

Tom squeezed the back of his neck. "Not directed toward her." And then he remembered the way he had lashed out at her before their guests had arrived and he winced. "Not usually, anyway."

Dan turned, paced toward the tree, then took another couple of steps back. Drawing a deep breath, he said, "I shouldn't have said what I did. It was completely out of line. I apologize."

Though he wasn't in the habit of graciously accepting apologies from anyone who had just slashed him in his most vulnerable spot, Tom remembered the way Melissa had pointed her finger at him. Somewhat grudgingly, he said, "Yeah, okay."

Giving a snort of laughter that held little humor, Dan sank heavily onto the couch, his hands clasped loosely between his knees, his shoulders a bit hunched. "I guess you wonder what the hell my problem is."

"I think it's obvious that you don't care for me." Tom shrugged. "I'm used to that. Usually I do something to deserve the hostility, but I guess you're entitled to the way you feel."

Dan was shaking his head before Tom even finished speaking. "It isn't that. I don't have anything personally against you. Like you said, I don't even know you. Despite what the press says about you sometimes, you seem like an okay guy. You've been real good to Debra and the kids today."

Getting confused now, Tom asked, "So why the attitude?"

After a long pause, Dan sighed. "Have you ever had a dream come true and then had it all slip away from you?"

This time it was Tom who gave the disbelieving laugh. "You did watch the season I just had, right?"

"Oh yeah. Sorry. Well, maybe you can understand the way I've been feeling lately."

Tom sat in a chair facing the couch. "Did you fall out of a championship race?"

"Not exactly. I started my own business. The one I've dreamed of owning for most of my life. A fishing resort on a lake in Southwestern Missouri."

Tom winced. "It, uh, didn't make it?"

"Oh, it hasn't gone under," Dan answered gloomily. "Yet. I'm breaking even, was hoping to even start making a profit within the next year or two."

"What happened?"

"A big storm happened. This past summer. Dropped some trees onto cabins, tore up the boat dock. No one was hurt, thank God, but the resort took a serious hit."

"You had insurance?"

"Yeah. High deductible, though, and of course the company wouldn't cover some of the damage. You know the fine print stuff you get into with insurance claims."

Scowling, Tom nodded. "Oh yeah."

"I sank every penny I had into that place. All our savings. I've been working sunup until long past sundown, 24/7, barely even have time to see the kids anymore. I didn't know anything about advertising or promotion, and not nearly as much as I should have about keeping books and records. Everything's a hell of a lot more complicated and expensive than I expected. The month of business we lost after the storm nearly put us under. I knew we'd have a lean Christmas this year, but the family seemed to understand. And then Debra won this contest."

Dan shook his head. "Don't get me wrong, I know she was lucky. The money's going to come in handy. Deb's getting to meet her hero, see this nice place of yours, and the kids are getting things there's no way I could have afforded this Christmas."

Light was beginning to glimmer for Tom. He nodded.

Suddenly stiffening again, Dan snapped, "I'm not asking for sympathy. I'm just explaining why I haven't been in the greatest mood today. I should be at home, working, and instead I've been wasting time here, watching…"

Watching his family enthuse over gifts and food provided by someone else, Tom silently finished for him. Couldn't be easy for a guy with any masculine pride. Especially when that someone else wasn't even the driver Dan rooted for, he added ironically.

"Anyway, now you know," Dan said, pushing a hand through his hair. "I'm a jerk, but I've got reasons. How about you?"

Tom shrugged thoughtfully. "I'm a jerk—but I've got reasons."

This time there was just a hint of genuine amusement in Dan's laugh.

A sound from the doorway made Tom look around. Melissa stood there, frowning suspiciously at them, Debra and the kids standing behind her.

Dan drew a deep breath and stood. "Call the photographer," he told Melissa. "I'll wear the danged coat."

Debra smiled a bit tremulously. The children were more vocal in their approval of their father's change of mood.

Melissa, Tom noted, seemed relieved—but he couldn't help noticing that she still wouldn't meet his eyes.

THE LAST ITEM on Melissa's agenda for the day was a special holiday toast. Eggnog was poured into fancy glasses and placed in everyone's hand. A RightTime Realty Christmas-themed banner was draped conspicuously behind them as they all posed with glasses raised.

"I'll make the toast," Tom offered without Melissa even prodding him.

Everyone looked at him expectantly.

"To dreams," he said, glancing from her to Dan. "And the obstacles that sometimes come with them."

Dan seemed drily amused, though everyone else looked as confused as Melissa felt. Before she could ask, Tom added more traditionally, "Merry Christmas."

"Merry Christmas," they echoed and sipped their eggnog while the camera shutter clicked to record the cozy scene.

As Melissa pretended to enjoy her own beverage, she couldn't help wondering if this would be the last Christmas toast she and Tom would share.

CHAPTER SEVEN

TOM HAD HIS HOUSE BACK. And it felt great. Turning from the door he had just closed behind his guests, he glanced around the paper-and-ribbon-strewn living room, deciding on the spot that he would never allow his home to be used that way again. No matter whose career it benefited.

Melissa returned then from the kitchen, where she had just checked to make sure everything in there was cleared away. Her expression was serene, but he thought he saw emotions roiling in her eyes. Despite her attempt to hide it, Melissa was still angry, he decided, studying her more closely.

He cleared his throat. "He started it."

Her voice was cool when she replied, "I'm aware of that. And you handled it pretty well, considering. Your publicist would be proud."

So it wasn't the confrontation with Dan that was still bothering her, he concluded. She was still steamed about the quarrel they'd had prior to the arrival of their guests.

Kneading the back of his neck, he said, "About the things I said earlier—"

"Actually, I've decided you were right," she surprised him by saying, bending to gather a handful of torn wrapping paper.

He watched her uncertainly. "About…?"

"About our relationship." Stuffing the paper into a garbage bag, she tucked a strand of hair behind her ear as she faced him, looking somehow nervous and resolute at the same time. "You were right."

Now he was just confused. "I'm not sure what you mean."

"We're too tied up in our careers, you and I. You're a driver, and I represent your primary sponsor. It's a complicated situation we should have acknowledged from the beginning."

"Okay, we've acknowledged it can get sticky. We'll just have to make sure it doesn't."

She shook her head, and now she looked more sad than angry. Which made his chest go so tight he found himself having a bit of trouble breathing. "It's not going to work, Tom," she said.

"What's—what's not going to work?"

"Us."

He tugged at his open shirt collar, wondering how it had suddenly gotten so tight. "Don't say that. We'll work it out."

"No." She blinked, as if forcefully keeping her eyes dry. "We can't. Not when you never know when I'm being your girlfriend and when I'm the sponsor. Not when you feel like our relationship depends on your performance on the track, or in front of the cameras. Not when so many people have wondered what would happen to us if RightTime and Shaw Racing decide to go their separate ways in the future—and neither of us could ever give them a definite answer."

"Whatever anyone might have said to you, I have never seen you as a way to secure my sponsorship," he said flatly, willing her to believe him.

"I know," she whispered. "We've hardly seen each other at all, have we?"

"Melissa—"

She moved abruptly toward the door. "I need to go. I'll send someone tomorrow to clear away the rest of the mess and the decorations."

He caught her arm, feeling as if he were in a spinning car over which he had no control. "Don't go. Let's talk about this."

She looked at his hand on her arm, and then slowly up at his face. "I'm sorry, Tom. I just really need to go."

To get where he was in his life, he had fought, schemed, sweated and persevered. He had never once begged. Because he found himself entirely too close to doing so now, he released her arm without another word. Catching her breath, she turned and rushed out the door, letting it slam behind her.

Sinking onto the couch, Tom looked at the Christmas tree, which looked rather bare and abandoned now that the holiday was pretty much over.

He knew exactly how that felt.

"IT'S A SHAME Tom couldn't join us today," Nancy Hampton said as she and Melissa sat in Nancy's living room, sipping hot tea in the glow of the tiny white lights that draped the massive tree and nearly every other part of the room.

Nancy's house had been professionally decked out for the holiday parties she'd given, every room coordinated in white and silver decorations. She hadn't had to lift a finger, which, to Melissa, wasn't nearly as much fun as doing the holiday trimming oneself. She'd had a lovely time doing Tom's house, she thought wistfully. They'd had an absolutely beautiful setting in which to break up.

"Yes, well, he said to send his regrets," Melissa fibbed, keeping her eyes on the bedecked fireplace in which a small gas fire burned tidily.

"I'm glad the contest came off okay," Nancy murmured, stretching her long, slender legs in front of her, her stocking feet crossed on a dainty footstool. "I have to confess I was concerned about it. There were so many things that could have gone wrong."

So many things had gone wrong, Melissa thought with a pang. She hadn't yet been able to tell her parents that she and Tom were finished. She just couldn't make herself say the words out loud yet. "Yes, it took a lot of work to bring it off. But the LeMays seemed satisfied and the PR photos will look great for the company. And for Tom."

"He certainly needed that." Nancy shook her head in tolerant exasperation. "To be such a nice man, he certainly has an unfortunate tendency to show his worst side when things go wrong, doesn't he?"

"Yes. He does. He's trying to do better."

"I know. He's worked very hard the past month to do everything his owner and sponsors have asked of him. Now if only he can keep this up next season, despite how he does on the track."

"I'm sure he will. And I expect that he'll have a good season next year. The new crew chief is working very hard to rebuild the team and get them back into Victory Lane. Tom's one of the best drivers in the sport. He won't stay down for long."

Maybe he would do even better this year, without the distraction of trying to maintain a long-distance relationship, Melissa thought sadly.

"You've always been his most ardent supporter," her

mother replied with a smile. "So, did the two of you have a chance to talk about the future while you were together, or did you let yourself get too bogged down in the details of the contest?"

"The, uh, future?"

"Yes. You don't plan to keep drifting along just seeing each other once a month or so, the way you have been, do you? It's obvious that you're good together. You're a positive influence on him—and the reverse is also true. He gives you something to think about besides your work. So when are you going to take things to the next level? Make the relationship more official?"

"I, um—" Melissa looked down into her teacup, unable to come up with anything coherent to say.

"Melissa?" Her mother set her own cup aside, an expression of concern on her perfectly made-up face. "What's wrong? Have you and Tom had a falling-out?"

Swallowing hard, Melissa confessed, "We broke up. Specifically, I broke it off."

"You? But, honey, why? You seemed so crazy about him."

"That hasn't changed."

"Then why did you break up with him?"

"He accused me of trying to control him. He told me he didn't know when I was being his girlfriend and when I was acting as vice president of RightTime Realty." And the very worst thing he had done was to let her leave, she thought, unable to say those words aloud because she knew exactly how irrational they sounded.

"Oh, my. That did get ugly, didn't it?"

Melissa nodded miserably.

Her mother rested a hand on her arm. "It isn't easy being an ambitious woman with a somewhat obsessive need to take charge, is it? I'm speaking, of course, from experience."

"I didn't try to control Tom," she answered defensively.

"Not consciously, I'm sure. But maybe you thought you had to remind him a few times what was expected of him during the Christmas event? And maybe sometimes you do slip into your professional persona when you should be concentrating on your personal life?"

Melissa shook her head stubbornly. "It isn't possible for me to compartmentalize myself that way. My job is a part of who I am. I don't leave it behind just because the clock strikes five or some other arbitrary quitting time. Tom's always a driver. It's who he is, the way he identifies himself. No one expects anything different of him."

"Nor should they of you. But we all have to prioritize sometimes between our careers and the people we love. I've had to do so often. There were times, I'm afraid, when I had to choose the job over a dance recital or a parent-teacher meeting or a family vacation. But on the whole, I hope you and your father have always realized that both of you will always come first for me when it truly matters."

"So you're saying that the problems between Tom and me were all my fault?"

Her mother smiled and shook her head. "Oh, no. I've met the young man in question many times, remember? I'm quite sure he contributed more than his fair share to the conflicts. I just want you to take your time and make sure you know exactly what you want before you burn any bridges behind you."

"I'll think about what you said," Melissa agreed quietly, subconsciously lifting her hand to the diamond pendant at her throat. "But the bridges may already be burned."

"That will be up to you and Tom to figure out, I suppose. Just know that I'm here for you, if you need me. Always."

"I love you, Mother."

"And I love you." Her mother kissed her cheek and then patted her arm again. "Why don't we go have some more of that delicious pecan pie the chef made for our belated Christmas dinner. I think we deserve to be sinful today."

"Sounds good to me," Melissa agreed with a slight smile, though part of her mind was preoccupied with the advice her mother had given her.

WATER LAPPED GENTLY at the rocks at Tom's feet. It was a chilly afternoon, but he was comfortable enough in his coat, sweatshirt and jeans, his hands shoved into sheepskin-lined pockets. He was a lot colder on the inside than he was on the outside, he thought glumly.

"Some would say the week between Christmas and New Year's is a strange time for a man to take a lonely vacation at a nearly deserted Missouri fishing resort," Dan LeMay said behind him. "Especially a guy who could afford to go to the Riviera or some fancy Mexican resort. Or, if he wanted winter fun, to some snooty ski resort in Colorado or Utah."

"I've never particularly liked fancy and I don't do snooty," Tom drawled, reaching down to pick up a rock and toss it into the wind-lapped surface of the lake. "Besides, I wanted to see this place you sank your life savings into. You made it sound pretty special."

"Well? What do you think?" There was just a hint of anxiety in the other man's voice, as if it mattered to him what Tom thought.

Because he believed it did matter to Dan, Tom took the time to look around before he responded. The resort was small, but tidy, with cozy cottages grouped around a central compound that held picnic tables and a playground area in addition to the pool that was closed for the season. Only a couple of the cabins were occupied at the moment by diehard fishermen who didn't mind the cold if there was a chance of landing a few bass. The boat dock and a combination office–convenience store–bait shop building sat lakeside, the entrance decorated with a big, cheery Christmas wreath. An immaculately kept, double-wide mobile home with a built-on wooden deck and rough cedar underpinnings served as the LeMays' home.

"It's a great place. I can see why you were willing to make the sacrifices you've made to own it."

Dan smiled. "Yeah. Maybe someday it will even be worth it all."

Tom shrugged. "Isn't it worth it now, really?"

"Yeah." Pride in his expression, Dan looked around. "I guess it is."

He turned back to Tom then. "You sure made my family's week by showing up here. The kids can't wait to brag about how their buddy, Tom Wyatt, came to visit them. And Debra's been cooking and cleaning all day for the dinner she invited you to this evening."

"I'm looking forward to it." Oddly enough, he sort of was. Even another meal accompanied by Dustin and Angela's squabbling was preferable to his own company just then.

"So, why are you really here, Tom? You didn't have any other plans for this week? A busy, famous guy like you?"

"I *had* other plans," Tom admitted glumly. "They fell through."

"So you just decided on the spur of the moment to come check out my resort."

"Something like that, yeah."

"Well, we told you when we left your house that you would be welcome here any time. I just didn't expect you to take us up on it so soon."

"Sort of surprised me, as well," Tom admitted.

"That you and I ended up kind of friendly?"

"That, too. Guess we had a few things in common, after all."

"Like both having tempers that get us in trouble sometimes."

Tom winced. "That's one."

Grinning, Dan added, "We also both seem to have a soft spot for bossy women."

Tom laughed, as expected, but this time there was a pang behind the humor. Because he didn't want to talk about Melissa then, he kept the conversation moving. "Another thing we have in common is both knowing what it's like to chase a dream with everything we've got. And how it feels to finally get there and find out it's not quite like what we'd expected."

Dan nodded. "I hear you," he muttered.

Shrugging, Tom looked around the resort again. "But still, you're living your dream. That's got to feel good to you."

"It does." Dan looked around with a smile when his children, bundled into coats and hats and scarves, tumbled from their home and pelted toward them, laughing in excitement as they ran. "It does feel good."

He glanced back at Tom. "But you should know about that. You're living yours, too. You're a NASCAR NEXTEL

Cup Series driver, man. You've won a championship. I guess you know how many people would give everything they have to be in your shoes."

The discussion came to an end when the children reached them, Angela throwing her arms around her father's waist with enough enthusiasm to knock a breath from him. Laughing, he swung her up in his arms, then set her back down, looking at that moment like a very happy man.

"Tom, come with me," Dustin said, motioning as he moved toward the boat dock. "I want to show you the carp that always come up to the dock for fish food."

Following obligingly, Tom thought about what Dan had said. There were a lot of different kinds of dreams, he mused. Dan was fortunate enough to have achieved several of them. As for himself…well, maybe he should spend the rest of the off-season deciding exactly what dream this former champion wanted to pursue next.

CHAPTER EIGHT

WITH LESS THAN AN HOUR left until the new year began, the party was in full swing. Laughter, conversation and music filled the air, not quite at a painful level but still fairly noisy. Plates of food and glasses of alcohol were steadily consumed, only to be judiciously refilled by discreetly efficient servers. Air kisses were exchanged, becoming more enthusiastic as the hours crept along and the booze disappeared.

Melissa crept out to her mother's patio at eleven-thirty, needing a few minutes alone in silence. This was just about the only place to find solitude in the house that was filled almost to capacity with her parents' guests.

Everyone inside looked and sounded so happy. Maybe a good portion of them were faking it, but if so, she didn't have their talent. She had kept up her phony smile for as long as it would hold.

She knew she had to go back inside soon. People would notice if she wasn't there for the big countdown to midnight. But, oh, how she dreaded it. There was no one in particular she wanted to kiss in celebration. No one in her parents' house, at least. She didn't want to celebrate the beginning of a new year that held little anticipation for her tonight.

"You seem to be the only person here not wearing a shiny party hat."

Her fingers tightened painfully on the wrought iron patio railing. She couldn't seem to make her head turn to look behind her. Maybe she was afraid she was only imagining the voice. "I didn't want to mess up my hair."

"That would be a shame. It looks very nice. You don't wear it up very often."

She swallowed. Hard. "Why are you here?"

He moved closer behind her, so close that she fancied she could almost feel his warmth through her too-thin black evening coat. "According to my very cool new watch, it's getting close to midnight. I was invited to be here to see the new year in."

"I know, but—"

"And I couldn't stand the thought of someone else kissing you at midnight."

Her eyes closed. "Tom—"

"You want me to leave?"

"No." She didn't even have to think about that.

His hands closed on the railing on either side of her, trapping her in front of him. And yet she knew that all she had to do was move away and he would let her go.

She decided to stay where she was. For now, at least, she told herself.

"Want to know where I've been the last couple of days?" he asked in a murmur, his breath ruffling the little hairs that had escaped her loose up-do.

"I—" She was having a little trouble talking. She cleared her throat. "I assumed you were at home."

"No. I've been in Missouri. At a fishing resort."

"A fishing resort?" she repeated, not sure if she should believe him. "Dan LeMay's fishing resort?"

He rested his cheek against the side of her head. "Yep."

Her skin tingled where their bodies came into contact. And that was almost every inch of her. "Um, why?"

"I just wanted to see it. He and I decided we've got a lot in common. Think we're going to be good friends eventually. I might even invest in his resort, though I haven't mentioned the idea to him, and I'm not sure he'd be interested in taking on a partner."

"Really?" She knew Tom didn't have a lot of close friends. He chose the ones he had very carefully. "What do you and Dan have in common?"

"We both like bossy women, for one thing."

For some reason her eyes filled with tears. "Do you?"

"Mmm." He brushed a light kiss across her nape, as though he couldn't wait any longer to do so. "And barbecue-flavored potato chips. We both really like barbecue-flavored potato chips."

"Sounds like a basis for a lifelong friendship," she whispered.

"We have something else in common. We both tend to get surly and say stupid things, especially when we're feeling like losers."

That made her turn to stare up at him, possibly a tactical error since it meant she was now standing in his arms, their faces very close together. "What do you mean?"

"Dan was feeling pretty bad because he'd sunk all his money into the resort, had a spell of bad luck, and couldn't provide a big Christmas to his family this year. The contest came along at a good time for them, but it also triggered his pride when his family carried on like I was the second coming of Superman."

"That's what he told you when the rest of us left the room?" she asked, surprised. She had wondered what had been said between the men that had left them in somewhat better moods for the rest of the afternoon.

"Pretty much. Words to that effect."

"So he lashed out at you because of wounded pride." She shook her head in disgust. "Men."

"Exactly. And I lashed back at him—and at you— because I've been feeling like a loser for a couple of years now. Worse after this season, of course."

"You are not a loser," she said heatedly, clutching the lapels of his beautifully tailored evening jacket in a fierce grip. "That's just a foolish thing to say."

"Maybe. But it was the way I felt."

Her grasp on his coat didn't loosen, but she looked at him in question. "Felt? Past tense?"

"For the most part, yes."

"What made the difference?"

"A little talk I had with Dan a couple of days ago. About dreams."

"What about dreams?"

"About all the work it takes to achieve them. About how scary it is when you finally get there, maybe a little too easily. A little too young. About how hard it is to hang on to that dream when you finally have it in your grasp, but you still have a lifetime ahead of you. About how easy it is to forget the successes when it suddenly occurs to you that every big dream comes with a big price tag."

"Haven't I told you some of those same things several times?" she asked, almost indignant now. "How many times have I reminded you that you are a NASCAR NEXTEL Cup Series Champion and that no one can ever take that away from you?"

"Yeah, you've said it. But maybe it was easier to hear it from Dan."

"Why?"

"Because he knows what it's like to have to fight for a dream. And what it feels like to worry about losing one."

Her grip loosened then. In shock. "You think I don't know what it's like to have dreams?"

"I didn't say that," he assured her more gently than was his usual habit. "I said you don't understand what it's like to have to fight and scratch for them. I know you've worked very hard for your job. You've trained, you've studied, you've sacrificed, you've given a hundred and ten percent. RightTime Realty is lucky to have you, and when the time comes for you to take the reins, you will be fully prepared. You'll be an amazing success.

"But the truth is…the job was always yours. Whether you deserved it or not. And it won't all be snatched away from you if someone decides to pull an ad. Or if someone decides you don't have the right look or personality or Q rating or star factor to represent RightTime."

He looked braced for her to explode in his face. She almost did. There was no subject she was more sensitive about than even the slightest hint that nepotism played any part in her career success.

And yet, something made her bite back the angry words that sprang automatically to her lips. Maybe it was the reluctant realization that he had made some valid points.

He looked as surprised as she felt when she said, "You could be right."

"I am right. I just didn't expect you to admit it," he said with a crooked smile.

She gave him a look that wiped the smile off his face. "Don't push it."

"Sorry."

"I'll grant you that there is a certain job security in the undeniable truth that my mother is president of the company. And no, she won't fire me, unless I go completely insane and somehow put the company in jeopardy. But you're wrong about one thing."

"What's that?"

She tightened her grasp on his coat again. "I know what it's like to be very close to a dream and watch it slip away. Without even understanding quite why."

She watched his throat work with a hard swallow. "You're talking about—"

"About us," she whispered. "About finding something so wonderful and being so afraid to watch it fall apart that it seemed easier to just walk away from it."

His hand rose to her cheek, and it touched her to realize that it wasn't quite steady. "Melissa—"

"You were pulling away from me," she said, letting the pain show now after hiding it from him for so long. "I didn't know why."

"When a guy feels like a loser, he doesn't think he quite deserves a woman like you. He keeps waiting for her to dump him, one way or another. So…it just seems easier to push her away."

"You are not a loser," she repeated, tugging at his coat until his face was less than an inch from hers. "Keep saying that and I'm going to do something very unpleasant."

He laughed softly. "Like I said, I love bossy women."

"Good. Because I love you. And that has nothing to do with whether you ever win another trophy or whether

RightTime Realty and Shaw Racing part ways or whether you decide to stop racing and chase the top prize for competitive knitting. Is that clear? I love you, Tom Wyatt. And I've decided I'm not letting this dream slip away so easily."

"I love you, too." He covered her mouth with his, kissing her until she was clinging to his jacket for support rather than emphasis. He raised his head only long enough to take a breath and repeat, "Competitive knitting?"

"Shut up and kiss me again."

He laughed. "Yes, ma'am."

"Melissa?" Nancy stood in the doorway, peering into the shadows from the brightly lit, people-filled living room. "It's almost midnight. You're going to miss the celebration—oh. I see you've already started."

Wrapping her arms around Tom's neck, Melissa said without looking around, "Happy New Year, Mother. I love you. Now please go kiss Daddy and see to your guests."

"At least you said please to her," Tom teased as the crowd inside began to loudly chant a countdown, beginning with "ten."

"I can say please," she assured him. "Please kiss me again, Tom."

"Happy to oblige."

They were still kissing when the new year was well under way.

EPILOGUE

TOM STOOD IN VICTORY LANE at the Chicago racetrack, his hair plastered to his head with a combination of July sweat and jubilantly sprayed champagne. A reporter stuck a microphone in his face, certainly not the first, nor would it be the last during this celebration.

"You've just won your third race of the season and you're only a couple of points out of first place in the championship race," the reporter said, as if Tom didn't already know all of that. "What would you say has turned your team around this year after the terrible season you had last year?"

"Len's doing a phenomenal job as crew chief," Tom said, giving a thumbs-up to his grinning teammate. "The whole team is working together like clockwork, and the hard work and spirit of cooperation is really showing out on the track."

"Your own attitude seems to have undergone a change this season," the reporter persisted, jostling to keep his prime position from the others eager to get a quote. "Even last week when Malloy took you out of the race with that aggressive move that sent you into the fence, you kept your cool and smiled through the interviews afterward. The Tom Wyatt from last year would have hid out in the hauler and avoided the press after a disaster like that. Can you explain the difference?"

"I guess I do have a new attitude this season," Tom admitted. "Maybe it's helping the team that I'm more positive now, which makes it easier for everyone to do their jobs."

"And what brought about that change?"

"I think I'd lost sight of why I started racing in the first place," Tom answered candidly. "It wasn't just for the championships or the fame or the money, it was for the love of the sport. I'm going to give everything I've got to win the championship again this year, but if it doesn't happen, then I'll start focusing on winning next year, knowing I've done my best."

And speaking of his job… "I want to thank my sponsors, RightTime Realty, Colby Oil, Hometown Building Supplies and Quench Cola," he recited smoothly. "My owner, Philip Shaw, and everyone at Shaw Racing. All the members of my team, who give me the cars and the support I need to win. The fans who've stood by me through the good times and the bad. My friend and business partner, Dan LeMay of LeMay Resort in Lake Ozark, Missouri. And my new bride, Melissa, who keeps me on track in both my professional and my personal life."

"So would you say you're a happy man now, Tom?" the reporter asked just as he was pushed out of the way by another impatient microphone-holder.

Tom grinned as cameras flashed all around him. "I'm the happiest guy on earth. It's like celebrating Christmas all year long."

"Lucky man," he heard someone say behind him.

Lucky, indeed, he thought as Melissa slipped through

the crowd to join him with the same loving smile she had given him the week before, when he hadn't even finished the race. Theirs was a partnership that had nothing to do with championship points—and everything to do with living a dream.

* * * * *

Coming in February 2008...
Watch for IN HIGH GEAR by Gina Wilkins,
the launch book for Harlequin's 2008
officially licensed NASCAR series.

TAKING CONTROL
Ken Casper

To Pres Darby,
An endless source of ideas and inspiration
Thanks, friend

CHAPTER ONE

"CONGRATULATIONS, you are now each the proud owners of one-third of Satterfield Racing."

"Humph," Estelle Satterfield grumbled. "What could I possibly want with a race car? My Bentley is excellent transportation—"

"Not nearly as fast, though," her daughter, Ellie, reminded her.

"I assure you, darling, comfort and style are far more important than noise and speed."

Ellie wasn't so sure. Oh, she definitely liked her comforts. The last time she'd returned home to San Francisco she'd been forced to fly coach instead of first class and vowed never to do it again. As for style, well…there was style and there was style. She'd take Wally's Ferrari over her mother's Bentley any day, even if she wouldn't take Wallace Carmichael IV to have and to hold as her mother had so fervently wished. Estelle considered the quality of a man's cummerbund—silk was the preferred fabric, of course—far more important than its girth. In this case Ellie was thinking of Sylvester Agincourt, another one of her suitors. But she really didn't want to dwell on the Pillsbury Doughboy. Even if the dough part also referred to mountains of money.

"Race cars," Estelle huffed. "Your father liked them, too. I never could understand why. Noisy, dirty and driven by men to match. If your uncle wanted to leave us a legacy, why couldn't it be something more dignified or at least more marketable? A house. A tract of land perhaps. Stocks and bonds are always acceptable. But a race car! We'll probably have to pay someone to tow it to the junkyard."

For just a fleeting instant Ellie thought she spied an upturned curl at the edges of the family lawyer's thin mouth, but she must have been mistaken.

"How soon can you dispose of our interests in this *jalopy?*" Estelle asked him peevishly.

Rupert Hollingsworth pulled back his double chins as if he'd just been served with a subpoena to appear as a witness for the defense in the case against the Hollywood Madam.

"Estelle, really. Hollingsworth, Diddlemeyer and Hollingsworth is not a company of merchants. We don't broker business deals. Should you find a willing buyer, I will, of course, be most happy to draw up the contract and see to the legal details of transferring ownership—"

For a hefty fee, Ellie mused.

"But the sale of a NASCAR racing team," he continued, "must be placed in the hands of people…with those sorts of skills."

Ellie perked up. "Did you say NASCAR?"

"Satterfield Racing is currently competing, I understand, in the NASCAR NEXTEL Cup Series."

Ellie let out a low whistle, earning a scowl from her mother.

"Surely you know someone—" Estelle argued.

"Mother, leave this to me."

"Sweetheart, what would you possibly know about selling an auto racing…whatever?"

"Team," Ellie supplied impatiently. And the answer was *nothing,* at least at the moment, but she was a quick study, and if her instincts proved right, this could be a very lucrative undertaking.

"Really, how difficult can it be?" Ellie went on. "You seem to forget, Mother, that I just received my Masters of Business Administration from Harvard University."

"Of course you did, dear, and I'm very proud of you, but managing a Fortune 500 corporation and selling cars, a used car at that—" she shuddered in a very ladylike way "—are hardly the same."

Except Ellie hadn't been overwhelmed with tenders to manage any Fortune 500 companies. Okay, one of the management trainee offers she had received from a burger-and-shake franchise was part of a fast-food conglomerate on the Fortune 500 list, but that hardly counted. The position hadn't exactly been what she would call executive level at corporate headquarters, either. Or anywhere close. Well, their loss.

"We're talking business, Mother, something I happen to be well trained in, an expert, as a matter of fact."

"I really don't think—" Estelle started.

"Tell me the provisions of the will again, Mr. Hollingsworth."

The senior partner heaved his massive chest and settled deeper into his oversize leather swivel throne.

"Your uncle, Walter Wilson Satterfield, left one-half of his two-thirds interest in Satterfield Racing to each of you."

"Two-thirds?" Estelle questioned. "Who'd he leave the other third to?"

Hollingsworth didn't like being interrupted. "He didn't leave it to anyone, madam. He only owned two-thirds."

Estelle picked a speck of nonexistent lint from her black skirt. "Must have fallen on hard times then. Can't say I'm surprised. He used to own the whole…whatever you call it—"

"Team," Ellie supplied again. "How do you know that?"

"Of course, that was years ago," Estelle rambled on, "when John was still alive."

Ellie glanced over at the elegantly overdressed woman in the chair beside her. Estelle rarely mentioned Ellie's late father, but when she did, there was always a note of wistful sadness in her voice, as there was now. John Satterfield died when Ellie was only a year old, so she had no personal recollection of him, only a romanticized portrait in a silver frame of a handsome officer in uniform.

"Perhaps he was sole proprietor at one time," Hollingsworth advised her mother, clearly annoyed at having his explanation challenged. "But at the time of his death Walter Satterfield owned only two-thirds of Satterfield Racing."

"Do you know who owns the other third?" Ellie asked politely.

The attorney shuffled through the papers on his otherwise unencumbered desk, came to a sheet, held it up to examine it and announced, "One Aidan O'Keefe."

"Who's he?" Estelle demanded.

Hollingsworth further perused the paper. "He's apparently the driver of the race car they own, identified as number 555. The will is quite explicit. Any one of the three partners can sell his or her share of the racing team with the concurrence of one of the other partners."

Estelle looked mystified.

"Which means," Ellie elucidated, "Mother and I can agree to sell one or both of our shares with the concurrence of the other. Neither of us needs Mr. O'Keefe's permission or approval."

"Quite correct," Hollingsworth stated. "It also means one or both of you can agree to his selling his interest to a third party."

"Or to one of us," Ellie posed.

"Indeed, since selling to one of you implies an ipso facto two-thirds sanction of the transfer of title."

"I don't understand," Estelle said.

"I'll explain it to you later, Mother."

Estelle scowled but only for a second. She wasn't in the habit of dwelling on trifling details and was perfectly content to let her daughter—her beautiful and brilliant daughter—handle them.

Ellie tapped her right front tooth with the polished nail of her right index finger, a habit going back to childhood, which her mother positively abhorred. Estelle was about to remind her how distinctly undignified it was when Ellie spoke up.

"Do you know when Mr. O'Keefe bought into this partnership with my uncle?"

"I do not."

"Or why?"

The lawyer shook his head.

"Or for what amount?"

Again the attorney dismissed the question without an answer.

"Surely it wouldn't be worth much," Estelle volunteered. "Probably sold it for a case of beer."

Ellie chuckled. "More like a brewery, Mother. Seems

to me the last time I read about a NASCAR team sale it was for over twenty-five million dollars."

Estelle had a sudden and very unladylike coughing fit. "Did you use the word million after twenty-five?" she asked at last, her brown eyes as wide and gleeful as Ellie had ever seen them. "So that would mean each of our thirds is worth eight million, three hundred thirty-three thousand, three hundred…. Whew!"

It was amazing how adept at numbers the woman could be with the proper motivation. Ellie winked at the man behind the desk, and this time she was sure she saw him holding back a grin.

"It seems to me," Ellie said slowly, thoughtfully, "the person who would be most interested in buying us out is Mr. O'Keefe."

"Write him a letter," Estelle directed. "Call him immediately. Tell him we won't settle for a penny less than eight and a half million apiece."

"I'm going to do better than that, Mother," Ellie replied. "I'll go see him personally."

AIDAN O'KEEFE STOMPED on the gas as he rounded Turn Four. He leveled onto the front stretch, the checkered flag fluttering wildly before him.

Twenty-two cars zoomed under it ahead of him.

Coming in twenty-third probably wasn't a bad ending in a race fraught with problems from the start. A front tire blowout in lap twelve. At least he'd been able to maneuver through the spinout without crashing, in fact with hardly a scratch. A sixteen-second pit stop that had cost him four more positions. And last but not least, a carburetor problem three laps from the finish line that made him look like a

Sunday driver in a funeral cortege. Not that it made any difference by then.

He pulled onto pit road, applied his brakes. No hurry now. This race was over. Phoenix was history. One race left for the season. Miami. No way was he going to win the NASCAR NEXTEL Cup trophy this year, either. He just didn't have the points. He'd been hoping for a better showing, though. For Walter.

He missed the guy. The heart attack that felled him the day after Aidan won at Talladega had come as a complete surprise to everyone. Aidan rushed to the hospital as soon as he received word of his partner's collapse, but it was too late. The man who'd been like a father to him was already gone.

He pulled into the garage area. Mace Wagner was waiting for him as he rumbled to a stop, and from the expression on his crew chief's weathered face he wasn't any more pleased than Aidan was. Their next team meeting would be a long one.

"We let you down," Mace said, as Aidan coiled himself out of the car's window.

"Stuff happens."

"You drove a good race."

"We all did our best," Aidan replied.

The members of his team, all in orange-and-green uniforms similar to his own, took custody of the car. He knew they were listening and would be beating themselves up without his adding a sucker punch to their pride.

"Fulton stopped by a few minutes ago," Mace muttered.

"Tell him to go—"

"I did." They marched side by side toward the hauler. "Got a call from the office this afternoon. Apparently Walter's niece is coming to Charlotte on Tuesday."

"Didn't Shirley explain I won't be there, that I'll be going directly to Miami on Thursday?"

"She tried to, but this gal, Ellie Satterfield, insisted she'll be arriving at our headquarters on Tuesday and expects to be shown around, whether you're there or not."

"Whoa. Throwing her weight around already, huh?"

"Shirley said she was very pleasant, very polite, but also very specific about her expectations."

"How about her mother? Is she coming, too?" Aidan asked. "From what Walter said, she's the one who flies the broom."

"No, the daughter said she was coming alone. She did have Shirley book a suite for her, though, at the Hyatt."

Aidan considered having flowers delivered but changed his mind. Wouldn't want the scent to go to the princess's head.

CHAPTER TWO

ELLIE'S PLANE SAT on the tarmac at San Francisco International for three hours before receiving permission to take off. Then it was diverted to Chicago because of a hurricane brewing off the Gulf Coast. Instead of arriving at Charlotte Douglas International at five o'clock in the afternoon as originally scheduled, Ellie wasn't able to deplane until nearly midnight. Even at that hour the terminal was chaos as other passengers, who'd also been diverted or delayed, occupied every available seat and even camped out like a bunch of vagabonds on the floor. The baggage claims area was pure bedlam.

"Miss Ellie Satterfield, please meet your party at the lost-and-found office in the main baggage claims area. Miss Ellie Satterfield…"

Her party? Sherrill or Shauna or whoever it was she'd spoken to at Satterfield Racing on Sunday must have arranged for a limo to pick her up. And they'd kept track of her flight! Well, that was the first positive thing to happen today…or was it yesterday?

She scanned overhead for signs to lost and found, saw one for the restrooms and was tempted to head in that direction first. The driver would wait. That was what he was paid to do.

"Paging Miss Ellie Satterfield. Miss Ellie Satterfield, please meet…"

Okay, okay. She followed the sign to lost and found.

No chauffeur, just a guy standing there in a black T-shirt and snug jeans. He needed a shave, but he was sort of cute. Actually more than sort of and more than just cute. *Hot and dangerous.* Too bad she wasn't into scruffy.

She stepped up to a room crammed with luggage of every description and condition, taped boxes, snow skis—in Florida? The man behind the counter was short, shaped like a sagging dumpling, bald-headed and sweat-stained. He made Mr. Scruffy take on the aura of a movie star.

"Excuse me," she called out, but the attendant ignored her while he checked tag numbers against a crumpled form in his hand. "Hey, you paged me."

"Miss Satterfield?"

She whirled around to the voice behind her and came face-to-face with Mr. Scruffy Movie Star. He was only a few feet away now. Taller than she'd realized, sinewy muscled, and even better-looking up close. Gorgeous blue eyes and a mouth that made her want to lick her lips…or his.

"Yes?"

He extended his right hand. "I'm Aidan O'Keefe."

The race car driver? The other third of Satterfield Racing?

She realized his hand was still extended and placed hers in it. "Ellie Satterfield. I certainly didn't expect you to come out personally to meet me, Mr. O'Keefe, especially at this hour."

"Call me Aidan. I'll take you to your hotel."

"That won't be necessary. I requested a limo—"

"Well, sure, if you'd prefer to wait," he said, gazing at

her with those heavenly blue eyes, "I reckon we can get one here in, oh, an hour or so."

He was smiling at her. Or was it laughing? At this point she wasn't sure she cared. She just wanted to get out of this madhouse. Although it was an exceptionally attractive smile. Sexy as hell, actually.

"I apologize, Mr. O'Keefe. I'm tired and out of sorts. Thank you for coming to get me. It's very kind of you."

"Do you have baggage?"

"Yes, of course." She dipped into her purse and pulled out her first-class ticket folder. "Three pieces."

He offered her the crook of his elbow. "Let's go see if they made it in as good a shape as you did."

Was he flirting? Was he saying she looked good or the opposite? While she was cogitating that riddle, it seemed perfectly natural to tuck her hand under his arm.

Oh, my. He wasn't just easy on the eyes. The touch…the feel of those warm, hard muscles… They made her think of raw power, strenuous physical exertion. Rumpled sheets.

Now where the devil had that come from? She seemed to have lost her mind somewhere around thirty-five thousand feet.

As they wove their way through the streaming crowd to the baggage carousels, they passed the restrooms. She excused herself and pulled away. She was breathing hard, or maybe hardly breathing, as she darted inside, only to find standing room only.

She was forced to wait in line. By the time she reappeared in the noisy claims area a mob had formed by carousel B, where her luggage was supposed to be coming in. Trapped in the center of the crowd was Aidan O'Keefe.

Well, maybe trapped was the wrong word, because he certainly didn't appear to be either downcast or anxious to get away. In fact he was talking and laughing with the people around him and signing autographs on whatever they shoved at him—pieces of paper, tickets, baseball caps. One woman had him sign her handbag.

Ellie stole a glance at the carousel behind him and caught sight of her handcrafted Italian luggage disappearing behind the rubber curtain at the far end.

Great. At this rate she'd be here all night.

Aidan's eyes caught hers. He grinned, winked and shrugged his big, broad shoulders. She didn't know whether to sigh or cry.

Her luggage did another rotation while he continued to mingle with people. Another ten minutes crept by before he was able to make his escape.

"Sorry about that," he told Ellie. "It's hard to say no."

"Does that happen very often?"

"They don't usually recognize me when I'm wearing a long beard and dark glasses. Didn't think it would be necessary this late at night."

She was at a loss. Was he serious or was this all a big joke to him?

"Why don't you just say no?" she asked.

He appeared positively appalled at the suggestion. "Why would I do that? Without fans where would we be?"

Her oversize pieces of baggage burst out through the curtain at the other end of the moving conveyor belt.

"There they are." She pointed needlessly. The three matching pieces in dark leather were the only ones left.

He gaped at the size of them and snorted. "Are you visiting or relocating?"

Before she could answer he long-stepped to the moving conveyor and manhandled the trunk-sized pieces to solid ground. A porter appeared with a cart.

"Can I help you, Mr. O'Keefe?"

Aidan blew out a breath. "Like a ten-second pit stop."

A ten-second pit stop? What in the world did that mean?

A minute later they were exiting the lower level of the terminal. A shiny orange Corvette convertible with green speed stripes glowed under the glare of nighttime floodlights. Another porter hovered nearby, obviously standing guard.

"Thanks, Lou. Appreciate your help." Aidan tucked some bills discreetly into the man's hand.

"Anytime, Mr. O'Keefe. My, she sure is a beauty."

For a moment Ellie thought he was referring to her and was about to take offense at his impertinence.

"New?"

"Got her a couple of months ago," Aidan replied.

He frowned over his shoulder at the luggage cart, confirming what he'd already deduced inside—there was no way these behemoths would fit in or on his car.

He peeled another bill from the roll he took from his pocket and handed it to the porter wrestling with the dolly.

"Load them in a taxi, will you, Frank, and have them delivered to the Hyatt. Tell the driver I'll meet him there."

"You bet, Mr. O'Keefe." He pushed toward the taxi stand.

Meanwhile the man who'd been serving picket duty opened the passenger door of the Corvette for Ellie and extended a hand to assist her into it.

Self-consciously she accepted it and dropped down into the very low, cream-colored leather bucket seat. While she reached for the seat belt, Aidan circled the front of the car, grabbed the top of the windshield and threw a long, denim-clad leg over the side and slid behind the wheel.

The porter closed Ellie's door, and Aidan turned the key that was already in the ignition. The engine roared to life, the smooth, rich, intimidating sound reverberating off the concrete walls and overhang.

Aidan waved to the porter and, without perceptibly checking his rearview mirrors, darted out into moving traffic. Ellie expected to hear horn blasts of protest, but he'd executed the maneuver so smoothly and efficiently no one objected. A moment later he shot left, around the van in front of them. It seemed to Ellie in no more than the blink of an eye they were on the open road.

She wasn't sure if she should protest his recklessness or just sit back and enjoy the ride. She opted for the latter.

OKAY, HE WAS SHOWING OFF, but Ellie Satterfield was having that effect on him. Damn, the picture Shirley had been able to scare up on the Internet of Ellie in cap and gown didn't look anything like her. Not much, anyway.

The short tawny hair was about right, but he hadn't realized her eyes were nearly the same golden amber. Like none he'd ever seen. And the gown she'd been wearing in the graduation photo gave no hint of the curvaceous figure beneath its folds.

A bit stuck-up, but he'd expected that. If Walter's description of her mother was close to accurate, the old lady was a harridan. Ellie had tried aloof disdain when she'd seen the 'Vette, but Aidan hadn't missed the fascination twinkling in her eyes before she'd taken control of her expression.

He hadn't missed the intriguing way her body tensed

up, either, when he goosed the gas pedal and shot into traffic. Or the tiny grin she tried so hard to suppress when he shifted into high gear and pulled away from the pack.

He continued to wend his way through traffic, then tapped the brakes as they approached downtown. Not many cars on the streets after midnight in the middle of the week, but traffic lights still stopped him.

She was surveying the scene, taking it all in.

"Ever been to Charlotte before?"

"No." She continued to rubberneck. Actually, he decided, it was a very nice neck. Long enough to be elegant.

"Ever been to a NASCAR race?"

She met his eyes this time, and he wondered what it would take to melt that brown sugar. "No, I haven't, Mr. O'Keefe."

"Aidan, remember? If we're going to be partners I think we can do so on a first-name basis. My condolences on the loss of your uncle."

That stopped the protest or whatever she was about to say.

"Thank you." She gazed straight ahead.

"He was a good man, one of the finest I've ever known."

She turned her head away, clearly uncomfortable with his remark.

The light turned green. Instead of stomping on the gas this time, he gently accelerated forward.

Less than three minutes later they were pulling into the driveway of her hotel. He halted under the canopy, catapulted himself over the door onto the pavement and rounded the front of the shiny sports car. A valet was already bending to open her door. She hadn't made an effort to open it herself, Aidan noted.

He tipped the valet, told him about the taxi that was following with the luggage and asked to be paged as soon as it arrived.

"Sure thing, Mr. O'Keefe. The minute it gets here."

Ellie had stood by. He took her gently by the elbow and escorted her toward the revolving door.

"Does everyone in town know you by name?" she asked.

"Probably not everyone," he admitted.

She glanced over at him again, not completely sure if he was serious.

He'd confirmed her suite reservation earlier, and the same clerk was still on duty, so there was no problem getting Miss Ellie Satterfield checked in.

"The lounge is still open," he said. "Would you like a nightcap while we're waiting for your things to get here?"

She let out a breath. "I think I could use one."

The cocktail lounge was empty, the bartender getting ready to close—until he saw them walk in.

"Evening, Mr. O'Keefe. Ma'am. What can I get you folks?"

Since he was driving, Aidan ordered a soft drink. Ellie inquired what white wines they had available, selected a label Aidan had never heard of and watched as the cork was pulled from the bottle.

He was about to ask if she ever got tired of being a prima donna when he was saved from the gaffe by the doorman announcing that the luggage had arrived. He left her, paid the taxi driver and had the bellhop take the three huge pieces up to her suite. She must have paid a king's ransom, or rather a princess's, in overweight charges, he mused. He stopped off at his car for a moment before returning to the bar. Coming in behind his new partner, he took his time, using the extra seconds to appreciate the view.

He also noted that half the wine in her glass was already gone and realized from the slope of her shoulders how exhausted she must be. He stepped up beside her stool, reported her baggage had been safely delivered, took a healthy swallow of his soda and placed the thick manila envelope he'd retrieved from his car on the bar beside her.

"I figured you'd want to review our financial status," he said, "so there are our last three annual reports, as well as our most recent audit."

She nodded. "Thank you."

He tossed a large bill on the bar. "I'll have someone pick you up in the morning at ten," he told her, "and bring you out to Satterfield Racing. We'll be going to the track, as well, so wear something casual with long sleeves. Oh, and comfortable shoes that are closed-toe. We take safety very seriously."

She extended her hand. "Thank you for picking me up and attending to everything, Aidan. You've been very kind."

Her hand was cool from her wineglass and slightly damp. But that didn't disguise the softness of her skin or the firmness of her grip.

"My pleasure, Ellie."

As they held each other's hands he had an urge to lean over and kiss her. On the cheek.

But he resisted.

CHAPTER THREE

As EXHAUSTED AS ELLIE WAS from the cross-country flight and light-headed from the single glass of wine she'd had in the lounge—at least she supposed it was the wine that had made her that way—she slept poorly. She kept picturing Aidan O'Keefe in jeans and T-shirt and the way both garments clung to his well-toned body. She kept recalling, too, the warmth of firm muscle when she accepted his arm.

In the sitting room of her suite she finished her croissant and poured more coffee from the silver pot room service had delivered, then she glanced at her watch. A quarter to ten. She'd reviewed the documents Aidan had furnished her and was pleased with what she'd found, assuming of course the reports were accurate. She could page through them again while she waited to be notified that her driver had arrived, but she decided not to.

She wasn't pleased with her performance the previous evening. She'd played a snoot—played it well, of course—but that had been the wrong approach. She might represent the controlling two-thirds of Satterfield Racing, but there was no point in alienating the other third.

Aidan, in contrast, had been easygoing, generous and considerate, and she'd treated him like hired help. It was unfair and decidedly didn't reflect well on her.

Shaking her head at her uncharacteristic lack of good judgment, she rose, went to the bathroom, brushed her teeth, patted her hair, adjusted the waistband of her slim jeans and returned to the living room. Giving herself one last appraisal in the full-length mirror by the door, she picked up her small shoulder purse, made sure she had her key card and left the suite.

No games today, she vowed, as she rode down in the elevator. Today was business. She had a multimillion-dollar enterprise to evaluate.

She was startled when she stepped into the lobby and found Aidan O'Keefe sitting in an upholstered armchair, long legs crossed, reading a newspaper.

He glanced up and a smile spread across his face. "Good morning."

No five o'clock shadow—or she supposed she could call it his midnight shadow—and without the dark whiskers the cleft in his chin was even more pronounced. Scruffy hadn't really been all that bad, but she decided she still preferred his naked skin. As the mental choice of words conjured up other images, heat began to flow into her cheeks.

"I thought you were sending someone else." Maybe it hadn't been the wine last evening after all, because that certainly wouldn't explain her slightly dizzy feeling right now.

"Everybody was busy," he replied easily, "so I thought I'd pick you up myself."

"Do NASCAR drivers normally moonlight as chauffeurs?"

He laughed, and the deep, male, rumbling sound stirred a fresh twitter in her midsection.

Uncrossing his legs—pressed jeans this morning and lace-up work boots—he dropped the newspaper on the table beside his chair and rose to his feet. "Shall we?"

He didn't offer his arm this time, which was disappointing but maybe just as well. She had to focus on things other than this man's muscles. They moved side by side toward the door and the bright orange Corvette parked at the curb just beyond it.

"Nice outfit," he said, as he held the door for her. "That green color brings out the gold in your eyes."

She was stunned, not just by the compliment, but by its specificity. This race car driver was more observant than she'd given him credit for. "It's teal," she said, then added, "and thank you."

He did the gentlemanly thing again and held the car door for her, but this time the courtesy annoyed her, not because he'd done it but because she'd let him. She wasn't a delicate blossom who had to be coddled, and the sooner he realized that the better.

The trip to Satterfield Racing was different from the ride from the airport the night before. Traffic was heavier, which meant more opportunities for him to weave in and out, but she was also better prepared for his driving skills now. Last night her reaction had been anxiety. This morning it was excitement.

She also had a better chance in the bright daylight, sunglasses in place, to check the guy out. She definitely liked what she saw. The elegant profile. His nose was aquiline and stately, but not overlarge. Somehow she'd missed the dimple in his right cheek last night. Now she found it fascinating. Then there was the athletic body, the dark hair. He, too, was wearing sunglasses, but she hadn't missed his eyes before he'd put them on. Last night they'd seemed darker. This morning they were mountain-lake blue.

By the time he pulled up in front of a modern, three-story, concrete-and-glass edifice beyond city limits, she decided she might as well forget everything her mother had ever told her about stock car racing. This was no greasy, ramshackle garage.

Aidan switched off the engine and as usual hopped over the door. It was hard not to stare at those long, denim-covered legs as she fumbled with her door handle. She had the door open—to make sure he understood she wasn't helpless—by the time he reached her side. She probably should have ignored his outstretched hand to help her out of the low seat, but…well, that would have been impolite. Besides, he was so close, she couldn't possibly avoid him. She slipped her hand into his, only to find her pulse quicken when he pulled her up. Suddenly they were standing face-to-face, mere inches apart. For a moment they froze in place, eye contact masked by their sunglasses.

Unnerved by his closeness, she had to force herself to swivel her head and look around.

The grounds were well maintained. The continuous rows of dark-tinted windows sparkled. The sign that identified the building as the headquarters of Satterfield Racing was prominently displayed and tastefully designed.

Just beyond the automatic, sliding tinted-glass doors was a reception counter, neatly decorated with colorful pamphlets and brochures, single-page handouts and fliers and a variety of decals. An attractively dressed woman of perhaps thirty-five sat behind the counter on a stool.

"Morning, Aidan."

"Morning, Nell. Nell, this is Ellie Satterfield, Walter's niece."

The woman's professional smile of welcome warmed, and she extended her hand.

"I'm real glad to meet you, Miss Satterfield. Your uncle was a wonderful man. We all miss him a whole lot. If there's anything I can do, you just let me know."

"Thank you," Ellie said, removing her glasses.

Aidan did the same and led her around the counter to the main lobby that had all the hallmarks of a museum. Stock cars formed a row down the middle and glass cases containing all sorts of items lined the walls. Uniforms, helmets, hats, gloves, emblems, along with mysterious pieces of equipment, which Ellie assumed were automotive parts. Written explanations accompanied most of them. In one corner was a video-viewing module.

Aidan pointed to a gaudily decaled stock car that gleamed under high-intensity pin lights. She knew it was a Monte Carlo only because the name was boldly emblazoned on the hood.

"That was my first car in the NASCAR Busch Series. It's been restored, of course. And that—" he motioned to a crumpled mess of distorted steel a few yards away "—was my first NASCAR NEXTEL Cup car." He grinned. "It obviously hasn't been restored. I flipped twice and rolled four times in that baby."

"My God," she exclaimed. "How badly were you hurt?"

"Hurt?" He shook his head. "Walked away without a scratch."

"I don't believe you."

He stanched the impulse to take offense at being called a liar. Instead he laughed and moved on.

They arrived at a steel door with a wire-mesh safety-glass window.

"This is where the real work gets done."

He used an electronic key card to open it. They were immediately greeted with the clang of metal being hammered, the shrill scream of pneumatic tools and a medley of smells—lubricants, electrical ozone and hot rubber.

Yet the bay she stepped into could have been a car showroom. The spotless floor was painted a shiny, light gray, and the fluorescent fixtures suspended from the steel rafters overhead flooded the high-ceilinged room with daylight brightness. After a few moments she realized the people she saw in clean white jumpsuits were actually working under the hoods. Nearby were tall, shiny red square containers on casters. Giant toolboxes with a myriad of doors and drawers.

Aidan introduced her to a man of about forty-five with a square face and ruddy complexion. Unlike the others, he was dressed in chinos and a long-sleeved collared cotton shirt of orange and green, which she now recognized as the team colors.

"Ellie, this is Mace Wagner, my crew chief. He's the guy who does all the work and gives me most of the glory."

Mace extended a warm, meaty hand. "Please to meet you, Ms. Satterfield. My condolences on the loss of your uncle. We thought the world of that man around here."

Over the following two hours Aidan and Mace walked her through a series of shops where they built stock cars, which, she soon learned, were not stock at all but meticulously crafted custom creations that only resembled the cars they were named after. Even then, she soon learned, appearances could be deceiving. They had no doors, no head- or taillights, and to her amazement, no speedometers or gas gauges.

As she observed men, and a few women, going about their work, she found herself drawn in, intrigued and fascinated by what they were doing, and it occurred to her that for none of these people was it a job. More like a proud calling.

She measured, too, their responses to Aidan O'Keefe. They liked the man, welcomed his company. She understood why. He was laid-back, a man without affectations or pretenses.

"SHARP WOMAN," Mace remarked when, a few minutes after noon, Ellie excused herself to use the ladies' room.

She may have come across as a spoiled brat the night before, but this morning, Aidan had to admit, she was a businesswoman who asked intelligent questions and listened attentively to the answers.

"Have you gotten down to the nitty-gritty yet?"

Aidan shook his head. "I gave her our financial reports and audit to review last night. She hasn't said if she has. It was pretty late and she'd had a long day, so maybe she hasn't."

"I wouldn't waste any time," Mace said. "You can be sure Fulton won't. And if she's as eager to sell as we suspect, she'll probably take the first offer that comes along."

Aidan disagreed. "She may be a spoiled rich girl, but she's not stupid. She'll play us off against each other."

"Which is a good reason for getting on her good side and staying there. Can I make a suggestion?"

"Fire away. At this point I'll consider anything. Well, almost anything. If you want me to kiss Fulton…"

"Please," Mace responded with a gagging sound. "It's lunchtime and I need my sustenance." He patted his belly, which was considerably wider than Aidan's. "No, what I'm going to suggest is a lot more palatable."

Aidan regarded him expectantly.

"Kiss Ellie."

"What?" Aidan stammered. "What the deuce are you talking about?"

"Well, kiss up to her. She's hot for you, Aidan. You probably haven't seen the way she looks at you, but I can tell you everybody else around here has."

"You're crazy." *Kiss Ellie.* The notion had crossed his mind the evening before. A silly impulse which he had nobly resisted.

Mace laughed. "More like she's crazy for being turned on by a goober like you, but she is. Take advantage of it. Woo her."

"Woo her? Have you started reading nineteenth-century romance novels or something?"

"I'm telling you she's got the hots for you, my friend. Okay, so maybe you don't have to bed her, though why you wouldn't—" he caught Aidan's chastising expression and retreated "—but you can certainly share some time with her."

"I've got a race to run and a daughter to raise," Aidan objected, "or have you forgotten those little details?"

"Why do they have to be mutually exclusive?"

"I'm not using my daughter—"

"I'm not suggesting you do. You know I'd never do that. What I am saying is spend as much time with Ellie as you can. Get to know her. Overwhelm her with your considerable charm, such as it is. Let her get to know you…and Annie. The better she likes you the less inclined she'll be to sell us out from under you."

Aidan wasn't pleased with the notion, but he had to admit it had merit. Not the part about wooing her but about being friendly, letting her see more of the human side of the business.

As for kissing her…

CHAPTER FOUR

AT THE END of the morning's tour, Aidan took Ellie up to the fancy office that had been her uncle's. He didn't tell her Walter hardly ever spent time there; he'd always been more interested in hanging around in the garage area or the pits. She met Shirley, who had been Walter's secretary for nearly twenty years, and who'd made Ellie's hotel reservation.

"This afternoon we'll go out to the track," Aidan told her. "You can watch practice laps."

"Good." She nodded. "I'd like that."

"And if you're interested, I can arrange for a demo ride."

The eyes of the cool socialite and businesswoman lit up like a kid seeing her first Christmas tree. "Really?"

He liked the gleam he saw, wondered what else might provoke that excitement. Funny how good the notion of eliciting it again made him feel.

Shirley had already called out for half a dozen sandwiches and now offered Ellie and Aidan first choice, saying she and the girls from accounting would split what was left.

Ellie selected the provolone and Black Forest ham, while Aidan went for the turkey-and-bacon club with

Swiss on sourdough. They ate off the paper wrappers in the maple-paneled office. Not the style to which his new partner was probably accustomed, he quickly surmised. Welcome to the world of racing.

"How long did you know my uncle?" she asked after wiping her mouth with a coarse brown paper napkin.

"Almost fourteen years. I was fifteen when he came to give a speech at the juvenile center where I was residing at the time. We talked afterward, and the following weekend he received permission to take me to a race he was sponsoring."

She eyed him, not sure if he was pulling her leg. "Why were you in a juvenile center?"

"My old man beat me one time too many and I ran away. Refused to go back to live with him and the lush he'd married after my mom died."

She took another bite of her sandwich. Crunched into the dill pickle, sipped her sweet tea, all the time avoiding eye contact with him.

"He was real proud of you," Aidan told her. "Harvard Business School. Top of the class."

"Third, actually."

"Close enough. I got my GED. Never went to college. But then, neither did he. Called himself the black sheep of the family."

"I'm sorry I never met him."

"You didn't?"

"Maybe when I was very young, but I don't remember."

"I figured since he and your mother were such close friends—"

"Friends? What are you talking about?"

"The cruises they took together every year."

She stared across the desk at him. "I really don't know what you're talking about. My mother didn't take any cruises with him."

He seemed to consider her reply. "She didn't take a Caribbean cruise every January?"

That caught her unawares and instantly put her on the defensive. "I don't think what my mother does is any of your business, Mr. O'Keefe."

He chuckled with amusement. "Ah, so it's back to Mr. O'Keefe, is it?" He bit into his sandwich to hide his smile. Apparently Estelle Satterfield had been keeping a secret.

Ellie's tawny eyes narrowed as she stared at him. "What you said about them taking cruises together…that's not true."

"Maybe you ought to ask your mother why your uncle left his racing team to her and you, since neither of you have ever come to a race."

She didn't respond.

They continued eating their sandwiches in frosty silence.

"Did you get a chance to review the papers I gave you last night?" he asked a few minutes later.

She nodded. "The team seems to be in very sound financial condition," she commented and almost added, *if the reports are accurate,* but decided questioning his veracity again would probably not be a good idea. "How long have you been a partner?"

"Three years."

"So the documents you furnished me are only since you've been involved."

He nodded. "Shirley can dig the earlier reports out of the archives if you want to examine them. I just grabbed what was most current and readily available."

"Is it standard practice for a driver to also be an owner?" she asked.

"It's not unheard of, but I wouldn't call it standard."

"So how did you come to be my uncle's partner?"

"Walter was a great guy, but he wasn't always a diligent businessman." At her wide-eyed expression, he held up his hand. "Nothing illegal or underhanded. I don't mean to imply that. Though the Internal Revenue Service did consider his failure to cross their palms with silver at the appropriate intervals to be a federal offense. But he wasn't trying to break any law or evade taxes. He just forgot to keep his accountant informed in a timely matter of some of his transactions, so when the tax bills arrived he didn't always have the cash on hand to appease them."

"Why would you enter into a partnership with someone who was so careless?"

"Because he was a good friend who needed help, and because I wanted to drive a stock car in the NASCAR NEXTEL Cup Series, and he happened to have one available. I did get him to agree to let someone else manage his money."

"You?"

Aidan laughed. "I have enough to do driving cars and raising my daughter, thank you very much."

He had a daughter? How about a wife? He wasn't wearing a ring.

"I wasn't about to play daddy to a man who was old enough to be my father," Aidan continued. "The last thing I wanted was to let money get in the way of our friendship. One of the accountants at the firm managed his checkbook for him."

"I presume an examination of the books will tell me how much you paid for your third interest."

He grinned at her. "Or you could just ask me."

She queried him with her eyes.

"One million dollars."

From reading the statements she knew Aidan hadn't been paid nearly that much cumulatively by the team in the past three years, but her personal research before coming out here disclosed that drivers earned substantially larger amounts from sponsors for promotions and guest appearances. Aidan could easily have made two or three times that sum in any one year.

She'd also calculated the team was worth considerably more than three million dollars, even assuming it had been debt-ridden at the time Aidan bought in. She estimated its current net worth to be anywhere from twenty-five to thirty million dollars.

"You bought cheap," she finally said.

"No question about it," Aidan replied, then smiled. "But Walter made me an offer I couldn't refuse."

"How much did he owe in back taxes?"

"About half that. He also had a couple of loans he was in danger of falling delinquent on that he wanted to clear up."

"You don't feel any remorse for taking advantage of him?"

Aidan stopped eating and raised his eyebrows. His beautiful blue eyes drilled into her. "Feel remorse?"

She kept chewing, though she wasn't sure she would be able to swallow.

"No, Ms. Satterfield," he said stiffly, "I don't feel remorse. He came to me and offered me a third of Satterfield Racing for a million dollars, if I could come up with the cash within thirty days. You don't have to believe me, but I asked him if it was enough, if he wanted or needed more. He said no, that he would eventually have given me a piece of the action anyway."

He crunched into a pickle. "Whether I took advantage of your uncle in a weak moment isn't the issue. It's history. Besides, I have enough witnesses who will testify that the deal was made freely and willingly. The relevant matter now is that you're here to sell Satterfield Racing." To the highest bidder.

"Is there something wrong with that?" she challenged.

Not wrong, he reflected, *just sad that Walter Satterfield's niece doesn't give a damn about something that played such a central role in his life.*

"There's nothing wrong with selling," he conceded, "if it's to the right buyer."

"And that would be you, I suppose."

Whatever he said would sound defensive, so he didn't say anything.

She continued to eat, while he studied her intently.

"I'm willing to offer you or your mother eight million dollars for one of your shares."

She shook her head. "We're not interested in splitting our ownership or giving up control. Both shares must be sold together."

In principle that suited him. There was only the little matter of cash on hand.

"How much?" he asked.

She closed her eyes and took a deep breath, as if there were no hurry. "I've studied the financial statements you gave me, Aidan, as well as the market. Twenty million."

It was too much, of course, and being the crafty businesswoman she at least thought she was, she didn't really expect to get that amount. But she wasn't being outrageous, only high, in her demand. They would eventually come to an agreement closer to what he expected to pay, and that gave him hope.

He shrugged sympathetically. "You won't get it, Ellie. I can sweeten my offer a little, but not that much. I'm willing to go to seventeen."

She was trying not to show overt interest, so she took another bite of her sandwich, chewed and swallowed before answering.

"I'll present the offer to my mother. If she's willing to accept, how soon could we conclude the deal?"

Here was the tricky part. "As you might expect I haven't got that kind of cash available right now, but by the end of the upcoming season—"

"Next season? That's a year off. I— We don't want to wait that long."

"We can sign a contract right now for seventeen million. I'll give each of you one million dollars down, the balance payable at the end of next season."

"And if you haven't raised the money by then?"

"You keep the million. Or we can negotiate a new contract."

He could see the wheels turning in her head.

"No," she said firmly. "Nineteen now, not next year."

She was backing off on the price. That was a start, but the time was the real issue. "Do you have other offers?"

"That's none of your business."

Which meant she didn't. But she would soon. Mitch Fulton hadn't gotten to her yet, but he would. Aidan didn't know if Fulton could come up with that kind of money immediately, but he might, and if he did, Aidan would be a goner.

"It is my business, Ellie. I have a vested interest in this team. I can't prevent you from selling to a higher bidder, but I have a right to know what I'm up against."

"Not legally," she pointed out.

She was right on that score. There was also the question of what constituted a higher bid. How did one calculate the value of a year, for example, especially if the market changed significantly during that period?

"I do morally, Ellie," he countered, "and that's more important."

She didn't respond.

"When you get another offer," he said, "let me know what it is and I'll do my best to meet or beat it. You can't get any fairer than that."

He gathered up the soiled wrappers and napkins, stuffed them into the paper bag they'd come in and deposited it in the wastepaper basket.

"Ready to go to the track?" he asked.

CHAPTER FIVE

HER FIRST INSTINCT was to curl into a fetal position and cover her ears.

Aidan handed her a headset and said something, but she couldn't make out the words above the unbearable roar of shrill engines screaming by, rattling every bone and joint in her body.

Gently he adjusted them on her head, closeting her ears. The din receded, not completely, but it was muted now, at a bearable distance.

"Better?" It took a moment for her to realize the voice was coming through the earpieces.

She nodded and the weight of the headset almost made it fall off.

Aidan, watching her, smiled. "You'll get used to them in no time."

She doubted it, but rather than disagree, she nodded again, more cautiously this time, and caught herself smiling back.

He proceeded to explain to her what she was seeing.

"These are test laps to evaluate a car's performance. We'll make adjustments based on the driver's analysis. Then, when we get to the track in Miami, I'll do my practice laps, and we'll make more."

"Haven't you raced there before?"

"Many times, but conditions are always changing. Track surfaces develop grooves, ruts. Or they may have been repaved since the last time I drove there. Sometimes they change the banking on curves and straightaways. Weather conditions also affect an engine's performance and a car's handling. Plus, this is a different car from the one I drove there last year."

He proceeded to explain about all the different adjustments they could make to the car based on conditions, loosening and tightening the suspension, changing tire pressures. She'd never considered herself mechanically inclined or interested, but listening to Aidan so enthusiastically describe the nuances of shock absorbers and springs, track bars and sway bars, she found it all suddenly fascinating.

Several men rolled out the shiny demo car, which resembled every other race car on the track in that it sported team colors. This one was emblazoned with the Satterfield logo, but it had no car number. Closer inspection disclosed an even bigger difference. This car had a passenger seat.

She should be afraid to climb through the window into this thing, and maybe she was just a little. *Maybe, too, fear added to the excitement. Or…it could have been the driver.*

"Will you be driving?"

"If you want me to."

She nodded. "Yes."

"Come on, then."

SHE WAS NERVOUS—he'd be worried if she weren't—but she followed directions meticulously without complaint. Her hands shook slightly as she put on the gloves he gave her, and she bit her lip—he was sure without realizing she was doing it. She didn't chatter, just concentrated on what she was doing.

"If at any point you want me to stop, just tell me," he instructed her.

He looked over at her, strapped snuggly into the passenger seat, and he realized she was at least as excited about this ride as she was apprehensive about it.

He slipped into First gear and let out the clutch with his left foot. Following track rules, he moved slowly and carefully between the garages, rolled past the low wall separating the garage area from the pits, turned left onto pit road, received the go-ahead through his headset and glided down the line to the entrance onto the track proper.

"Here we go."

He rammed his right foot to the floor.

The g-force pressure of acceleration flattened them against the backs of their seats. He glanced over. Ellie had her hands at her sides, gripping the seat in pure terror, then he saw the corners of her mouth twist into a grin.

They did three laps before she said anything.

"How fast are we going?"

"About one-fifty."

"Is that all?"

He chuckled and pressed down on the right pedal.

"One-sixty," he announced.

"You said you normally cruise at one-eighty."

"In a race."

"Will this car go that fast?"

He was enjoying this, enjoying her unexpected appetite for speed. "It will if I tell it to."

"Tell it to," she urged.

He laughed and flattened the pedal to the floor.

"Wow!" she said, not even trying to hide her wide-eyed grin.

He drove more laps, taking turns wide and tight, high and low, before finally pulling onto pit road again.

Back in the garage area his crew helped her through the window on her side of the car. She was astounded to discover she was wobbly legged, but he wasn't surprised. In a little while, when the adrenaline faded from her bloodstream, she'd be so weak she'd be worried she'd injured herself.

"Thank you," she said. "That was…fantastic."

"You're welcome."

Something happened when they made eye contact this time. It was a strange sensation, as if for that twinkling of time they had ceased to be two people. A second later the connection was broken, but the bond wasn't. He took her hand, led her aside, out of the hub of activity, and they talked about NASCAR. Later he wondered what he had said, what she had said, if she herself knew. A change had taken place. He couldn't define it, but whatever it was made him feel good.

LATER THAT AFTERNOON Ellie was in Mace Wagner's office getting a rundown on his staff, what they did and how they were organized and compensated, when her cell phone went off. She expected it to be her mother wanting to know when she could expect her multimillion-dollar check. The image made Ellie smile. Estelle wasn't as bubbleheaded as she acted, but there was no doubt she liked money—or more precisely, spending it.

Viewing the caller ID, however, the name that appeared on her screen wasn't her mother's. Without realizing she was doing it—a sign undoubtedly of fatigue after her stress hormone–pumping ride with Aidan—she muttered the name: Mitch Fulton.

The instantaneous wave of hostility that washed across the desk from the crew chief put her nerves immediately on edge.

She answered the phone. Fulton identified himself and, wasting no time on small talk, requested they meet at her earliest convenience.

"About what?" she asked. Sitting across from her, Mace made no pretense of not listening, nor did he offer to leave the room to give her privacy.

"I'd rather wait until I see you to go into details," Fulton replied.

"I'm not asking for details, Mr. Fulton. All I'm asking is what you want to see me about."

"Perhaps you don't know who I am. I—"

"You own Q Racing. But you still haven't answered my question. Why do you want to see me?"

"To discuss the sale of Satterfield Racing, of course."

The announcement came as no surprise. "I'll be leaving in the morning for Miami. Perhaps after the race, on Monday."

"I'd prefer not to delay this conversation that long. Would it be possible for us to get together this evening? Someplace private."

She waited a beat before answering. "I'm staying at the Hyatt. If you can be there at eight this evening, we can meet in my suite. Will that be convenient?"

"That'll be fine," he said.

The conversation ended, Ellie closed her phone and slipped it into her handbag.

"There are a few things you need to know, Ms. Satterfield, before you meet with Mitch Fulton," Mace said, clearly tight-jawed.

She sought a more comfortable position in the stiff-backed visitor's chair and took a fortifying breath. "Fill me in."

"If you sell Satterfield Racing to Fulton, Aidan will be the first to go."

"You mean fired? Why would Fulton do that? Aidan's the team's star."

"Because Fulton hates O'Keefe, has for years, and has been waiting for a chance to get back at him."

"For what? I don't understand."

"Jenny, Aidan's late wife. The three of them, Aidan, Mitch, and Jenny went to high school together. Aidan and Mitch were both racing dragsters back then. Jenny was going with Mitch at the time, until one race when he got caught cheating. She dropped him and started dating Aidan. Mitch continued to get in trouble and a few years later was suspended from racing for an entire season. Meanwhile Aidan advanced to the NASCAR Busch Series and finally the NASCAR NEXTEL Cup Series. By then Mitch had inherited a pile of money from his rich daddy, bought into Q Racing and eventually forced the original owner, Quint Quintana, out.

"Three years ago Jenny was diagnosed with terminal cancer. There was a new drug available the doctors suggested trying. Aidan was desperate for anything that might save her, so he and Jenny agreed she should take it, but it was too late. She died a month later. Mitch blamed Aidan, claiming that by forcing her to take an unproven, experimental drug he accelerated her death. It wasn't true. You never saw two people more in love than Aidan and Jenny...."

"That's terrible," Ellie said. "And Mitch would fire Aidan if he had a chance."

"In a New York minute. Not that he'd get a chance. If Fulton takes over Satterfield Racing, Aidan will walk."

AT TWO MINUTES TO EIGHT that evening Ellie's hotel phone rang. The clerk at the desk announced Mr. Fulton was there to see her. Since her suite was on the concierge level and required key access in the elevator, permission was required before a bellhop would bring him up.

The digital clock on the mantel over the gas log in the fireplace showed exactly eight when her doorbell rang.

Mitch Fulton appeared slightly older and grayer in person than he did in his professionally touched-up portrait on the Q Web site. He handed the bellhop a tip and greeted her.

"Please come in." Ellie's voice was flat.

After the door was closed they shook hands. She led him from the small foyer to the living room and offered him a choice of drinks from the bar or coffee from the tray room service had delivered five minutes earlier. He declined both.

He was taller than she'd expected and leaner, almost too angular to be considered good-looking. As they sat on opposing couches in front of the fireplace, Ellie noted he had large hands with long, straight fingers. He was dressed in a suit, probably an Armani.

"Since you know who I am," he said, in the pleasantly modulated voice she remembered from the phone, "I don't have to give you a long-winded introduction, and I'll get right to the point."

She nodded.

"I'd like to buy Satterfield Racing from you and your mother."

"You already have Q Racing, which has teams in both the Busch and NEXTEL Series," she said. "Why acquire another team?"

"Growth. It's the nature of business to expand."

"That's a true enough statement, but it doesn't tell me anything. Why Satterfield Racing?"

"I should think it would be fairly obvious. Because it's available."

"And you're sure we want to sell."

The thin smile that appeared on his lips came close to a smirk, but it disappeared almost as quickly as it had appeared. His eyes met hers unflinchingly.

"Please don't take me for a fool, Ms. Satterfield. I know that in all the years your uncle owned Satterfield Racing neither you nor your mother ever attended a single race. You've come here as an ingenue, ignorant of even the most rudimentary facts about NASCAR. You and your mother now own the controlling interest in a racing team, but neither of you has the least desire, much less the expertise, necessary to manage it successfully. You're here to sell, and you want the best price you can get for what you see as a commodity."

Ellie's breath caught in her throat, and it was only by the greatest force of will that she kept from lowering her gaze.

She should throw him out. The crack about being an ingenue—an artless innocent, an actress playing a part—both offended her and frightened her. Mitch Fulton hadn't raised his voice. In fact his tone throughout his brief diatribe, all the facts of which had been completely correct, had been downright friendly, and that only seemed to make him more intimidating.

"Touché, Mr. Fulton." She resisted the urge to laugh nervously, smiling with narrowed eyes instead.

"You and your mother will undoubtedly entertain other offers. When you have received what you consider to be the best one, call me and I'll top it."

He clearly wanted Satterfield Racing every bit as much as Mace had said he would. She wondered if she should mention Aidan and perhaps make a stipulation that he was not to be fired. But this was, after all, a business decision, not a sentimental one. Besides, she couldn't stop Aidan from quitting.

"That's a generous offer, Mr. Fulton, and a dangerous one. You could find yourself paying a highly inflated price."

His smile this time intimated how naive she was. "Not if I'm dealing with someone of integrity. It's also acceptable practice in a case like this to see such a bid in writing. Naturally, if I had any doubt of the sincerity of the offer I would verify that the other party had the wherewithal to follow through on it."

The man certainly knew how to insult with finesse.

"Just so there is no misunderstanding, Ms. Satterfield, I am prepared to pay one million dollars in cash over your highest offer for all rights to Satterfield Racing. All rights means just that. Upon signing the contract of sale and electronically transferring the money to the account or accounts of your choice, onshore or off, you walk away and I take complete control of Satterfield Racing."

"Will you put that in writing?"

He reached into his jacket's inside pocket and removed a vellum-type envelope which he placed on the coffee table separating them. "It's all there. Short and sweet. We can conclude this transaction within twenty-four hours of your concurrence."

He didn't mince words. A bid in writing was hard to ignore.

"I've specified no time limit on this offer, but naturally the sooner the better, before the first of the year is preferred. That'll give the team adequate time to adjust to the transition before we start the new NEXTEL season."

And bring in a new driver.

He rose from the couch. She did the same. They both moved toward the foyer.

"Good luck on Sunday." He extended his hand to her.

She smiled. "See you at the races."

He grinned back. "Race, Ms. Satterfield. There's only one left."

He opened the door himself and was gone.

CHAPTER SIX

"WHAT'S WALTER'S NIECE like?" Beth Wagner asked, as they drove from the airport to the racetrack Thursday night. A storm had delayed their arrival, so Aidan's daughter and Mace's wife and sons were getting in much later than planned. "Mace hasn't said much about her."

Aidan's first impulse was to say sexy, followed by beautiful, intelligent, stuck-up and insecure. But his mind didn't seem to want to go past the first word.

"Not much like him," he said.

"I miss Uncle Walter," Annie said from the backseat, where she was securely belted in between ten-year-old Kevin and twelve-year-old Lief. The boys' heads were bobbing to their iPod music.

"We all do, honey," Aidan replied, "but he's still here in spirit. All you have to do is picture him and there he is."

"I do, but sometimes I forget what he looks like. Like I forget what Mommy looks like."

"That's all right, sweetheart," Beth said, reaching back and patting the girl's knee. "People's looks change, but their love never does."

Annie nodded and continued gazing out the window. The infield was packed with vehicles and RVs of every variety. People were milling around. Music was being pumped from stereos, and the scents of food being cooked on grills permeated the air.

"Are we going to meet Ellie tonight?" Annie asked a minute later.

"Not tonight, but in the morning."

It was already after nine locally, well past Annie's bedtime.

"I invited her to stop by and meet you in the morning at eight. She's using Uncle Walter's RV."

ELLIE SHIFTED the cell phone from one ear to the other as she told her mother about Aidan's offer to buy their interests but with the stipulation that full payment be delayed a year.

"I was hoping you'd be able to settle this ridiculous matter quickly," Estelle complained.

Ellie didn't tell her about Mitch Fulton's offer to top it or any other offer by a million dollars, payable immediately. It was a no-brainer, yet she hesitated. This was a business deal, and that meant accepting the high bid and getting out.

She should have stayed in California and handled it from a distance. The decision would have been easy then. Now she was faced with Aidan O'Keefe, and he was hard to ignore. Time to change the subject.

"When was the last time you saw Uncle Walter?" Ellie asked her mother.

Silence on the other end.

"Mother? Are you still there?"

"Just thinking, dear."

"Could it have been last January? Aboard a ship in the Caribbean?"

The sound on the line had an uncanny resemblance to a muffled gasp.

"Why didn't you ever tell me you were seeing him?"

"I wasn't *seeing* him," Estelle objected. "We just happened to be on the same cruise."

"Every year?" Ellie laughed. "I'll say this for you, Mother. You've been discreet. Why didn't you ever bring him home, let me meet him?"

"He wasn't suitable, Ellie. For one thing, he was my brother-in-law. Your father—" there was that pause again "—your father was refined, educated, sophisticated. An achiever. Walter... Well, Walter was the wild one, the renegade—"

"The bad boy," Ellie supplied.

Estelle sighed. "Exactly."

And bad boys can be very attractive, even seductive, Ellie reflected. Of course, a lot depended on how you defined good and bad.

"He didn't do too shabby, though," Ellie reminded her mother. "He got to own a multimillion-dollar NASCAR racing team."

Estelle didn't respond. Instead she asked, "What's this Aidan O'Keefe person like?"

Sexy, Ellie almost blurted out. *Dangerous.* "An experienced driver and an astute businessman, as well as a dedicated family man."

"Family man? I didn't know—"

"He has a six-year-old daughter. I haven't met her yet, but I will tomorrow."

"And his wife?"

"Died two or three years ago."

"Oh, I'm sorry. And he's bringing his daughter up all by himself? Can't be easy."

Her mother's comment took Ellie a bit by surprise.

Estelle didn't usually dwell on other people's lives, except as they impacted her own, but having been a single parent, she could appreciate the challenges a widower faced.

Ellie knew her mother's self-absorption was largely a defense mechanism. She suspected the young Estelle, who'd married the handsome air force captain, had been a different person from the mature woman she'd developed into. John Satterfield's sudden and tragic death had traumatized Estelle and made her afraid to get too close to people, at times, even to Ellie. Still, Ellie never had any doubt she was loved.

What, then, of Estelle's relationship with Walter? Ellie wouldn't be surprised if it had gone beyond a once-a-year assignation, but this wasn't the time to probe deeper.

What she had to do now was figure out how she was going to handle the sale of Satterfield Racing. More particularly, how she was going to deal with Aidan O'Keefe.

EARLY THE NEXT MORNING Ellie tried, not wholly successfully, to prepare coffee in the galley of her late uncle's motor coach, which, she had to admit, blew her away. This wasn't your weekend camper but a home away from home.

Among the things she'd found in inventorying the coach the day before, after flying in from Charlotte, was a doll. Very different from the dolls Ellie had grown up with, the kind dressed in finery and lace, wearing wide-brimmed hats and a myriad of crinolines. This doll wore denim, clunky shoes and a long-sleeved shirt displaying Satterfield Racing colors. Only the length of the yellow hair and painted fingernails identified it as a girl.

Was this doll commonly available at the many souvenir booths that lined the parking lots and roadways to the huge racing stadium? Since it was not in a box, and there were no labels on it or any of its garments, Ellie suspected it was a handcrafted one-of-a-kind. For Annie? From what Mace had told her, Walter had been very close to Aidan and his daughter, virtually a member of the family.

She could hear the whispered roar coming from outside of engines being gunned and tuned. A few days ago she would have frowned at the *noise,* but this morning it called out like rock music at a concert. There was something about speeding along at a hundred and eighty miles an hour, feeling the grumbling vibrations of engine and road shivering through her flesh that excited her soul as well as her body.

The air was charged as she exited the coach and walked toward Aidan's RV. This was the last race of the NASCAR NEXTEL Cup season. The people she encountered along the way, men—and a few women—in team uniforms, family members—mostly women and children—all displayed the same kind of nervous energy she felt, that jittery anticipation of an important event.

She mounted the steps of Aidan's coach and was about to knock when the door opened and he was facing her.

Unexpected exhilaration swept through her. She wasn't supposed to have this kind of response to the mere sight of a man, but he was so close.

"Good morning."

Returning his smile was easy, unconscious, uncontrollable. "Good morning."

"Come on in." He widened the door and stepped back.

Waiting to greet her were a woman and a girl. Ellie focused instantly on the six-year-old. She had straw-blond hair, brushed straight back off her shoulders, and her father's mountain-lake blue eyes. A lovely child with smooth, flawless skin and pleasant features, but Ellie's experienced eye immediately discerned bone structure and a sensuous mouth that would one day make her a beauty.

"This is my daughter, Annie," Aidan said with obvious pride, "and Mace's wife, Beth. She helps with Annie's homeschooling."

Ellie greeted Annie first, extending her hand. The girl was understandably reserved but not bashful. She took Ellie's hand firmly and said hello in a strong voice.

Reaching up, Ellie shook Beth's hand, as well. She was an attractive woman in her late thirties with short dark hair and intelligent brown eyes. Her greeting, though pleasant, was more wary.

"Can I get you some coffee?" she asked.

"Oh, please," Ellie responded gratefully. "I tried fixing some in Walter's RV, but what came out…you could have read the fine print of a sales contract through it."

Beth laughed. "Well, you can't read anything through the mud this guy concocts, I promise."

"I like my coffee strong," Aidan declared in self-defense.

"First, though," Ellie said, "I have something for Annie. I found this in the coach. I think Uncle Walter was going to give it to you for Christmas, but that's more than a month away, and I thought you might like to have it today."

She removed the doll from the bag.

Annie peered at it for a moment before her eyes lit up.

"Oh, isn't that nice!" Beth exclaimed.

Shyly now, Annie took it, as if it were a sacred object.

Ellie caught the smile on Aidan's face and realized he wasn't studying the doll but his daughter. The love in his eyes almost brought tears to her own. What would it have been like, she wondered, to have had a dad who looked at her that way?

"What are you going to call her?" he asked Annie.

"We can play with names today until we find the right one," Beth said.

"Can we call her Walter?" Annie asked.

"That's pretty much a boy's name," Aidan told her.

"How about—" Ellie stroked her chin "—how about Waltera? You could shorten it to Tera."

Annie gazed up at her and a new grin brightened her face. "Tera! That's a nice name. Isn't it, Daddy?"

"I think it's a perfect name." He glanced over at Ellie and the warmth of his smile this time threatened to melt every bone in her body. Her heart skipped a beat.

Aidan checked his watch. "I've got to run." He bent down and planted a kiss on top of his daughter's head while he clasped her small shoulders. "Have a good time with your new doll."

"Daddy, I know you're going to win the pole today."

He stroked her cheek. "Keep those positive thoughts, kid. I can't promise I'll win, but I can promise I'll do my best."

"That's what really counts," she replied, proud of her wisdom.

She walked him to the door and stood on the raised platform to bid him farewell and good luck.

Ellie stared at the retreating figure, at the wide set of his broad shoulders, at the way the jumpsuit hugged his narrow hips. She was probably imagining rather than seeing the play of leg muscles as he dodged around people.

"Shall we finish our coffee?"

Ellie jerked sharply to her right at the sound of Beth's voice, only then realizing she'd been so mesmerized by the man running away from her, she'd forgotten about everybody else.

"I think you should kiss my daddy," the six-year-old declared.

After a moment of shock, Ellie asked, "You do? Why?"

"'Cause he likes you."

"He does, huh? Did he tell you that?"

"Yep. He said it's hard not to like someone who's so in love with herself."

Ellie decided she should have quit while she was ahead.

Beth chuckled.

CHAPTER SEVEN

MACE OFFERED Ellie the opportunity to watch practice and qualifying laps from the top of the pit box, and for a brief time she did, but then she decided to sit in the stands and experience events as a spectator, since Annie was too young to be in the garage and pit areas. Ellie enjoyed wearing a headset, now that she knew how, and listening to the chatter between driver and team, but spending time with Aidan's daughter today seemed more important and more fun.

In her twenty-four years, Ellie had spent very little time with young children. She'd never had a babysitting job. A few of her friends had married, but once their kids were born, she either didn't get to see them very often or when she did it was in situations where the children were left with others so the parents could get away for a few hours' respite.

Now she felt entranced by this precocious six-year-old who could rattle off statistics, explain rules and keep up with what was happening on the track while Ellie could barely distinguish one car from another as they zipped by in a blur.

"She's something, isn't she?" Beth commented during the lull between practice laps and qualification trials. "Definitely her father's daughter."

They watched the qualification laps and were ecstatic when Aidan did indeed take the pole.

Ellie said goodbye to Annie and Beth after that and sat in on the team meeting that followed. When it was over, Aidan invited her to have dinner with him and Annie. She didn't take long to accept.

She expected it to be in a restaurant, but Aidan grilled chicken pieces on the stovetop hibachi in their motor home, baked sweet potatoes in the convection oven and popped in a tray of homemade biscuits at the last minute. Annie prepared the green salad—actually she took it out of its plastic bag—while her father mixed his own vinaigrette dressing. Ellie, whose culinary skills didn't go much beyond scrambling eggs and putting presliced bread in a toaster, was impressed and humbled.

"You don't know how to cook?" Annie asked.

Ellie scrunched up her mouth. "Afraid not."

"Daddy can teach you. He's really good."

"I can see that."

"You should ask Santa to bring you a stove for Christmas," Annie said.

Ellie laughed. "I already have a stove, a pretty good one, too. I just don't know much about using it."

"Maybe Santa will bring you a cookbook then."

They ate leisurely and talked about everything. The upcoming race, of course. Annie's schoolwork. The places Ellie had visited in Europe and North America.

Ellie started to help Aidan clear the table, but he would have none of it. She was a guest. She started to protest. She didn't want to be treated like a guest.

"Why don't you teach Ellie how to play Clue," Aidan suggested to Annie, "while I load the dishwasher."

"Will you play with us, Daddy?"

"If Ellie isn't too tired." He smiled at her, and she felt her insides flutter.

"I'll do my best to keep my eyes open," she commented.

Ten minutes later he joined them on the floor around the coffee table. Over the next couple of hours they laughed and conspired. When Aidan announced it was time for Annie to get ready for bed, Ellie felt as disappointed as the child.

Annie said good-night and gave Ellie a big hug. Ellie hugged her back with more enthusiasm than she would have expected. Spending the day with the girl had been fun, but it had also been satisfying in a way Ellie had never experienced before.

SATURDAY WAS the NASCAR Busch Series race. Ellie spent part of the morning at the garage with Aidan, Mace and the team, listening to them discuss the upcoming competition, who were the favorites, the tactics they could expect to use and how they might impact the next day's race. She didn't understand much of what they were talking about— hardly any of it, in fact—and shied away from constantly interrupting them for explanations. So she joined Beth, her boys and Annie in the stands.

She'd seen tapes of races with big crack-ups, but seeing them live in front of her was more scary and exciting than she could ever have imagined. Later, Beth invited her to join them for supper at their RV.

Aidan showed up just before nine o'clock to take Annie home. She and the boys were stretched out on the floor watching TV. He looked tired, yet keyed up, motivated. Tomorrow was the last race of the NASCAR NEXTEL Cup season.

"Why don't you walk Ellie to her RV while I get Annie's things together?" Beth suggested. "The program they're watching won't be over for a few minutes."

Ellie was about to protest. She didn't need an escort, but of course that wasn't what this was about.

"Thanks for giving Annie two such wonderful days," Aidan said when they were outside and beginning their stroll to Walter's motor home a few spots away. "She really enjoyed being with you."

"I'm the one who needs to say thank you," Ellie replied. "I can't think of the last time I had so much fun. She's a great kid, Aidan. You can be very proud of her and of yourself. You're a good daddy."

The poses they'd each assumed on their first meeting were gone now, replaced with a contented humility she wouldn't have believed possible for either of them.

"She's the world to me."

"And she adores you. It can't be easy for you bringing her up by yourself."

He didn't protest or try to minimize the challenge. "You do what you have to do, Ellie, and pray it's the right thing."

They reached Walter's RV.

"Have you got time to stop in for a few minutes, or do you have to get back right away?"

"I think Annie will forgive me if I'm a few minutes late, as long as I'm there to tuck her in."

As Ellie had noted, he was a good daddy. She opened the motor coach door, went in, turned on the light, deactivated the alarm and motioned him inside.

"Since you're not driving tonight, can I offer you a beer or glass of wine? I noticed the coach driver left the refrigerator and bar well stocked."

Aidan chuckled. "Walter liked a toddy or two before turning in."

"Apparently with a host of friends," she said.

This time Aidan laughed. "He wasn't a big believer in solitude."

"I have a feeling I would have liked him. What can I get you?"

"Beer is fine."

"Coming up." She went to the fridge, got out two bottles and used an opener to remove the caps.

"You're having beer, too?"

She snickered. "My tastes aren't all champagne."

"I didn't mean—"

She laughed as she clicked the neck of her bottle against his. "Yes, you did. And well deserved, too. I owe you an apology for that first night. I'm not usually such a stuck-up—"

She didn't get a chance to finish, because his lips were suddenly pressed against hers.

Her eyes widened in shock, then closed in welcome surrender. The two of them fumbled to place their untouched bottles on the counter behind her, then his arms were around her and the kiss became more than the mere touching of lips.

Her breath caught. Her senses were filled with the taste of him, the stimulation of his body pressed against hers.

Both were breathing heavily when they finally broke off.

He grinned. "I've been wanting to kiss you since the night you arrived. I almost did in the hotel lounge—"

"I wished you had. But I can understand why you didn't."

"It would have been wrong then," he said.

"And it's right now?" she asked playfully.

"You think we ought to make sure?" His blue eyes glittered in a teasing smile.

"I hate uncertainty, don't you?"

"Absolutely."

If the first kiss was tantalizing, this second one was earthshaking. She'd been kissed before. She was no ingenue in that regard, but Aidan's kisses were so much more intense.

Sleep that night was fretful after that mind-blowing second kiss. It wasn't fair, she told herself, for him to taunt her like that and then leave. His fingers had dragged through hers as he went through the door, as reluctant to go as she was to see him leave. The tingling spark he'd left behind certainly hadn't died down. Her active mind kept replaying the way his lips met hers: the way his mouth covered hers; the sensation of his arms surrounding her; the feel of his tall, strong, hard body pressed against her.

No, she decided, over and over again, she'd never been kissed like that.

SHE FOLLOWED THROUGH on his parting invitation and showed up at his coach Sunday morning to join him and Annie for breakfast. Aidan greeted her with eyes that said he wanted to kiss her again, and Annie literally jumped at her arrival. It was a strange and wonderful phenomenon, one she'd never encountered before, being made to feel so welcome, so special for just being herself.

"Daddy is making blueberry pancakes," Annie announced. "My favorite. He lets me put the blueberries in and mix it all up."

"I bet they're going to be good."

"There's a cup," Aidan said with a cockeyed grin. "Help yourself." He nodded to the corner of the counter where a team mug sat in front of the coffeemaker.

Ellie prepared her first morning shot of caffeine with cream and sugar. She usually drank the second cup black, although, on her first sip, she decided she may have to reevaluate that strategy. She added more cream.

She'd just taken an invigorating mouthful of coffee when he served up a huge stack of the purply flapjacks, along with a second platter of sausage patties, a tub of butter and a small pitcher of warm maple syrup.

They sat down to eat, Ellie taking a seat next to Annie, across from Aidan. She was uncomfortably aware of him glancing up at her as he piled his plate high.

"Are you really going to eat all that?" she asked.

He answered with a laugh. "I'll lose about ten pounds out there today on the track, most of it water, but a lot of nutrients, too. A man needs his carbs to keep up his strength."

Ellie raised her brows in amusement and took another mouthful of fruity pancake. "Carbs to keep up your strength, huh? I'll have to remember that."

She could feel the slow, knowing grin building across from her, but she didn't dare raise her head to confirm it. It was difficult enough not to blush at the thoughts going through her mind.

Twenty minutes later, they were finishing their breakfast, when Mace, Beth and the boys showed up. Aidan gave Annie and Ellie each a kiss on the cheek, then the two men left.

Beth smiled as Ellie watched them go, rubbing her cheek where Aidan had kissed her so fleetingly.

This last day of the season, Ellie divided her time between the grandstands and the garage and pit areas.

When Aidan got caught up in a multicar pileup, her heart was in her mouth. The spinout slowed him down temporarily but didn't stop him.

Halfway through the race, after four caution flags had been raised and three cars eliminated, Ellie leaned over to Beth and asked, "Are you sure this is fun?"

Beth just laughed. "Doesn't make any difference. You're hooked."

Ellie grinned back. The woman was right. "I'm that obvious, huh?"

Beth's eyes twinkled. They both knew they weren't talking just about NASCAR. "Some things are hard to hide." Then she added, "And some people aren't very good at hiding them."

Aidan came in third. A good, strong ending, even if it wasn't a win. They'd known from the outset he had no chance to take the NASCAR NEXTEL Cup Series this year, but finishing third in this race ensured he'd have a sponsor for the upcoming season, and that he would be in a strong position during contract negotiations. It also increased the value of the team.

CHAPTER EIGHT

MOST OF THE MOTOR HOME drivers had started pulling their RVs out of the infield shortly after the race began in order to get a head start on the traffic that would jam the roads for hours afterward. Race car drivers, their families and crews would leave later by car and plane, eager to get a start on their long winter vacations. Those who chose to hang around would put up at local hotels.

"Annie—" Beth addressed the little girl "—how would you like to come on home with me and the boys? Your dad can pick you up tomorrow."

"Can I? Did Daddy say it was all right? I want to play with Ruckles."

Ruckles was the Wagners' young cocker spaniel. Because she and Aidan were on the move so much, Annie wasn't able to have a pet of her own, but Beth's parents lived right next door to the Wagners and were able to take care of their dog and goldfish when the family was away.

"I haven't talked to him yet, but I bet he'll say yes," Beth said. Annie had stayed with the Wagners before.

"Yippee!"

Beth smiled at Ellie. "You might call a local hotel to see what's available. With everyone leaving here you shouldn't have too much trouble finding accommodations, but the sooner the better."

"Uh, yeah," Ellie responded. "Good idea."

Two hours later Annie was in the van with Beth and the boys, headed for Charlotte.

"I was able to get us a suite at the Stanford," Ellie told Aidan. "Their last one."

"You mean we won't have to sleep in the car?"

"Who said anything about sleeping?"

They dined in a quiet restaurant and were interrupted only once by someone seeking an autograph. Later they danced in the hotel lounge before going upstairs.

The next morning, Ellie announced she was returning to San Francisco.

"Why?"

"Thanksgiving," she said.

"I was hoping you'd spend it with us."

She brushed her hand along his cheek. "That's sweet of you, and I wish I could, but Thanksgiving's a big deal for my mom, bigger even than Christmas. My dad died between Thanksgiving and Christmas, so Thanksgiving was the last big family occasion they shared together. She doesn't talk much about him, but I know how important this holiday is for her. She'll be really upset if I'm not there."

"I understand—" he wrapped his arms around her waist "—but I'm going to miss you." He kissed her on the lips. "When will you be back?"

"The week of the Christmas party."

"That's not until the middle of next month."

"Knowing my mother, she hasn't opened a single business envelope since I left, and I have a couple of meetings

I have to attend. Annie asked me to take her Christmas shopping, so I'll be back in time to do that before the party."

At his gloomy expression, she added, "It's not like we'll be incommunicado. There's the telephone, e-mail, instant messaging. We'll hardly know we're apart."

He grinned up at her under knitted brows. "I can't kiss you over e-mail," he said. "I can't—"

She crossed his lips with her finger. "I'm going to miss you, too. More than you can imagine. But it's only for a few weeks."

"A few weeks," he repeated. "Why does it sound like an eternity?"

She kissed him then, and time stood still.

ELLIE INVARIABLY FOUND San Francisco a beautiful, vibrant and friendly city, the place that in her mind was synonymous with home. But not this time. She felt like a visitor, a foreigner, someone out of place when she arrived there from Florida. She missed Aidan so much it hurt. She missed Annie, too. She'd always taken it for granted that she'd have children when she got married, but both had been abstract concepts somewhere off in a hazy future. Until now.

In an ironic way her mother contributed to her feeling of being an outsider. Not surprisingly, among the dozen guests Estelle had invited to share their holiday dinner was an eligible bachelor, Chaz Howard. He was a nice enough guy, three years Ellie's senior and a junior associate in a large, prestigious law firm. Chaz was good-looking, athletic, well-mannered and well-read. He and Ellie got along fine and could probably become friends, but there was no spark between them, not the kind Estelle was undoubtedly hoping to kindle. At the end of the evening Chaz invited Ellie to dinner the following week, but she declined. Maybe another time, they agreed.

Fortunately there was plenty to keep Ellie busy while she was home. Her mother's investments had done fairly well, but Estelle's propensity for extravagant spending did more than keep up with her income.

Ellie was also beginning to receive offers for Satterfield Racing; Mitch Fulton's standing offer trumped them all. She'd assured her mother she'd get them the best possible price for the racing team, and, she told herself, she had a fiduciary obligation to do so. That meant selling to Fulton.

There was a complication, however. One she had never anticipated. She'd fallen in love with Aidan O'Keefe. Fallen in love with the man and his daughter.

Business was one thing. In this regard the right thing to do was clear and unequivocal. It came down to two people bidding for controlling ownership of Satterfield Racing. One offer was indisputably the better.

So how was Ellie going to solve this dilemma? If she sold to anyone but Mitch Fulton, she would be selling for less than she could get for the team. And if she did sell to him she would be effectively betraying the man who had helped build the team and made it valuable. The man she loved.

AIDAN AND ANNIE SPENT Thanksgiving with the Wagners at their house. Beth's parents were there, along with some other friends and their kids, one of whom was a seven-year-old girl who bonded instantly with Annie, so the house was filled with noise and laughter. The family atmosphere was as warm as Aidan could ever hope for.

Except, of course, it was someone else's family, and Ellie wasn't there.

Recalling what he could of Walter's comments about his sister-in-law, Aidan doubted Estelle would ever be the cuddly grandmother, so even if he and Ellie were to get married, Annie would not be blessed with grandparents like the Wagner boys were.

That he was actively thinking of marriage both excited and worried him. Was he in love with Ellie? He'd experienced love once. With Jenny. And he'd expected it to last a lifetime. Ellie was nothing like Jenny. She wasn't a cookie-baking homebody as Jenny had been. Ellie admitted she didn't even know how to cook. Was it simply the allure of long-denied female companionship?

Certainly that was an attraction. But what he felt about Ellie was more than physical.

He thought about her constantly. Reminded himself a dozen times a day to tell her things, recount events past and present, ask her opinion about various matters, seek her advice. When he daydreamed about being with her it wasn't just in the bedroom…well, not exclusively, anyway. He thought about the gold that glittered in her pale amber eyes when he touched her. The feel of her skin as his fingers explored her planes and curves. The surge of vitality that rocketed through him when he was in her company. The sweet sound of her voice. Even the way Annie looked up at her.

Just because she couldn't cook…

They could still be a family, and who knows, maybe if she tried, she could learn to bake cookies.

ELLIE WAS FEELING GOOD. She'd worked out a solution to the dilemma of Fulton's offer. It wasn't all that complicated and she wondered why it had taken her so long to figure it out. Have Aidan buy Estelle out first. There would still be a few kinks to iron out, like the size of his down payment, but that was negotiable.

Ellie was sure she had a smile on her face the entire trip from San Francisco to Charlotte. It was a toss-up whether it was because of her brilliant strategy or anticipation of seeing Aidan and Annie again. Either were good reasons, and combined she felt just plain happy.

She'd hoped Aidan would be able to meet her at the airport, maybe even wearing a black T-shirt and the tight-fitting jeans that molded to his very sexy body, but he was at a promotional event all day. He'd offered to have someone else pick her up, but she'd rejected the idea. She was perfectly capable of getting to where she was going on her own. She also didn't have nearly as much luggage with her this trip.

It was a little lonely in the terminal this time. No great milling crowds, no Aidan, no bright orange Corvette. But the porters were friendly and helpful. She got her rental car, had her luggage loaded and took off for Satterfield Racing.

She parked in the nearly empty parking lot behind the building and, coming around the corner of the garage, heard voices. She was about to call out a greeting when one of them mentioned her name.

In spite of herself, Ellie stopped and listened.

"I heard she's coming back for the Christmas party." Ellie recognized the voice as that of Nell, the lobby receptionist. "You think she's going to announce she's selling to Fulton?"

"I sure hope not. If she does we might as well all start looking for new jobs." It took a moment for Ellie to realize the second woman was Shirley, Walter's secretary. "Fulton will probably fire half of us, and the other half will quit. No way am I going to work for the jerk, I promise you that."

"When she left here she had it pretty bad for Aidan, so maybe she won't."

Shirley chuckled. "Yeah, he did a good job on her."

"What do you mean?"

"Oh, nothing."

"Come on. You can tell me," Nell insisted.

"Well…" Shirley hesitated. "What I heard… Mace suggested he put the make on her, woo her, so she wouldn't sell to Fulton."

"Aidan wouldn't do that," Nell objected. "He's not that kind of guy."

"You ever seen him act around other women the way he was around her? You don't really think he's interested in a stuck-up California girl, do you? She's not his type."

"You have a point there, but I just can't see Aidan—"

"Hey, he loves this team. He and Walter put a lot of time, energy and money into it. You think he'll let this sweet young thing, who doesn't know the difference between a spoiler and a sway bar, sell it out from under him without a fight? He knows he can't outbid Fulton, so the only alternative is to make the prim Ms. Satterfield refuse to sell to him."

"He does have team loyalty, but still… You don't think Aidan's really interested in her?"

"He's a man, so I'm sure there's a certain attraction, if you know what I mean, but he's not about to take her home to play mommy with his little girl. He's got better tastes and higher standards."

CHAPTER NINE

"THANKS FOR DOING THIS," Aidan said, and placed his hand on Ellie's shoulder, preparatory to drawing her into his arms.

She hadn't called the night before and hadn't answered her cell phone. He'd left messages at the hotel, but she hadn't called back. She'd just shown up this morning to take Annie Christmas shopping.

She eased away from his attempted embrace. He told himself it was because his daughter could come bouncing out of her room any minute.

"Beth usually takes her shopping with her, but Annie insisted you had to do it. I have to warn you, she'll run you ragged."

"I don't mind."

But she didn't sound all that enthusiastic about it, either.

"If you'd rather not—"

"I said I'm glad to do it, Aidan."

"Is something wrong?"

"Nothing's wrong."

His expression was leery, uncertain. "You could have fooled me. Why didn't you return my calls last night? I was going crazy worrying about you. Is it something I did or said? Something Annie—"

"I'm ready," Annie announced as she emerged from her room wearing red cowboy boots, tucked-in jeans and a bright red sweater. "Can we have pizza for lunch?"

Ellie's face, so somber a moment earlier, was now beaming at the girl. "Pizza's a great idea. What kind? Pepperoni?"

"I don't want any of that green stuff on it. Yuck."

"Bell pepper," Aidan supplied.

"Pepperoni, hold the pepper. Got it. Okay, grab your coat, kid, say goodbye to your dad, and we'll be on our way. We have a busy day ahead of us."

"Any idea what time you'll be home?" Aidan asked.

"When we get here," Ellie said casually. "Shopping is very serious business. It can't be rushed."

Aidan accompanied his daughter to the hall closet, where he helped her into her green quilted jacket and red knitted cap. The weather had turned sharply colder in the past few days.

"You girls have fun," he said, giving Annie a peck on the cheek. He wanted desperately to kiss Ellie, too, but she turned away before he could make the overture.

He watched them walk down the path to Ellie's rented car.

What the devil was going on?

Had she decided to sell to Fulton but was afraid to tell him? He hoped that wasn't the case, but if it was, he couldn't imagine her not having the courage to own up to it. Probably in a very businesslike fashion.

I want you to know, Aidan, this is nothing personal. It's simply a business decision.

The past three weeks since the end of the NASCAR NEXTEL Cup season had been busy ones for him. He'd been on the road a lot at various sponsor events, but that wasn't unusual. More important, he'd been exploring ways to raise the cash needed to up his ante to the Satterfields. He had a reasonable offer for his RV. He didn't relish the prospect of staying at hotels for the upcoming season, maybe the next two, or giving up the lease on his private jet, but they would be well worth the inconvenience if he could get control of Satterfield Racing.

He still wouldn't be able to match an all-cash offer, but maybe, if he could sweeten his down payment and match Fulton's bid, Ellie and her mother would be willing to accept his terms.

Ellie brought Annie home later than he'd expected, and he was disappointed when his daughter told him they'd already had supper. He'd gotten a couple of thick steaks out of the freezer, thawed them, cut them into smaller chunks, then marinated them and made shish kebobs, one of Annie's favorites, with fresh mushrooms, small onions, green and red bell peppers and cherry tomatoes. It would all keep until tomorrow night, he told himself, but even if it tasted as good or better, it wouldn't be the same. Not for him.

"Go brush your teeth, honey," he told Annie, "and get ready for bed."

"I'll be going," Ellie said.

"Hang around," Aidan said. "We need to talk."

"I have other plans," she stated.

"No, you don't," he countered quietly but firmly. He didn't want to alarm Annie to the friction between them.

Ellie glared at him. He tried to read her expression, but the signals he was getting were mixed. Anger, hurt, contempt, mortification.

"Besides," he said, "I'm sure Annie would like you to

help tuck her in." He hated using his daughter this way, but he didn't have any choice. "Wouldn't you, honey?"

"Yes, please," Annie said. "We really had fun today. We went to—"

"Shh—" Ellie put her finger up to her lips. "It's a secret, remember?"

"Oh, yeah." Annie smiled up at her father. "You're going to really like it, but I can't tell you what it is, 'cause it's a secret."

"Going to surprise me, huh? I can't wait. Now, why don't you get into your pajamas, then Ellie and I will tuck you in."

"Do I have to? I'm not tired."

"You have to." He gave her a hug and a kiss in her hair. "Now go on."

"Oh, okay." She trudged heavily off to her room.

"Little Miss Drama Queen," Aidan said fondly. "Take off your coat," he instructed Ellie.

"I really—"

He shook his head. "No games, Ellie. At least have the courtesy to talk to me."

He'd never been this domineering with her, this arrogant, but he wasn't going to let her walk out on him without an explanation.

She slipped out of her cashmere coat and draped it over the back of a chair.

Ten minutes later, the rituals of childhood bedtime completed, Annie was in her room, her door closed.

"What do you want to drink?" Aidan asked. It wasn't a question of whether she wanted anything, just what it would be. "I have beer, wine, Scotch and bourbon…."

She shook her head.

"Coffee, tea, soda, even milk, if you prefer."

"Decaf coffee, if you have it."

"Come on out to the kitchen while I fix a pot."

She sat on a stool at the counter. He got out fresh beans and ground them.

"Tell me what's going on, Ellie." He measured out a lighter portion of pulverized beans than he would normally use for himself into the paper filter of the coffee machine. "What happened in San Francisco?"

"What are you talking about?"

"You left here a few weeks ago after we'd spent the most wonderful night together, and now you're treating me the way you did the night you arrived, like hired help. What happened to you in San Francisco? Did you meet someone else, someone with more money and sophistication? Someone your mother would approve of?"

"Don't be ridiculous. Of course not."

"Don't be ridiculous," he repeated, still managing to keep his voice low. "Is that what I'm being, Ellie? Ridiculous? You don't understand, do you? I'm in love with you. I thought you were in love with me. You certainly acted that way, but then you're the real drama queen, aren't you? Yeah, how ridiculous of me to think that behind all those poses, all those Hollywood airs, there might actually be a real person there."

She averted her head and didn't answer.

"Why have I become the enemy?"

"I don't like being played for a fool."

He frowned. "Now it's my turn to ask what you're talking about."

"You've been cozying up to me, *wooing me,* in the hope that I won't sell to someone else."

His stared at her openmouthed. Someone had over-heard Mace and him talking. Never mind that he'd rejected the advice.

"Who told you that?" he demanded.

"Does it matter?"

He took a long, deep breath. "Since you apparently believe it…no, I don't suppose it does."

The coffee machine sputtered to a finish. He poured two cups, moved one toward her, took down the sugar bowl from an overhead cabinet, went to the refrigerator and got out the container of half-and-half, set it in front of her, as well. All the busywork done, he picked up his steaming mug, held it between his hands and leaned against the counter by the stove.

"Are you going to?" At her questioning glance, he added, "Sell to Fulton?"

She took her time fussing with her coffee, adding a little cream and a half spoonful of sugar, making him wonder if her delaying tactics were because she was unsure of the answer or didn't know how to phrase it.

After sampling the brew, she placed the mug on the counter but left her finger in the handle.

"You said I have a moral obligation to tell you if there is another offer so you can bid against it. You're probably right."

He raised an eyebrow.

"Okay, you *are* right. The problem is, you can't bid against it."

"I don't understand."

"Fulton gave me an offer in writing, promising to pay a million dollars over any other offer I might receive. In cash, within twenty-four hours of notification."

Aidan digested the information. Slick. It was foolproof. No matter what he offered, Fulton's was better, especially since it was for immediate payment in cash.

"You don't have to accept his offer."

"It's not just me. There's my mother. I might be willing to forgo the profit, but I can assure you she isn't."

It was a tangled mess. Given that Fulton would have the controlling interest, Aidan wouldn't be able to realize nearly as much from a sale to a third party as he might now. If he could sell at all, since Fulton would have to give his chop on any deal.

On the other hand, if he kept his third interest, even though he wouldn't be driving for Satterfield Racing anymore, he would share in the profits. It wasn't likely Fulton would bankrupt his own team just to deny Aidan income on his investment, though he wouldn't put it past the man to cheat him out of his due. As a minority partner, Aidan would have to watch everything that was going on to keep Fulton honest. That in itself could be expensive.

"Thank you for telling me," he said now.

TWO DAYS LATER Ellie received a telephone call from her mother.

"I'm ecstatic about the sale, Ellie, but I'm also a bit confused."

For Estelle to be ecstatic or confused, separately or together, was not exactly a new phenomenon. But the phrase "about the sale" had Ellie on full alert.

"Well, Mother, if you'll tell me what you're ecstatic about, perhaps I can share the ecstasy with you, and if you'll tell me what's got you all confused maybe I can explain it to you. But first you're going to tell me what you're talking about."

There was a three-second pause on the other end. "Are you all right, dear? Is something wrong?"

Everybody seemed to want to know what was wrong.

Let's see, I've fallen in love, really in love, for the first time in my life, only to find I've been used, made a fool of. I've been backed into a corner by another guy who called me an ingenue and proved it. Now I'm faced with a business decision that will make me rich and leave me poorer for the rest of my life. So why should anything be wrong?

"Sorry, Mom. I've been wrestling with some software and it's put me in a mood." Since Estelle didn't understand computers, that was always a safe excuse. "So what's up?"

"I got the contract approval forms by courier just a few minutes ago and am getting ready now to take them to Rupert Hollingsworth to review and to notarize my signature. I'm just wondering why they came directly from O'Keefe instead of from you? And why we're going with separate contracts. I thought we were selling jointly."

Ellie's mind was racing at a hundred and eighty miles an hour. This sharp turn wasn't something she'd anticipated. She tried to think. Aidan had sent Estelle a contract for her to sign authorizing him to sell. Obviously Ellie wasn't buying, so who was Aidan selling to?

"Mother, is there a cover letter with the contract? Would you read it to me, please."

A minute later Ellie knew the answer and her heart sank. Aidan was selling his share of Satterfield Racing to Mitch Fulton.

She tried to assemble all the pieces. Why would Aidan sell out to his archenemy? By beating Ellie and her mother to the punch he would probably be able to negotiate a good price for himself, which was fine, but Aidan's share wouldn't give Fulton control. It would, however, give him leverage. Fulton would now be in a position to buy out Estelle independently, and given her hunger for money, she'd sell, especially if Fulton was generous in his offer. It wouldn't make any difference to him, because he could easily deduct it from what he would offer Ellie for her share, if he ever bothered to offer her anything. With control of Satterfield he wouldn't need her share. Is that what Aidan had in mind, getting back at her because she hadn't sold to him promptly on his terms?

"Don't sign it, Mother."

"But, dear—"

"This isn't what Uncle Walter would want. Trust me on this."

"But, darling—"

"Put the contract back into courier and send it to me, unsigned."

"Are you sure this is what Walter would want?"

"I'm absolutely positive. Put it in courier today, Mother, so I'll have it in the morning."

"If that's what you want, dear."

"That's what I want."

CHAPTER TEN

"ELLIE IS GOING TO BE at the party, isn't she, Daddy?"

"I expect so, honey. She was invited like everybody else."

"But a lot of people don't come to the Christmas party because they've left to go to other places, and she lives way out in California."

"We'll just have to wait and see, sweetheart."

"She said she was coming to the party," Annie persisted.

"Then I bet she'll be there."

"Yeah." But the girl didn't sound all that convinced. Even though Aidan had told Annie that he and Ellie were still friends, she had figured out something was wrong between them, and it worried the girl.

The annual Christmas party was held in the middle of December in order to give people enough time for their own holiday plans. Not many people missed it, however. Some teams had the parties on team grounds, some at private residences. Walter had always preferred hiring a hotel party room. That way someone else did the serving and cleaning up, and the hotel itself was convenient for anyone who wanted to stay over. The highlight of the festivities was the exchange of gifts, most of which were gags rather than serious. Walter had enjoyed playing Santa for that portion of the program, but Mace, who always organized the party, refused to say who would be playing the jolly fat man this year.

As usual, team families had gotten together and decorated the hall with all the appropriate emblems of the season. A big Christmas tree stood colorfully decorated in one corner of the ballroom. Behind it was 555, pulled by nine reindeer, red-nosed Rudolph leading the way with a checkered flag. A jolly, bearded Santa, much slimmer than his stereotype, wearing a red-and-green NASCAR jumpsuit that resembled no other, was leaning out the driver's window.

In the other corner of the room a small combo was playing traditional music of the season. Occasionally people would join in and sing with them.

Each of the round tables, some with red tablecloths, others with green, had Yule logs as centerpieces.

There was stunned silence when gift-giving time arrived and Mrs. Claus came in from a side door and walked up on the stage. Below a snow-white wig, she wore wire-rimmed half-glasses on the tip of her nose, a colorful, full-skirted, ankle-length, neck-high gingham dress and wraparound apron. The moment people realized it was Ellie Satterfield, the place exploded with laughter and applause.

"Santa's busy supervising the elves this afternoon," she said into the microphone, "so he asked me to come in his place. I hope that's all right."

Approving cheers and hand claps resounded.

If anyone had doubts about her commitment to the team and her growing knowledge of NASCAR, it was dispelled over the next hour. She distributed presents with verve and a surprising sense of comedic timing, adding little personal notes with each one.

Aidan and Annie sat at a table with Mace and his family, laughing at her jokes and occasional good-natured jabs. All the time he felt detached from what was going on, an outsider peeping in.

At last it was his turn to receive a present.

"Since his daughter helped pick this one out," Mrs. Claus announced, "I think she should be the one to give it to him. What do you all think?"

Applause confirmed her conclusion.

Aidan and Annie walked jauntily up onto the stage.

Annie, who was rarely shy, stared out at the sea of faces uncomfortably, until she realized she knew all or most of them. Then she grinned and took the gift-wrapped box from Mrs. Claus.

"Merry Christmas, Daddy," she said, holding it out to him.

It was about the size of a shoe box. With everyone looking on anxiously, he began removing the colorful ribbon and paper. He felt a frisson of nervousness as he stared at the trademarked box in his hands. Trying to match the upbeat atmosphere, he gave the crowd a sidelong grin and prolonged the suspense by very slowly removing the lid.

Inside he found a handmade scale model of 555, precise in every detail, every decal, even the gauges on the dashboard.

A model of the car he would never drive again. He glanced over at Ellie, who was grinning at him rather complacently.

"Wow!" he exclaimed and held the model over his head for all to see.

"Do you like it, Daddy?"

He gazed down at his daughter, the greatest treasure in his life.

"Honey, I love it, but not as much as I love you."

Without thinking he handed the model to Ellie, bent down and picked up his daughter and held her in his arms. The two of them waved to the crowd like a couple of celebrities while everyone hooted and cheered.

Aidan gazed at his little girl. Just beyond her in his line of vision was Ellie, looking beautiful and proud in her Mrs. Claus outfit.

"You want to give Ellie her Christmas present now?" he asked Annie in a whisper.

Her face lit up. "Yeah."

He motioned to Mace at the table where they'd been sitting. The crew chief passed up a gift-wrapped package.

"This is for Ellie," Annie said, holding it out to Mrs. Claus.

"Maybe you can deliver it to her," Aidan said into the mic.

Everyone laughed.

Caught off guard, Ellie accepted it.

"Open it," Annie instructed her.

Carefully, Ellie slit the seams of the paper. "Ohhh."

She blushed, bit her lips, hugged the book to her breasts, then held it up.

"Cooking Made Easy," she read the title, *"Simply Elegant Recipes for the Novice."* She laughed. "I guess I'm going to have to learn to use that fancy stove I have at home."

She kissed Annie and hugged Aidan at the same time, unbearably aware of the scents of child and man.

This was the last presentation. As the crowd settled back into small groups, Annie darted off to be with her friends and Aidan started to leave the platform.

"There is one other thing," Ellie said to his back. "But I think I ought to give it to you in private."

She smiled playfully at him when he turned to face her.

"Why don't we go sit in the lounge," she suggested.

He narrowed his eyes, suspicious, or at least mystified.

The hotel bar wasn't open this time of day. Aidan accompanied her to a small table around the corner from the cordoned-off entrance.

"What's up?"

She handed him a flat package.

He scrutinized her rather than it as he accepted it from her hand. Responding to her nod, he removed the ribbon and tore open the shiny wrapping paper. Beneath it was a manila envelope. He turned it over and released the metal clasp, reached inside and withdrew a sheaf of papers.

He recognized the top page of the contract release form he'd sent to Estelle. Was Ellie actually presenting him with what amounted to the sale of his team to his worst enemy as a Christmas present? That seemed rather cold.

He flipped to the last page and stared.

Estelle Satterfield's signature block was crossed out with a bold black *X*.

"I don't understand," he said.

"No, I guess you don't." She was smiling, a little smugly, he thought. "You accused me of playacting, of playing games. And I'm sorry to say you're right. My mother is even worse, but I don't want to talk about her."

He waited.

"I've had a hard time figuring out who I am, what I want to be when…if I grow up. But I've learned something since I met you. I've learned that I love NASCAR. I love the speed, the noise, the controlled chaos, and I don't want the team that my uncle—and you—created to be destroyed, which, of course, is what Fulton will do if he gets his hands on it.

"So I had to come up with some way of keeping him

from getting control. You'll have to forgive me for being so slow, so stupid about handling this, but I'm sort of an ingenue…a novice at this."

She smiled in a self-satisfied way that he still didn't understand, and it made him all the more uncomfortable.

"I learned something even more important while I was away. I learned that I love you."

His heart stopped.

"I love you and I love Annie."

He rose, moved over to her, stroked his hands down the length of her arms, setting off firestorms of need in their wake.

She gazed at him. "I've never been in love before," she said softly. "I've been fascinated, infatuated, but not in love." She raised her hand and caressed his face. "But then I've never met anyone like you. Youthful but mature. Responsible but fun-loving. Skilled yet modest. I've never met that combination in one person. I guess what blew me away was that those qualities could be combined."

He covered her upraised hand with his, brought it to his mouth and kissed the palm. "I'm not a saint, Ellie. Don't make me out some sort of hero."

She laughed. "That's exactly what makes you so lovable. You have no idea how rare humility is."

He shook his head. "I'm a man, Ellie. Nothing more."

"Oh, you don't have to convince me of your gender. But let me move on. I learned something else being with you. I learned to love Annie. I've had almost no experience with children. Even as a kid I didn't have close friends my own age. Other kids were competition. That was all. Annie…Annie is special." She smiled at him. "But then I don't think I have to convince you of that."

He kissed her, but not on the mouth. He gently touched his lips to her forehead in a gesture that was endearing, protective and reassuring...and promised more.

She bit her lips to control the ache welling inside her. "Why did you send the contract release form to my mother?" she asked.

He wasn't expecting the question, or at least not at this moment.

"When you suddenly gave me the brush-off, I figured you'd decided to sell to Fulton and you just didn't want to deal with me."

She appeared momentarily offended, but then she nodded in recognition of the logic. Her change in attitude toward him had been abrupt, irrational.

"Once you sold out," he went on, "I knew I was finished. I wouldn't be able to sell to anyone without his permission, and I knew he wouldn't give me a dime on the dollar if I offered to sell to him. It seemed to me the best thing for me to do was sell to him first. That wouldn't give him control of Satterfield Racing, but it would get me out with at least some dignity. Fulton would then have to either buy one of your shares to control the team or be a silent partner. I couldn't see him doing that, but according to the agreement you and your mother had, whoever bought would have to buy both shares. That would put you in a power position."

"Slick," she conceded.

"So what do we do now," he asked, "since you won't let me sell?"

"We team up, of course."

"I thought you and your mother wanted the money?"

"Oh, Mom wants the money, all right. Your noisy sport may have won me over, but it's never going to turn her into a fan. So I propose you give her a hefty down payment, a million or two ought to do it, and at the end of the season buy her out. At a fair price, of course." She studied those deep blue pools. "Trust me, Mother will survive. In spite of her crying poor, she's actually quite well-off. I know because I manage her accounts and her investments."

"What about Fulton's offer of a million more?"

"He bid on two shares, controlling interest. If we sell separately—or only one of us sells—his tender is void."

"That's pretty slick, too."

"A master's in business administration should be worth something."

"So we draw up a new partnership agreement," he mused, his gaze off in space somewhere, as if he were contemplating legal clauses. "Probably need a new name?"

"New name? You want to change Satterfield Racing?"

"Why not? Your mother won't be a partner, and you won't be a Satterfield anymore."

"I won't?"

"Not if you marry me."

Marry you?

"How about O'Keefe Racing?"

"Or Annie Motors?"

He shook his head. "That won't work. The other kids will get jealous."

"Other kids? What other kids?"

"The ones we're going to have." He gazed into her amber eyes. "Will you marry me, Ellie? Will you be my wife and a mother to my daughter?"

"Will I have to learn to cook?"

He laughed, and this time when he kissed her it was more than just reassuring.

* * * * *

Coming in June 2008…
Watch for HITTING THE BRAKES by Ken Casper,
part of Harlequin's 2008
officially licensed NASCAR series.

THE NATURAL
Abby Gaines

For my sister-in-law and one of my first
and most loyal readers, Anne Latham

CHAPTER ONE

DANNY CRUISE was all "Jingle Belled" out. And it was only December 1.

Unconvinced of the fun to be had riding in a one-horse open sleigh—anyone could see it would be too damned slow—he stabbed the stereo's Off button. The cheery music died, and a blessed silence filled the cab of his Ford F-150 truck. With the darkness outside and the North Carolina freezing rain glazing the windshield, the truck felt like a cocoon.

Danny needed solitude right now, every bit as badly as he needed it in the lead-up to a NASCAR NEXTEL Cup Series race. On race days, his team knew better than to talk to him in the half hour before he went out on the track.

"Smile. Shake hands. Congratulate." He reiterated aloud the routine he'd planned for tonight. Tried to convince himself it was no different from any of the other routines he employed as a race driver: *Fasten harness. Insert earpieces. Put on helmet.*

The great thing about routines was that you could do them without thinking. If Danny could greet Trent Matheson, winner of the NASCAR NEXTEL Cup Series, without thinking, *It should have been me,* he'd probably emerge from tonight's party a better human being.

But he'd still be the guy who'd lost the championship to Matheson in the last seconds of the last race at Homestead.

The rain pelted down harder, in perfect sync with Danny's mood, and he set the heater to full blast to prevent the windshield icing over. Even in good weather, visibility wasn't great on the winding country road that connected his house near Kannapolis with I-85 to Charlotte. He eased off the accelerator in deference to the road conditions—it wasn't as if he was in any hurry to get to the party.

The sooner I get there, the sooner I can move on. The road straightened, and Danny sped up. He would do the right thing tonight, with a smile on his face and a gracious attitude. He would listen, with forbearance, if not acceptance, to the observations and advice that everyone from the waiters to rival drivers and team owners would feel compelled to offer him. Then he'd move on to the next season of NASCAR NEXTEL Cup Series racing. Next season, he would win.

Another vehicle, the first he'd seen since he left home, rounded a bend up ahead, coming toward Danny with its lights on full beam. Danny squinted, momentarily blinded, then the other guy dipped his lights.

That's when Danny saw the dog—so huge it could have been a small horse—darting out from the foliage at the side of the road, into the path of his truck.

Danny stomped on his brakes, estimating he had maybe fifty yards to stop. Any NASCAR driver knew that wasn't technically possible from this speed, in these conditions. The dog apparently lacked the ability to perform that calculation. Either that or it was confused by the car lights coming from both directions, because it paused in the middle of the road.

"Move it!" Danny yelled, knowing the animal couldn't hear him. He gripped the wheel tighter to counter the truck's shuddering as the antilock brakes kicked in.

Not fast enough.

Just as Danny came to a halt, there was a thud of dog-meets-truck.

As Danny cut the engine, the oncoming car sped past him on the other side of the road. All he could hear was the fading rumble of its engine, the tattoo of the rain, the swish of the wipers. No barking, howling, or any other sound that might emanate from a still-alive, justifiably enraged dog.

"Damn." He got out of the truck, ignoring the icy pellets that drove into his face.

The animal lay against the front bumper, its tongue hanging out, panting. Alive.

"Hey, buster." Danny knelt down, put his hand in the region of the dog's nose. The animal didn't seem interested in sniffing it. Its eyes held Danny's. Danny leaned in closer, and in the light of his headlamps saw blood caking the animal's fur. "We'd better get you some help."

There were no houses nearby, so he couldn't think where the animal had come from. Nor where he'd find the owners to confess he'd run over their pet. He'd better get the dog into his truck, find a vet.

Picking up a creature that must have weighed a good hundred pounds wasn't easy, no matter that Danny regularly bench-pressed more than twice that in the gym. The animal put up a heck of a lot more resistance than a barbell. Its legs flailed and it flung its head around, tongue lolling, jaws uncomfortably close to Danny's face.

"Quit fighting," he grunted as he staggered around the truck.

After he'd hefted the dog onto the truck bed, Danny climbed back into the cab. He ran his hands over his face to clear away rain and grime and dog spit. When he pulled off his tie, the overhead light revealed dirt and blood on the shirt of his tuxedo. Thankfully he'd stowed his jacket on the passenger seat for the journey; he'd keep it buttoned at the party.

A call from his cell phone retrieved the number of an after-hours vet clinic on the edge of Charlotte, whose answering machine assured him the clinic was open until midnight, even though "our staff cannot take your call right now."

Danny read the time on his phone. Seven o'clock. He could drop the dog at the clinic and still get to the party in time to offer warm congratulations to his number one rival.

MADISON BEALE FUMED as she typed the notes on her last patient, a cat suffering a distended stomach from gorging itself on a rat almost half its size. The owner had delayed bringing it to the clinic because she didn't want to miss her favorite TV show. When Madison had said pointedly that if the show had been a double episode the cat would have died, the woman had been shocked, but not repentant.

The sudden slam of the clinic's outside door sent Madison's hand skittering across the keyboard.

"Anybody there?" The masculine voice that called from the waiting area sounded strained.

When she hurried out, she saw why. The man was tall, but the dog struggling in his arms, while undeniably a mongrel, looked to have more than a passing acquaintance with a Saint Bernard somewhere up the family tree. "Keep still, dammit," the man snapped at the animal.

Madison bristled. "That's no way to talk to your pet."

"It's not a pet, it's a road hazard. Where can I put him?"

She shifted a display of flea treatments before the writhing animal overturned it. "Just lay him on the floor."

The guy let out a grunt of relief as he lowered the dog gently to the floor. Madison crouched down, too, her face just inches from the stranger's, giving her a close-up of strong cheekbones, well-molded lips and a square jaw. She sat back on her heels.

"You found him on the road?" With calm, firm strokes, she soothed the dog.

"I, uh, ran him over." When she looked up, startled, he added, "He ran out in front of my truck. I'd pretty much stopped when I hit him, but I think he got cut by the winch on my front grille."

She scratched the dog under its chin. "Okay, gorgeous," she crooned, "let's take a look." She darted a quick glance at the man. "*Gorgeous* is the dog, obviously."

"Obviously," he said drily.

Examining the dog, Madison found a deep laceration to his thorax, but no broken limbs, no sloughed skin, no indication of blunt trauma. "He'll be fine, but this cut on his chest will need stitching."

The guy didn't reply, and Madison looked up to find him frowning at her.

"You're a vet, right?" he said. "Not a student, or something?"

"Of course I'm a vet." She knew she looked younger than her twenty-seven years.

"You have a stocking on your head," he said abruptly.

Instinctively, she put a hand to her hair. She'd forgotten she was wearing the red wool Christmas stocking, complete with pipe-smoking snowman, that the grateful owner of an epileptic German shepherd had knitted for her. "It's a variation on the Santa hat—I wear it at Christmas to cheer people up. Most folk who come here after hours have an emergency on their hands. I like to help them relax."

"Did it occur to you they might find a white coat more reassuring?" He eyed her green chenille scoop-neck sweater and slim black pants as if they were a clown costume.

"What's most reassuring is when I treat their pets' problems," she retorted. "My name is Madison Beale, and I've been a vet here four years—you'll see my diploma on the wall." She jerked her head toward the counter, behind which hung all the staff's qualifications. "I've treated plenty of injuries like this, and I promise you this one isn't too bad, Mr.…"

It was the perfect opportunity for Mr. Slow-Brakes to introduce himself, but he didn't.

"Fine, you're a vet," he said, as if he'd just made it so by personal decree. "That means you can stitch him up, right?"

Madison felt through the thick brown fur of the dog's neck—at odds with his short-haired jowly face—for a collar. Nothing. "Do you know where he lives?"

He ran his hands through his dark hair, flattened by the rain. "I was in the middle of nowhere."

The movement showed the flex of muscle beneath the white shirt plastered to his chest, courtesy of said rain. His shoulders were broad, and where his collar was unbuttoned, Madison glimpsed a strong throat.

When she met his dark eyes it occurred to her he looked familiar. "If we can't find the owner, will you pay for the treatment?"

She'd treat the dog regardless, but her boss objected—loudly and often, despite the clinic's robust financial health—to the amount of free care Madison dispensed. This guy was wearing dress clothes and, if she wasn't mistaken, that chunky steel watch on his wrist was a Rolex.

He glanced at the Rolex, and, guiltily, she jerked her gaze back to his face.

"Sure." He pulled out his wallet, put a credit card on the counter. "I have to go, but I'll give you my details—"

"You're leaving?" Madison said, confused.

"Yeah." He looked around. "Is there somewhere I can wash up?"

"But—what about the dog?"

Displaying considerable ability to read the moment, the dog whimpered and his head slumped forward.

"You said he'd be fine." A business card joined the credit card on the counter. "Call me tomorrow if you like, tell me how it went. Right now, I'm late for a party."

"You're going to a *party?*" Madison's voice rose. He might as well have said he had to get home to a TV show. "You ran over a dog. You can't walk away from your responsibility."

Danny observed with some alarm the flashing of Madison Beale's tawny brown eyes, the clenching of her fists on her hips. She looked like a fairy that had toppled off the Christmas tree in the corner, with her petite figure and that ridiculous stocking on her head. She'd been all tender concern while she examined the dog. Now she looked at Danny as if he'd lined the animal up for target practice.

"I checked that you're qualified to treat him and I said I'd pay. That's as responsible as I get." He didn't have time to argue, so he fixed her with the hard stare that he used to intimidate his rivals before they went out on the track.

"That's not good enough—" She stopped, and he saw recognition dawn. "You're…Danny Cruise," she said hesitantly, and he noted with satisfaction that her hands unclenched. "You're The Natural."

As always, the nickname grated. Danny had been tagged with it the first time he climbed into a race car and never managed to shake it off. Yeah, he'd won a lot of races, and yeah, he was more at home behind the wheel of a stock car than anywhere else. But nothing about those "effortless" wins, as the press called them, had been natural. He'd earned every inch of pavement through hard work, grit and one hundred and ten percent focus. He never got into a car certain of victory. But people didn't like to hear that, so he said neutrally, "That's me."

"I didn't recognize you without your uniform." Her eyes narrowed, as if she still wasn't certain he was Danny Cruise. "Seems strange that a NASCAR driver couldn't brake in time to avoid a dog."

"Have you seen the roads tonight?" he demanded.

She pursed her lips. "I guess you don't have much experience driving in the rain—you're probably no better than the average Joe in bad weather."

He snorted. "Even blindfolded with both hands tied behind my back, I'm a *lot* better than the average Joe."

She huffed as if she suspected that was exactly how tonight's accident had happened.

"Look, I feel bad about the dog," he said, though in fact he was more worried about NASCAR's new chassis specifications. "But I'm on my way to Trent Matheson's victory celebration."

Trent Matheson was a homegrown star, and now that he'd won the series, he was Charlotte's undisputed hero. Madison softened visibly.

"I'll bet Trent could have stopped in time," she said.

Danny bit down on a rude comment. "If I couldn't stop, no one could."

"Be that as it may—" she was all snooty disbelief "—you can't go now. I need help moving this fellow. And he may need calming while I stitch him up." She eyeballed Danny, presumably trying to look tough. Someone should tell her that with that chestnut hair peeping out from under her stocking, with her eyes wide and her chin tilted, she could make a killing selling Girl Scout cookies. "You might have hundreds of people wanting to see you tonight, but right now, this dog has no one."

Which meant Danny and the dog had more in common than she would probably believe.

CHAPTER TWO

MADISON HAD RESIGNED herself to ruining a colleague's evening off. It took a few seconds to realize that her powers of persuasion were greater than she'd dreamed. She'd called Danny Cruise, NASCAR star, on his bad attitude, and now he was unbuttoning his shirt-cuffs, rolling up his sleeves to reveal strong forearms sprinkled with dark hair.

"Uh, right," she said, not as crisply as she'd have liked. "How about you carry him into the treatment room down the end of the hallway?"

When the dog was safely on the stainless steel treatment table, she administered an intravenous sedative. The animal panicked as the liquid went in, but Danny did a good job of holding him still. That, coupled with the same diamond-hard glare he'd directed at Madison earlier, seemed to have at least as much effect on the animal as the drug.

"We need to wait five minutes for the sedative to take effect," she told Danny as she threaded her needle.

With most clients, she'd make casual conversation while they waited. But Danny's "Uh-huh" wasn't encouraging and the dog wasn't a beloved pet whose diet and exercise regime they could discuss. Madison trained her gaze on the clock above the door, watched the second hand's staccato journey around the dial.

Funny how twenty seconds of silence could feel like an hour.

She glanced at Danny. He was looking right at her, yet she could tell he didn't see her. His dark brows were drawn together, his lips clamped as if he might say something he regretted. She'd always thought his mouth was his best feature, whenever she saw him in close-ups on TV. It was the sort of mouth a woman might— She jerked her gaze back up to the clock. Thirty-four seconds.

"I'm sorry to make you late for Trent's party," she told him in a desperate bid for conversation.

He cocked a skeptical eyebrow and didn't reply.

"Trent's my favorite driver," she said. "That race at Homestead was incredible." She winced, added apologetically, "Not for you, I guess."

Danny shrugged. "You can't win 'em all." It came out casual, relaxed, just as he intended.

"And the way Trent proposed to his girlfriend right after the race…" Madison sighed, a faraway look on her face.

"That was smart," Danny agreed. It had been a PR masterstroke. Not only did Trent's win score huge coverage in the newspapers, his marriage proposal made the cover of several women's magazines. Small wonder Trent's sponsor was footing the bill for tonight's extravaganza, a combined victory and engagement party.

"I'd call it romantic," Madison said sharply.

"That, too," Danny said.

"This is the second year in a row you were runner-up in the Cup, isn't it?"

Great, his favorite subject. "Yep." He'd been second last year, third before that. This year, he should have won.

"It's an incredible record."

"Thanks," he said automatically. Then he added warmly, "It's great, the whole team was thrilled."

Madison's sudden chortle took him by surprise.

"What's so funny?" he demanded.

Madison's eyes met his, brimming with amusement, and Danny felt an unexpected tug of attraction.

"The whole team was thrilled," she mimicked him. "You so don't mean that."

"I do, too," he said, outraged. He'd practiced that mix of pride and delight out loud, over and over. If a woman he'd never met before could see right through him, what chance did he have of sounding gracious in defeat when he got to the party?

"Maybe the team was thrilled," she said, "but *you* weren't. I've seen you on TV."

"Oh, well, in that case..." he said sarcastically. People who'd seen him on TV had told him he was vitamin A deficient, that he was ambidextrous, that he was the metaphysical twin of a Tibetan monk. Why shouldn't a vet with a stocking on her head be able to read his mind over the airwaves?

"Before the race, during the invocation and the national anthem, you have this look on your face," she said. "A kind of set, fixed gaze, and your mouth goes into a thin line." She colored slightly as she looked at his mouth. "It's like you're not really there, your mind has gone on ahead."

Okay, so she was right about that. Everyone got lucky sometimes. Intent on disconcerting her, Danny looked right back at her mouth, and discovered her lips to be full and well shaped. He ended up resorting to a childish, "So what?"

"Winning matters to you...."

"It matters to every driver out there," he shot back.

Her "insight" was nothing more than a bad case of stating the obvious.

She tutted. "You didn't let me finish. Winning matters to you *more than anything.*" She smirked. "No way were you happy with second place."

"You don't know me," he said flatly.

"During my training I worked with racehorses."

Danny closed his eyes against a sudden throbbing in his head. "Please tell me this isn't part of the same conversation."

"You soon learn that although they're all there to race, some want to win more than others. You start to see it in their eyes."

"So why haven't you retired on your winnings?" he said.

"I placed a few mental bets that would have paid big money," she admitted, "but other times I read them wrong."

"Ha," said Danny, satisfied. He looked down at the dog. "Surely the sedative is working by now."

"Yep, I'll give him a dose of local anesthetic at the wound site, too." Madison picked up a syringe and bent close over the patient. "And there's some grit I'll have to flush out with a saline solution before I stitch him."

When she'd done that, she told Danny she needed to neaten up the edges of the wound to make stitching easier. It was a painstaking process executed with great care, and it seemed to prohibit speech, which he at first counted a mercy. He liked that she was so focused on her work, just as he was. Then he found himself wanting to argue with her about her conclusions.

At last it seemed she'd finished. "Okay, gorgeous, now we can sew you up."

The dog, which until now had been droopy to the point

of semicomatoseness, made a sudden movement in response to her voice, and Danny soothed him. "Easy, buster."

Madison's head jerked up, and Danny realized she'd forgotten he was there. The unexpectedness of her reaction—when every minute of every day he had people vying for his attention—made him smile. The creasing sensation around his eyes felt unfamiliar, and he realized it had been weeks since he'd felt anything other than tension. Madison blinked twice, then smiled back, her lips curved generously, sweetly. For a sudden, still moment something hung in the air between them.

Then she dropped her gaze back to the dog, made her first stitch, knotted it. "Even though I'm a fan of Trent's, I really thought you'd win the Cup."

Danny shook his head to clear away that odd sensation. "The racehorse thing, right?"

"That…and you did actually drive better most days."

"The most sense you've made all night," he approved.

She continued her work in silence. When she'd knotted the last stitch and put a dressing over the wound, she pulled off her latex gloves. "If you'll carry the patient through to the recovery room, you can go to your party."

Danny looked at the clock. "The speeches will be starting right about now. If I walk in during Trent's speech, it'll look as if I'm trying to upstage him." He pulled out his cell. "I'll ask my girlfriend to make my excuses."

Kristal would be furious. Twice since he'd lost the championship, Danny had forgotten about dates they had scheduled.

"She's the model with the navel ring that you rub before each race, right?" Madison said blandly.

Last year at Daytona, he'd teasingly patted Kristal's

navel ring. When he won, people said the gesture had brought him good luck. Danny didn't believe in luck. But he did believe in getting his share of camera time for his sponsors, so he'd played to the media by rubbing Kristal's navel ahead of every race after that. It wasn't his classiest moment, but it got attention.

"That ring is just one of her many excellent qualities," he assured Madison. He turned away as he dialed Kristal. She answered right away. "Hey, baby," he said. He heard a snicker behind him.

"Where the hell are you?" From the way Kristal whispered into the phone, Danny deduced the speeches had already started. "Do you have any idea how late it is?"

She had an annoying habit of asking questions designed to lead him to an admission of guilt.

"I had an accident."

"It'd better be serious," she hissed.

So much for playing the sympathy card. "I hit a dog and I had to bring it to the vet. I can't walk in there now, so if you can explain to everyone—"

"Don't you dare." Her voice rose, then quickly dropped. "You've been jerking me around for weeks, Danny. I don't give a damn about the dog, just get here fast."

The thing he'd liked most about Kristal was that she was as wrapped up in her modeling career as he was in his racing. Neither of them depended on the other. But on this occasion, he could do with her giving an inch. "I'm not going to barge in on the proceedings now," he said. "I just need you to—"

"That's it, Danny, we're finished," she snapped.

"Kristal, listen, I—"

The phone went dead. Bemused, Danny hit the Off button.

"Patience not one of her many excellent qualities?" Madison suggested.

"She dumped me," he said slowly, trying to decide how he felt. One thing was for certain, his heart was still in one piece. His relationship with Kristal would have ended sooner or later—maybe now was a good time. He had to win the NASCAR NEXTEL Cup title next year, even if it meant two hundred percent focus. If he wasn't with Kristal, he could spend his evenings watching reruns of every race from last season, trying to work out where he went wrong….

"I'm so sorry," Madison said.

Danny shoved his brain into reverse, tried to figure out why she was chewing her lower lip in that cute, anxious way. Oh yeah, Kristal. "I'll be fine," he said.

But Madison felt awful. She'd made Danny stay here, and as a result his supermodel girlfriend had dumped him. Not that she personally thought the loss of Kristal Kane was a tragedy. Call her a short woman with a grudge, but Madison had always thought Kristal looked stuck-up and self-centered. But it was Danny's opinion that mattered, and he'd dated her right through last season. Poor guy.

"Where do you want this thing to go?" Danny indicated the dog.

Madison excused his calling the animal a "thing" on account of his broken heart. "Two doors down on the left."

She went ahead, opened the door to the recovery room. Danny deposited the dog in the cage she indicated.

"So long, buster," he said. The dog licked his hand.

"He likes you," Madison encouraged Danny, mindful of his fragile state.

Danny rolled his eyes. As he stood, he wiped his hand on his pants. "It's too bad he's a guy, otherwise I'd date him."

She felt herself flush. "Animals can sense feelings of rejection and hurt, and many people derive comfort from—"

"Are we done here?" he asked.

Madison pursed her lips. "You are, I'm not. I noticed his pupils are uneven—there's risk of a rise in intracranial pressure."

"Wow." Danny sounded impressed. "He's that worried about my feelings of rejection and hurt?"

"I'm talking about a swelling of the brain, resulting from a head injury," she said repressively. "A head injury caused by someone *running him over with a truck.*" She patted the dog. "Wait right here, gorgeous." Then she headed out of the room toward reception, saying over her shoulder, "I'll stay to observe him. Hopefully it'll come to nothing. If the owner doesn't come looking for him, I'll send him to a shelter when he's well enough, probably later next week."

She pulled Danny's credit card from the drawer behind the counter, where she'd left it for safekeeping. "I'll put this through."

Danny nodded, but Madison could tell his mind wasn't on their conversation. He must be fretting about Kristal. She put the charge through on his card, had him sign.

Then it was time to send him back out into the rain. She found herself oddly reluctant to say goodbye. *Not* because of that weird sensation she'd had when he smiled at her. She felt sorry for him, that was all. He was obviously still smarting from losing the NASCAR NEXTEL Cup Series championship, yet he'd helped Madison, then been dumped by his girlfriend for his pains.

She handed the credit card back to him, and as he took it, she wrapped both her hands around his. Surprise and faint alarm flashed across his face. He jerked his hand back, but she didn't let go, even though the contact heated her right through.

"You're looking at me the way you looked at that dog," Danny said suspiciously.

She said, "I know you've had a rough couple of weeks, but it won't last—Christmas is right around the corner. If you take a break, you'll find—"

The incredulity in his dark eyes told her she'd let the sympathy that dogs, cats and rabbits responded to so readily go too far. She swallowed, fell silent. Slowly, deliberately, he extracted his hand from hers.

"Forget Christmas," he said, his voice colder than the rain that lashed the clinic's windows. "You get what you want in this life the same way you win races. By running hard and never stopping." He took a step backward, and it was as if a gulf had opened between them. "You go ahead and have a Merry Christmas if that's your thing—" she discerned contempt in the gaze that flickered to the stocking on her head "—but don't tell me what to do."

The clinic door banged behind him, cutting off the gust of icy air that blew in. Despite the central heating, Madison rubbed her arms. So much for trying to dispense a little Christmas cheer. Darned cynical NASCAR driver. It was all very well for him to say forget Christmas, but not everyone wanted to. Not everyone had that luxury.

Her mom had phoned today, tense and anxious, to report that Madison's father would be "home" for Christmas. Her parents had divorced years ago, thanks to her dad's infidelities, which had all but destroyed Mom. That didn't stop

Dad phoning every other year to invite himself for Christmas. Mom always gave in, and each time it ruined their holiday.

Madison pulled the stocking off, ran a hand through her hair to fluff it up. She couldn't forget Christmas, but she could darned well forget Danny Cruise.

"Is Cruise a Bad Sport?" Danny read the headline aloud, then tossed the newspaper down on Hugh Naylor's desk. "Dammit, Hugh, you know I'm not."

Danny's team owner leaned back in his chair, steepled his fingers. "I know it, but I sure as heck wish you'd turned up to that party last night so other people would know it, too."

Danny gritted his teeth. The Sunday morning summons to the SouthMax Racing headquarters hadn't been all that unusual—the habit of working on Sundays was hard to break, and in the off-season he and Hugh often spent the day at the office. He hadn't expected his PR representative, Sandra Jacobs, to be here. He certainly hadn't expected to be handed several newspapers, all with headlines along the same theme—that Danny Cruise's failure to show up at Trent's party meant he was sulking.

"Didn't Kristal explain about the dog?" he asked.

"What dog?" Hugh's forehead creased in perplexity.

By the time Danny finished telling him, Hugh was shaking his head. "Next time, don't ask a woman who's just dumped you to pass on a message. Kristal told everyone you weren't coming and she wasn't surprised because you've been depressed ever since you lost to Matheson." He tapped the newspaper. "It turned a boring party into a great story."

"John from Sports Force America called me at seven

this morning," Sandra said. "He wants to know how we plan to kill this thing."

Damn. Sports Force America, the chain of sporting equipment stores, was Danny's primary sponsor. He only had to think the name to have the jingle from their radio and TV ads run through his head, relentlessly upbeat: Sports Goods for Good Sports.

"Having their spokesman labeled a bad sport in the middle of the Christmas shopping season is not good," Hugh said, in the kind of understatement that would have betrayed his British origins even if his clipped vowels hadn't.

Christmas. An image of Madison clutching his hand, her brown eyes worried, that stupid stocking on her head, flashed into Danny's mind, as it had more than once since he left the clinic last night.

"If we don't fix this, we'll lose Sports Force America," Sandra said. "And chiming in late with a story about a dog won't do it." She held up her hands against Danny's indignation. "I know, it's not a story. But it's going to look like we're covering our butts."

Danny had a lot of respect for Sandra; she knew her stuff. He glanced across the desk at Hugh, who had become pretty much the most important person in Danny's life over the fifteen years since his parents had died. If he couldn't have his own father, Hugh Naylor would be his next choice.

But Hugh wasn't his father. He'd invested unstintingly in Danny's career, not out of paternal love, but because he trusted Danny to deliver results. Danny had felt as bad for Hugh as he did for himself after the race at Homestead.

"We've already lost a couple of smaller sponsors to Matheson Racing," Hugh reminded him.

This time last year, they'd been turning sponsors away—there was no more room on Danny's car. If they lost the Sports Force America sponsorship, it would be a disaster for Hugh, for Danny, for the whole team.

"What if I produce the dog?" Danny said.

Sandra perked up. "You know where it is?"

"The vet planned to keep it at the clinic a while. We could take a reporter to visit."

"Or a whole bunch of reporters." Sandra began making notes. "A photo opportunity. Was it a good-looking dog?"

"Definitely not," Danny said.

"You're handsome enough for two. We'll snuggle you up together." She ignored Danny's shudder. "I'll call the clinic and tell them we're coming. We'll ask the vet to corroborate your story."

"I'll make the call," Danny said. He had the sudden, uncomfortable feeling he might have left Madison in a frame of mind that wasn't conducive to her cooperation.

CHAPTER THREE

TURNED OUT forgetting Danny Cruise wasn't that easy. *You shouldn't have held his hand,* Madison scolded herself as she ran through her list of appointments in the small office behind the clinic's reception desk on Monday morning. She chewed on her pen as she summoned her focus to the list.

If she hadn't touched him, she wouldn't be struggling to remember the exact nature of Mrs. Barrett's poodle's breathing disorder, yet at the same time be able to recall with perfect clarity the strength of Danny's long fingers, the firmness of his flesh.

It was nuts—and the final proof of her insanity was that, despite the man's rudeness as he left, she'd spent the rest of the weekend imagining there'd been some connection between them.

"Danny Cruise," said the receptionist with a kind of gasping excitement.

Madison's head snapped around—was she somehow broadcasting her thoughts to the entire clinic?

No, it was worse…or better. When she craned her neck she saw Danny standing at the reception desk. He wasn't, to Madison's regret, wearing that rain-dampened white shirt. But the black polo emblazoned with the Sports Force

America logo showcased the breadth of his shoulders, tapering to narrow hips in well-fitting black jeans. Madison's undisciplined mind immediately set about memorizing this new incarnation.

"Is Madison Beale here?" Danny said.

He was here to see her! What's more, he was carrying a bunch of flowers, deep gold roses and red gerberas wrapped in red paper and tied with gold ribbon. Was it possible that Danny Cruise, NASCAR star and dater of supermodels, had felt the same connection?

Okay, would whoever put those butterflies in her stomach please remove them immediately?

He's here to inquire about the dog. She pushed her chair back from the desk, stood slowly, allowing time for the heat to wash out of her face before she stepped into the reception area.

"Hi, uh, Danny." Halfway through the greeting she realized she hadn't addressed him by name before. Her tongue felt thick in her mouth. Around her, silence fell as every person in the waiting room realized *the* Danny Cruise was here. Her boss, Roger Smales, stiffened to attention.

"Madison, good to see you." Danny stuck out his hand.

Don't make me hold his hand again. I won't sleep for a week. But, of course, she shook it, then accepted the flowers he offered.

"I hardly recognized you without your stocking." He cast an appraising eye over the hair she wore loose and wavy over her shoulders.

She remembered his contempt for that stocking. "I hardly recognized you without your bad manners."

The receptionist gaped and Roger Smales made an

anxious sound, but Danny was unfazed. "I want to apologize for my rudeness on Saturday night." He nodded at the flowers he'd just given her. "I called yesterday, but you weren't here."

"Apology accepted," she told him, pleased that she managed to sound gracious rather than grateful.

"And, uh, I also came to ask for your help." He handed her a newspaper clipping.

Madison unfolded it, scanned it. Seemed the media had misinterpreted Danny's absence the other night. Seemed his appearance here today had nothing to do with a sudden urge to apologize.

"I've invited a few journalists here to verify my story about the dog," he said.

"You mean the dog whose progress you haven't bothered to ask about?" Her foot tapped the floor.

"Uh, Madison…" Roger, who'd witnessed Madison berating substandard pet owners before, called a nervous warning.

Danny didn't appear to notice her tension. He shrugged. "You said he'd be fine. Is he?"

"He's doing as well as can be expected." Madison didn't mention that she *expected* the dog to be alert, playful and champing for his freedom. She added less truthfully, "Subjecting him to the attention of a crowd of journalists might set back his recovery."

Danny looked downright skeptical. "I get that I should have asked about the dog," he said. "But caring about animals is your job. Mine is to win races, and I won't apologize for putting that first. That newspaper article has done a lot of damage. If I don't produce the dog, my main sponsor will walk."

She folded her arms. "You're asking me to care about that *and* the dog?"

His eyes narrowed. "If I lose my sponsor, I can't race. If I can't race, my team loses their jobs. That's thirty-three people who work on my car. Unemployed." He paused, then delivered the coup de grâce. "Right before Christmas."

Darn it, he had her.

She didn't even get to make him sweat a little longer—Roger shouldered his way into the conversation. "We'd be honored to help you out, Danny. You're our favorite driver."

Danny's gaze met Madison's and she telegraphed, "Not mine," with her eyes. One side of his mouth quirked.

Roger insisted on leading the dog out to the reception himself. The animal tugged on the leash—like most patients, he wanted to be more active than his injuries permitted. At times like this Madison wished she could speak Dog. She'd woof, "Take it easy." And maybe, when he got close to Danny, "Bite him."

The dog responded to Danny's "Hey, buster" with joyous welcome.

Then a tall woman arrived, introducing herself as Sandra Jacobs, Danny's PR representative. Fifteen minutes later, the place was overrun with reporters and photographers, even a couple of TV crews. Danny pulled on a Sports Force America cap and posed hunkered down with an arm slung around the dog. He grinned as if they were long-lost buddies, and didn't flinch when a long, slobbery lick landed on his cheek.

In response to the journalists' questions, Danny recounted the story of how his truck came to hit the dog—

his publicist jumped in and emphasized the wet road and terrible conditions.

Madison chipped in with answers to questions about the dog's health. From the corner of her eye, she saw the reception grow increasingly crowded—no one wanted to go into their appointment while Danny was there. The backlog would likely last all day.

A reporter asked, "What happens to the dog now?"

"I hope the owner will see this story and come forward," Madison said. "If not, he'll go to a shelter, probably at the end of the week when his wound is more healed."

At last they ran out of questions, and the media left. While the PR lady thanked Roger for the clinic's cooperation, Danny turned to Madison. "You did great."

She shrugged, her earlier annoyance dissipated by the realization that the media interest could be useful. "If it helps find the dog's owner, I'll be happy."

He glanced down at the animal lying at his feet. "I'm glad he has someone like you looking out for him." He smiled, with his eyes not his mouth, as he stuck out a hand.

"I'm a sucker for a stray," Madison said lightly, trying to get the handshake over with as fast as possible. But he caught her with his other hand, trapping her fingers between his, the way she'd done to him the other night. She wondered if his bones had melted then.

For a long moment, he looked down at her hand as if he could feel her liquid response. Mortified, Madison tried to tug free. He tightened his grip. "How about I buy you dinner tonight?"

The words swam in her head in a delicious sea of temptation. Dinner with Danny… "Why? Are you planning another photo shoot tomorrow?"

He laughed. "Nope, but you never know what might come up." A pause. "Dinner would be to say thanks for helping out when I didn't deserve it."

She'd bet he knew there was nothing sexier than a man acting humble. Then he glanced at his watch, and she remembered this man would happily forget Christmas, would forget anything that didn't help him win races. He would forget her long before she forgot him.

"Thanks," she said, "but I'm getting together with my mom and my sisters tonight to plan Christmas. It's important."

His eyes gleamed an acknowledgment of her put-down. At last, he relinquished her hand, and immediately she felt the loss of contact.

"It was interesting to meet you, Madison Beale."

Before she could even regret the finality of those words, he was gone. Madison squelched a pang of disappointment as she headed to the reception desk, picked up her clipboard.

"Mrs. Barrett," she called. A stout woman with a blue rinse and a black poodle heaved herself out of a chair. Madison smiled a greeting. "Come this way." As she headed down the corridor, she tried not to stew over Danny's description of their encounter as "interesting." Surely he could have managed "fun" or "great." She'd even settle for "nice."

ON WEDNESDAY AFTERNOON, Madison gave in and picked up the phone to call Danny. She ran a finger over the cell phone number on his business card. *He must have minions to answer the phone. I probably won't even get to talk to him.*

She pressed in the number.

"Cruise." No minion had a voice that sexy.

She cleared her throat. "Hi, uh, it's—"

"Madison, hi."

It felt darned good that he'd recognized her voice.

"How's the dog?" he asked.

She collected her thoughts. "Do you really care?"

"No, but I'm too scared not to ask."

She heard his smile, couldn't help smiling back. "He's fine." She paused. "The story came out well in the papers. On TV, too."

"The 'bad sport' theory has gone away," he agreed. "And my sponsor's thrilled to have so much off-season publicity."

"Hold that thought, because it's my turn to ask you for help."

A moment's silence. Then a cautious, "Uh-huh?"

"I wouldn't ask if I had a choice," she said. "We've been flooded with e-mails and phone calls since that story came out."

"People wanting the dog's autograph," he guessed.

"NASCAR fans wanting to adopt him," she corrected. "His real owner hasn't come forward, but there must be five hundred people who want him."

"That's great."

She tsk-tsked. "I don't have time to deal with them. You must have people who handle your mail. They can sift through these inquiries and give me a short list of potential owners."

Danny's silence seemed contemplative rather than reluctant. Madison was learning he didn't talk until he had something to say. She personally found it difficult to say nothing, so she added, "It's just I have a—a patient about to arrive for lifesaving surgery."

"I'll deal with it," he said abruptly. "I'll see you soon."

"I only wanted—" But she was talking to dead air.

CHAPTER FOUR

TWENTY MINUTES LATER, Danny walked into the treatment room where Madison was working.

"How did you get in here?" And how come every time he turned up she had something odd on her head? Today she wore a pair of magnifying goggles that made her look bug-eyed.

"There was no one at reception. Nice specs." He stepped toward her…and stopped, his eyes fixed on the patient she held in one hand, the needle poised in the other. "Don't tell me," he said in a strangled voice, "this is the lifesaving surgery?"

"Yes, it is. And I don't have a lot of time, so you'd better leave."

She bent over her tiny patient. Danny came closer.

"I realize," he said conversationally, "this is probably some rare species on the verge of extinction, but it looks just like a goldfish."

Madison bit down on a twitching of her lips, prayed her hand would stay steady as she made another tiny stitch. "It *is* a goldfish," she admitted. "His name—" a little snort of laughter escaped her, and she paused in her work "—is Goldie."

Danny guffawed, a noise to which Goldie thankfully seemed oblivious. "What happened to him?"

"Cat," she said briefly, intent on her last two stitches.

When she was done, she dropped the fish into his bowl. After a wrenching moment of immobility Goldie flexed his tail experimentally, then swam a circuit. Madison sighed with relief as she pulled off her goggles. She rubbed the skin around her eyes, where the goggles had left an imprint.

"Did you ever think," Danny said, "about just flushing the little guy?"

"Goldie is a child's pet," she said, shocked. She picked up the bowl. "She's waiting in reception, very worried. I'll be right back."

WHEN SHE RETURNED, Danny jumped right in, aware this was his best chance to convince her. "I've found a new owner for the dog."

Madison's face lit up. "Who is it?"

"Me."

Her face darkened.

"What's the problem?" he demanded.

"Am I wrong, or did you just suggest flushing away an animal?"

"A *goldfish*," he corrected. "A dog is very different."

"Too big to flush, you mean?" Superciliously, she added, "Leaving aside the latest research proving that goldfish have considerable social and memory skills, you made it very clear the dog is low on your list of priorities."

"He's growing on me. I've realized a pet would make me a more rounded individual."

"You don't want to be rounded," she pointed out. "Racing comes first and you're proud of it."

Danny had noticed how that statement of his had rankled with her the other day. He figured it was why she'd turned down his offer of dinner. He should have been relieved—he didn't have time to date her—but instead he'd had that empty, gnawing feeling that hit when he lost a race. Unlike racing, where he could throw himself into his efforts to do better the following week, he'd been stuck with this feeling.

"Besides," she continued, "you're too busy for a dog. You spend half the year traveling."

"Plenty of NASCAR people take their dogs with them." He added, "I have a huge backyard, and if he doesn't come with me I can hire a dog-walker. When I'm home, he'll be good for my fitness."

"Big dogs don't need as much exercise as you think," she warned.

"He'll keep me company." Danny wished he hadn't said that. It made him sound lonely. Still, it produced the first softening he'd seen—Madison's brown eyes warmed up a fraction.

"I don't know," she said doubtfully.

"Dogs help people deal with hurt and rejection," he reminded her. Though, truth was, he hadn't thought about the breakup with Kristal with anything other than relief.

Danny knew for certain it would be a dumb idea to tell Madison he'd had such great publicity from the dog that he wanted to keep the story going. Even dumber to mention that a dog food company had approached the team about becoming a sponsor. Dumbest of all would be the revelation that Danny and the dog were getting as much media coverage as Trent Matheson and his fiancée—

a level of coverage that drivers usually attracted only by getting married or having babies.

All Danny had to do was own a dog. It was a no-brainer.

Doubtless Madison wouldn't see it that way. She wasn't one of the many people who would roll over just because Danny Cruise asked her to.

"A dog can be a good friend," she agreed.

Danny didn't have a lot of time for friendships—and that was the beauty of dog ownership. Instant friendship of the best kind, where he didn't have to do more than pat the creature's head every so often. Hell, he wished more of his girlfriends had been like that.

"I don't have a lot of friends," he admitted. If that's what it would take to get the dog...

Her mouth softened. But her eyes fastened on his, as if she could see into his thoughts. Danny blocked her by mentally rerunning last February's race at Daytona.

"What happens," she mused, "if the dog's real owner turns up?"

"I don't know," he said cautiously. It sounded as if she was considering letting him have the animal, but this might be a trick question. He threw it back to her. "What happens?"

"It might be a kid who doesn't see TV, who doesn't know we've found his pet," she said. "He could be crying himself to sleep every night."

Danny figured it was futile to point out that these days there weren't any kids who didn't see TV.

"The poor child has lost his pet right at Christmas," she continued.

The goldfish incident had shown Danny how seriously

Madison regarded children and their pets. Which gave him the answer to her question.

"If the real owner comes along, I'll give the dog back," he said triumphantly.

She sighed with relief. "You're right, of course."

"So I can have it?" Maybe it would be well enough to go for a walk, even chase after a stick, on Sunday. Sandra could tip off the newspapers about where he'd be.

"On one condition," Madison said.

Danny groaned inwardly. Was any publicity stunt worth dealing with a woman this difficult?

"I'll want to check the dog's living conditions and monitor how you're looking after him the first few weeks."

She had nerve, suggesting he wasn't a suitable dog owner. Then he remembered he hadn't been honest about his motives. He spread his hands in capitulation. "Fine."

"What are you going to call him?"

It took him a second to realize she'd conceded. He grinned, light-headed with relief. "Buster, of course." When she frowned, he teased, "You didn't think I'd call him Gorgeous, did you?"

She laughed, and her brown eyes danced. "Buster will do. I can give you some information sheets that will help you get started. He won't need a lot of exercise at first—he should take it easy until he's healed. Next week I'll take those sutures out."

She walked briskly to a filing cabinet in the corner, found what she wanted, then passed Danny a sheet of paper. "Here's a list of what you'll need to buy before you take him home—a bed, food and so on."

Danny hadn't had more top-five finishes in the NASCAR NEXTEL Cup Series than any other driver last season without taking advantage of every single gap open to him. And right now, he saw a gap that would allow him to get rid of the feeling that had bugged him since Madison had turned him down for dinner the other night.

But sometimes, the best way to attack a gap wasn't the most obvious. The gap might be between your rival and the wall—but if you sensed he would try to close the high gap, the smarter move was to run low. Danny sensed the less obvious approach was required here.

"I may need help to be sure I get the right stuff. How about I pick you up after work and we go to that pet emporium next to the mall?"

She frowned. "The list is pretty specific."

He scanned it. "It says I need a lead and collar. How long should the lead be? A soft collar or a leather one?" The chewing of her lower lip told him she was wavering. "It won't take long—Buster and I could really use your help." Relying on a dog to swing a date arguably repre- sented a new low in Danny's career. But as always, he'd do what it took to win.

"Fine," she said at last, and he was conscious of that release of pressure that came when he successfully sneaked through a gap out on the track. "You can pick me and Buster up tonight, if you're happy to leave him in your car when we're anywhere other than the pet store."

"No problem. Uh…he *is* potty-trained, right?"

Mischief lit her eyes. "We'll soon find out."

AS THEY WANDERED the pet store that evening with Buster on a leash, Danny insisted on pointing out which owners looked most like their pets. Nine times out of ten Madison disputed any resemblance, but there was one very funny instance of a Bichon Frise-toting blonde with an Afro.

"Wait till you start to look like Buster," she warned him.

He grinned. "It might improve my love life." As if every woman in the store hadn't turned to look at him, even those who didn't know who he was. But he didn't seem to register the attention—he was always one hundred percent focused on the task at hand. Which was what made him a great race driver, Madison guessed.

By the time Danny had bought out half the pet store, it was seven o'clock.

"I'll take you to dinner," he said as he loaded his purchases onto the truck bed.

Five harmless words. But Madison's imagination rampaged past dinner and didn't stop until it found a scenario that involved the two of them getting much more personal. Maybe she was coming down with a fever. She must be, because her brain lost its capacity for original thought and told her mouth to say, "Sorry, I have to wash my hair tonight."

He chuckled, ushered Buster into the backseat of his truck. He slanted her a half smile as he held her door open. "I insist."

Madison blew out a long, cooling breath and got a grip on herself. Why not see dinner as an extension of their shopping trip—she had to eat.

At a steak restaurant a couple of blocks from the mall, they agreed to share an appetizer of breads and dips, and ordered individual entrées. After the waiter had brought Danny's beer and Madison's glass of white wine, Danny leaned back on his side of the cowhide booth, his arms clasped behind his head, surveying Madison with an un-nerving satisfaction.

"What are you smirking at?" she demanded.

He raised his eyebrows at her assertive tone. "Can't I be pleased we're out on a date?"

"We—we're not," she said, as her imagination took off on another wild ride.

He pursed his lips as he looked around the restaurant. Following his gaze, Madison saw most tables were occupied by couples. Much of the lighting was supplied by candles. And sometime in the last few minutes the background music had switched from country to a popular love song.

"It's not a date," she said again. "You're not my type."

"Ouch." Yet he didn't look overly concerned as he leaned forward. "Where did I lose out? Is it my looks?"

Spoken like a guy who knew he was gorgeous. "You're okay," Madison admitted, her eyes fixed above his head.

His lips quirked. "Not rich enough for you?"

"Irrelevant."

"Hmm." He rubbed his chin. "My sense of humor?"

"Passable." She'd discovered she loved his deadpan, dry humor.

"Just no spark, huh?" He reached across the table, took her hand. His thumb traced her knuckles, and heat coursed through her veins, up her arm, suffused her whole body.

"That's right," she managed, slightly breathless. "No spark."

His smile widened. He held her gaze as he turned her hand over, and now his thumb found her wrist, its thudding pulse. He drew a circle, a trail of fire. Danny's eyes darkened as they dropped to her lips.

"Okay, okay, there's a spark," Madison said crossly. She wrenched her hand away, whipped it into her lap so he wouldn't see the trembling. "Sparks happen, no big deal. I can't imagine you really think this is a date. You're too one-dimensional for me."

Annoyance flickered in his expression. "Focusing on my racing doesn't make me one-dimensional. I want to win the NASCAR NEXTEL Cup Series championship. I've worked hard for years and that's put me in a position to achieve my dream."

The waiter arrived with their appetizer, and Danny waited until they were alone again before he continued. "I've seen how you are with your work, Madison. Don't tell me, with all that passion you feel for those animals, you don't have some kind of dream."

She did, but she never talked about it. Her boss would see it as treachery, her mom would worry about the risk involved, her sisters wouldn't understand why it was so important. Danny, who spent his life following his dream, would understand.

"I want to open my own clinic," she admitted. "I'd work with animal shelters half the time, private clients the rest. The private work would fund the shelter work."

"Sounds like something you'd be good at." He snapped a bread stick in half. "How's it going?"

"Excuse me?"

He bit into the bread stick. "What progress have you made?"

"I—uh…" She stared at him. "It's not like I'm planning to do it tomorrow."

"You'll never do it if you don't start working toward

it." He folded his arms. "Unless you get a little more one-dimensional."

"I don't have a lot of free time," she protested. "Roger, my boss, often needs me to work extra shifts. He promised he'll send me to a Clinic Management course next year—it's expensive and it'll help with setting up my own business. If I refuse shifts, he might back out." She could tell by the way Danny's lips clamped together he didn't think much of her reasoning.

Yeah, well, she didn't have a whole team of people helping her focus on her dream. "Your family must be proud of your racing," she said.

His eyes shuttered. "They would be if they were still around. My parents died when I was sixteen. They were driving through a flooded area. Their car got washed away."

"Oh, Danny." Instinctively, she reached across the table, put her hand over his.

For a fleeting moment, she saw stark pain in his eyes. Then he shook his head briskly and said, "Up until then I had a great childhood. Mom and Dad were the best, we did everything together."

Which would only have made the loss harder to bear.

"Did you have other family who could look after you?"

Danny eyed her with irritation. He never had this conversation with people; he hated talking about his past. "No one I wanted to go to. I already worked as a gofer for SouthMax Racing after school and during summer, and I was racing a midget for Hugh Naylor on weekends. Hugh said I could live in the apartment over his garage if I agreed to work for him full-time after I finished high school."

"So he adopted you? Fostered you?"

He shook his head. "I applied for emancipation as a minor, rather than go into the foster system."

Madison's eyes misted over.

"Hugh and his wife, Marj, were great." Danny took a hearty swig of his beer. "I had a place to live and an income. And I got to do what I love—drive race cars. If I hadn't been with Hugh I wouldn't have gotten into the NASCAR Busch Series as early as I did, and from there into the NASCAR NEXTEL Cup Series."

Madison made an inarticulate noise.

He slammed his empty glass down onto the table, rattling silverware and making her jump. "Dammit, Madison, quit looking like you're about to cry. Save your pity for dumb animals that can't help themselves."

CHAPTER FIVE

MADISON'S BROWN EYES filled with hurt—which was a welcome change from that damned pity she seemed to feel for anyone and everyone at the drop of a spanner.

Danny scanned the drinks menu, so he wouldn't have to look at her. So what if he'd had fun shopping with her tonight…and even more fun teasing her about the attraction between them? Somehow he'd ended up asking about her dreams, then blabbing about his parents—those things wouldn't help him win races and they left him feeling even more unsettled than he'd been lately. He decided she was right; this shouldn't be a date.

Their steaks arrived, along with steak knives that would have come in handy cutting the tension at the table.

For a while, they ate in silence. Danny took the opportunity to observe Madison as she cut her steak, speared pieces of salad with her fork. Her cheeks were flushed—no doubt because she was mad at him—and her hair looked soft and touchable. Her sweater was a chunky gold knit that crossed in a V over her breasts. At the pet store, Danny had noticed how the sweater skimmed her trim, jean-clad derriere.

His gaze traveled back up to her face and locked on her lips. He imagined leaning across the table and kissing her right now. Bad idea, given he didn't plan to see her again.

Then he heard himself say, "I have to go to New York for the NASCAR NEXTEL Cup Series awards ceremony on Friday. I wouldn't know where to start finding a place to board Buster—any chance you can look after him overnight?"

Madison put down her fork, happy to talk, it seemed, when it concerned the dog. "I'd love to look after him, but my condo rules don't allow me to have a dog. Even if it's just for one night, one of the neighbors is bound to make a fuss—it's hard to sneak in an animal as big as Buster."

Danny drummed his fingers on the table. He couldn't believe what he was about to say, yet there was an inevitability about it he couldn't fight. "You can stay at my place."

She recoiled. "I'm a stranger. Why would you invite me to stay?"

"You care about Buster. You're more likely to let him destroy my garden than you are to steal the silver." Danny realized it was that caring side of Madison that had grabbed him and wouldn't let go. Looking at it dispassionately, he could admit he was vulnerable right now. It might not be a bad idea to give in, temporarily, to his need for the kind of care Madison offered—even if it was aimed at his dog, not at him. It might make the holiday season less…solitary.

In the end, he convinced her, which he chalked up as another victory for Danny Cruise. Then he swiftly wrapped up the evening—before his runaway mouth and his lonely soul invited her to move in with him permanently.

He drove Madison back to the vet clinic to pick up her car. He got out of the truck to open her door. She was so close he could smell her hair, lemons and something spicy like cinnamon. She looked up at him. Man, she had a nice mouth.

"Good night, Madison." He leaned in, kissed her briefly,

just long enough for the softness of her lips to tantalize him into wanting more. When he pulled back, she was smiling and frowning at the same time.

She got into her car, lowered the window. "Thanks for an interesting evening, Danny."

After she drove away, Danny climbed back into the truck, slamming the door. "Interesting!" he expostulated. "What kind of word is that?"

In the backseat, Buster lifted his head and yawned.

Suddenly, Danny wasn't sure who'd won tonight.

AT SIX O'CLOCK Friday evening, Madison keyed in the entry code Danny had given her, and let herself into his stone-and-cedar home near Kannapolis.

"Wow." Slowly, she turned to take in the double-height entryway, the open-plan living and dining room with vaulted ceilings. It was so large, it might have been intimidating, but Danny's house was homier than she'd have imagined. Warm colors delineated the spaces and created intimate corners. The enormous fireplace was piled high with logs and pinecones.

Then she noticed the Christmas decorations everywhere. A tree in the living room, swathes of red and gold ribbon. Obviously Danny hadn't done it himself—the decor proclaimed a professional touch. But even so, why would a guy who wanted to forget Christmas have someone make his house look like this? As she headed to the kitchen, she noticed mistletoe hung above every doorway. Which took her mind in the obvious direction…

It was the shortest kiss in history, she scolded herself. Yet she only had to close her eyes to feel Danny's mouth on hers again. Impatient with her mental meanderings, she yanked the back door open. Buster's chain rattled on the back porch as he got to his feet.

"Come in, boy," she invited. "Come and distract me from Danny Scrooge."

After Madison fed Buster and ate the microwave meal she'd brought with her—despite Danny's insistence she should help herself to the contents of his family-size fridge—she turned on the TV.

The NASCAR awards show started at nine. As she watched the opening credits roll, an awful thought struck her. What if Danny was taking a date to the ceremony? Surely he would have said something…but Madison was the one who'd insisted the dinner they'd shared wasn't a date.

She watched various drivers, team owners and sponsors arriving on the "Yellow Carpet," the men in their tuxedos, the women glamorous in evening dress. Pretty much everyone was in a couple.

The voice-over said, "And there's NASCAR NEXTEL Cup Series runner-up Danny Cruise, The Natural."

He appeared on her screen—alone. Immediately, for his sake, Madison wished he wasn't. Because she couldn't help feeling that, whatever he said about his focus on his racing, Danny was lonely.

She watched the ceremony right through. Danny won the Most Dramatic Moment Award, when viewers voted his knife-edge win at Daytona as the most nerve-racking highlight of the last NASCAR NEXTEL Cup Series season. And, of course, he won the award for finishing second in the series.

On that trip to the podium, he said, "Winning the NASCAR NEXTEL Cup Series championship is the pinnacle of any driver's racing career. I want to congratulate Trent Matheson on his deserved victory. And to give him some advice for next season—watch your back."

The crowd laughed and applauded. Back in Danny's living room, Madison added graciousness and self-possession to the list of things she liked about him. *The only list I should be making is my Christmas shopping,* she thought.

After the program finished, Madison took Buster outside, where they both shivered in the freezing night air, then she showed him to his basket in the utility room before she headed upstairs. The guest room Danny had told her to use was spacious, decorated in aqua and teal colors that lent a restful feeling.

She brushed her teeth, donned her pale blue flannel pajamas, which featured gamboling kittens. Buster had been fine tonight—if she managed to dig up enough willpower, she would leave right after breakfast, without waiting for Danny to get home.

Bad idea to start thinking about Danny as she climbed into bed. Madison slept fitfully, waking several times, and each time it took her a while to get back to sleep. On about the fifth occasion, the bedside clock read four-thirty. She went to the bathroom, then, restless, wandered to the window, peeked through the curtains. It was still pitch-dark outside. Maybe a soothing cup of tea would put her back to sleep.

Downstairs, she stuck her head around the utility room door—Buster slept the sleep of the innocent, lying on his back, legs in the air. Madison chuckled as she put the kettle on the stove.

Then she saw the slow, silent movement of the back door. Opening.

The sensible thing would have been to run for a phone and dial 911. Madison froze to the spot and let out a squawk.

The door flung open, and Danny raced into the kitchen. "Madison? Are you okay?"

"No, you jerk, I'm having a heart attack." She clutched at her chest, where her heart had almost leaped out of its cavity. Her other hand gripped the back of one of the pine kitchen chairs, because her knees threatened to buckle.

"Hold on." He grabbed her upper arms, half supporting her, half hauling her toward the phone. Then he computed that her condition was the result of his unexpected appearance, and stopped. "Dammit, you gave me a scare."

"*You* gave *me* a scare." She thumped him lightly on his chest. He was wearing a tuxedo again, and his white shirt looked just as good dry as it did damp. "What are you doing here?"

Apparently satisfied she was in no danger of imminent cardiac arrest, he relaxed his grip. "I left right after the awards ceremony. I flew up on my own plane, so it was no big deal."

"Oh." That was all Madison could manage, because Danny's hands were caressing her upper arms. Awareness scattered and regrouped—awareness of the scant few inches of space between them, that she was wearing her pajamas, that she'd failed to fasten the top three buttons, giving him a generous view of her cleavage. Fortunately, he wasn't looking down.

Now he was.

His eyes lingered on the swell of her curves, and Madison thought she really should do something to get his attention. Something other than removing her pajama top.

"I watched the awards on TV." Her voice came out husky.

He brought his gaze back up. "I hoped you were."

The simple words had Madison's heart thumping again.

"It wasn't much fun being there on my own," he admitted.

"Too bad they don't let you take a pet," she joked.

He inched closer. "I wasn't thinking about Buster." He fingered the lapel of her pajamas, touched one of the kittens. "Cute pj's."

Without waiting for a reply, he grasped her other lapel and tugged her toward him so they were touching almost the entire length of their bodies. Surely that lightest of contact couldn't explain the explosion of heat that rippled through Madison?

"Your house is gorgeous," she babbled, feeling as if her face was on fire. "It's so comfortable, so warm."

"I had a good decorator." One arm slipped behind her back.

She swallowed. "You must have told her what you wanted."

He nodded. His other arm went around her, just loosely, but now she was wholly in his embrace.

"And the Christmas decorations," she said urgently.

"The decorator again," he murmured, tucking a strand of hair behind her ear. His fingers lingered there. "All part of the service."

"The tree looks fantastic."

"Uh-huh." His eyes told her he thought something was fantastic, but it wasn't the tree. "What did you think of the mistletoe?"

"It, uh…" The words dried up under the scorching heat in his dark eyes. He tightened his embrace enough to move her backward to the doorway. Madison couldn't resist looking up at the mistletoe.

"Let's see if it works." Danny lowered his mouth to hers.

From the first touch, it was nothing like that swift kiss he'd given her the other night. He kissed her hard, seeking a response that Madison gave willingly. She wound her arms around his neck, pressing herself closer to him.

If they didn't stop now, the next step was bed.

She tore her mouth from his. "Danny, wait." She put a hand on his chest, creating a space between them.

He was breathing heavily, just as she was, and his eyes glinted with a hunger she recognized. He ran a hand through his hair. "You're going to say this is a bad idea."

"You know it is." She ducked her head aside as he leaned toward her again. "I should go back to bed. Alone."

He sighed as he released her, then smoothed her pajama top back into place with an efficient intimacy that had her blushing. "If you're sure that's what you want."

"It is," she lied.

His hands rested on her hips. He glanced over her head and said regretfully, "Best damned mistletoe I ever bought."

WOULD DANNY KISS any woman he found in his kitchen in the early hours of the morning? Or only a woman he…liked?

The questions plagued Madison as she showered. She'd fallen asleep after she came back upstairs this morning, and she hadn't woken until nearly eight.

She toweled herself dry, pulled on jeans and a clean long-sleeved cherry-colored T-shirt.

"I don't think he'd kiss just anyone," she said out loud. Danny wasn't one of those drivers who had a reputation as a flirt. From what Madison knew of him, he wasn't overly impulsive. In which case, he liked her.

"Why shouldn't he like me?" she asked her reflection. She might not be as glamorous as his other girlfriends, but she was attractive. He'd described their dinner the other night as a date. Did he want to keep dating her? If he did, what would she say?

Madison tried to picture herself as Danny Cruise's girlfriend.

Will I have to get a belly button ring?

She lifted her T-shirt and checked out her navel above the low-slung jeans. Imagined a gold stud or hoop—very tasteful, nothing flashy—glistening there. She rather liked the idea.

Of course, she couldn't let her mom see it.

Just like that, the bubble burst. Who was she kidding? She liked Danny, he was a great guy—but he was never going to fit into her ordinary life. He wasn't going to spend time with her mom and her three younger sisters when they had their boyfriends over for a family Sunday dinner once a month. He wasn't going to help them move furniture and paint walls.

Why start dating him when she'd end up dissatisfied? To avoid any risk to her heart, she should end it now.

But…maybe she'd let him kiss her good morning first.

CHAPTER SIX

WHEN MADISON WALKED into the kitchen, Danny was using a knife to extract something from the toaster.

"I picked up some bagels from the all-night store on my way home this morning," he said.

Electrocuting himself seemed an unnecessarily severe way to end their relationship. Madison moved swiftly to unplug the toaster from the wall.

He looked up, surprised. "Thanks, but I was being careful."

"Wouldn't want to deprive the female species of one of the best kissers I ever met." *Good,* she told herself. *You're keeping it casual, but giving him the opportunity to kiss you again.*

"Is that so?" His eyes on Madison's mouth, he freed the bagel from the toaster, tossed it onto the counter. He took a step toward her, just as Buster rose from his position under the kitchen table and came to check if the stray crumbs that fell to the floor constituted his breakfast.

Danny nudged the dog with his knee. "Out of my way, mutt."

When Madison tutted, he broke off a piece of bagel and fed it to Buster, then patted him on the head. As a vet, Madison disapproved of feeding dogs anything other than dog food from anywhere other than their bowl. As a dog lover, she approved of Danny's conciliatory effort.

He sidestepped around Buster. "Now, where were we?" From the heat in his eyes, he hadn't forgotten. He took Madison in his arms. She had the crazy thought that she'd been created to fit this particular space.

He dropped a kiss on the top of her head, one on her forehead, one on her nose. "I've been thinking about this ever since you went upstairs."

Keep it casual. "You're a guy. Guys always think about sex."

"Who said anything about sex?" he asked, amused.

Betrayed by her own big mouth! Embarrassed, she tried to wriggle out of his embrace. He tightened his grip.

"I'm not saying my thoughts wouldn't have got there in the end," he assured her. "But they weren't rushing." His lips skimmed hers. "They were enjoying the journey."

Madison quivered with need for more of his mouth on hers. But she made a supreme effort. "Let's be sensible about this, Danny. You and I have nothing in common."

His quizzical gaze met hers. "Apart from this raging attraction and our mutual love of dogs."

"Attraction doesn't necessarily mean anything. I admit, I don't usually kiss guys I'm not dating." She struggled to remember her point. "But I'll bet you do—you probably kiss lots of women without it meaning a thing."

"All the time," he said. She felt a twist of jealousy, which only served to remind her Danny wasn't the man for her. "You could say I'm an expert on the subject."

"How interesting," she said frostily.

He chuckled, glanced at her lips again. "And in my expert opinion, that kiss you and I shared this morning was not meaningless." Broodingly, he added, "If kisses were NASCAR NEXTEL Cup cars, that one would have been first over the line."

"Really?" She couldn't help betraying her pleasure.

He narrowed his gaze. "Are you sure you don't get a lot of practice?"

She shook her head.

"Then you're a natural." His lips descended toward hers.

"I had help," she reminded him modestly, her eyes riveted to his mouth. "Expert assistance."

"True." He paused, tantalizingly close. "Or it might have been beginner's luck."

She licked her lips. "You think?"

"A repeat would help us determine that."

"I guess…if you think it's necessary," she murmured.

The pressure in Danny's lungs told him if he didn't kiss Madison right now it would be bad for his health.

"It's essential," he said authoritatively.

With a little sigh, she tilted her face to his. Something soared through Danny—the same blend of relief and elation that hit him when he was first past the checkered flag—and he claimed that essential, sustaining kiss.

When it ended, he was surprised to find he wasn't quite steady. He held on to Madison. "You can't tell me that was meaningless."

She rested her head on his shoulder, and Danny's hand moved involuntarily to stroke her hair. "No—" her voice was muffled "—but I wish it had been."

His hand stilled. "You're going to be difficult again, aren't you? Can't you just take this…whatever it is…at face value? Enjoy it?"

"I did enjoy it—" she pulled away "—and now it's over. Admit it, Danny, you're not interested in me."

He ran a hand through his hair. "I'm very interested in kissing you some more." He didn't want to lie to her about how far he was willing to take this.

"You date models, actresses, women who look good on a NASCAR driver's arm."

"I date women I like," he corrected. "I happen to meet a lot of those types of women, and I happen to like some of them."

"You don't date ordinary women." Before he could protest, she added, "And why should you? You're an extraordinary guy. I'll admit I find that exciting. But I don't want to get sucked into thinking you and I might have a relationship that lasts after the new season starts."

"We could date until then. It's only a couple of months until Daytona."

"I don't want to risk falling for you, getting sidetracked from what I really want." She chewed her lower lip. "I want a man who's part of my life, as well as me being part of his. I just want a regular guy."

Any desire Danny had to argue evaporated. If there was one thing he could never be—would never want to be while he was racing NASCAR—it was a regular guy. Regular guys didn't win the NASCAR NEXTEL Cup Series championship.

Danny was a race driver—nothing more, nothing less.

Maybe further down the track, when he was done racing, he'd have space for the kind of relationship Madison was talking about…. Of course, she'd be snapped up long before that. He shoved the thought aside.

"You're right," he said.

She let out a breath that he would have thought was relief if he hadn't seen the shadow of disappointment in her eyes.

He turned away before he did something stupid, and started spreading butter on a bagel. But he couldn't resist rubbing in the consequences of her decision. "It's too bad we're not good for dating," he said, "because that was one hell of a kiss."

MADISON CHECKED on Buster twice the following week, and each time she had to fight the impulse to relax too much in Danny's company. He and the dog were getting along okay, and after she removed Buster's sutures at the clinic on Friday morning, she decided she no longer needed to monitor Danny's dog-owner skills. When she told him, he eyed her thoughtfully. But he didn't protest, just kissed her goodbye—she thought he was aiming for her cheek, but at the last second it turned into a hard kiss on the mouth—and left.

On Sunday, he phoned to invite Madison over for lunch.

It wasn't fair, making her listen to his sexy voice on the phone while he talked about cooking his specialty dish for her.

"We're not dating," she reminded him, one hand on her stomach to ease the hunger pangs that weren't at all related to food. "I want a regular guy, you want a supermodel."

"Buster needs you."

"He was fine two days ago."

"He had a relapse last night and is at death's door," Danny said cheerfully.

She'd given a refusal her best shot. But she was only human, and two days of thinking the nearest she'd get to

Danny again was her TV set had her cursing her lifelong common sense.

"In that case," she said, "I'd better come over."

She made herself wait until midday before she drove to Danny's. It took him a while to get to the door after she rang the bell.

It was worth the wait.

He'd obviously been working out—he wore sweat shorts and a T-shirt with cutoff sleeves. The man was a picture of athletic hunkdom. Biceps, triceps and quads gleamed with perspiration, his hair was mussed, the way it might be if she stepped forward and—

Madison swallowed a wave of desire. "How's Buster?" she managed.

"A miraculous recovery." Danny hauled her into his arms, kissed her hungrily. Madison kissed him right back, reveled in his male heat, the hard strength of his thighs against her legs, strong hands that sought her curves.

"I'm all sweaty," he murmured some time later.

"So am I now." She kissed him again. "I just want to point out that we're still not dating."

"Right." He nuzzled her ear.

"I'm here for lunch."

"Nice appetizer," he murmured against a sensitive spot on her neck. His warm breath sent shivers through her.

"Maybe you should start cooking," she prompted.

"I guess." Reluctantly, he let her go. "First, I'll go take a shower."

Oh, yeah, just leave her with *that* image.

DANNY SERVED THE PASTA with tomato-based sauce and spicy chorizo sausages that was one of his personal favorites. Today, it came with a kick of self-criticism and a side order of guilt.

He hadn't wanted to go another day without seeing Madison, but given what he had planned for this afternoon, his timing stank.

Madison mopped up the last of her sauce with a slice of Italian bread. "Who would have thought you could cook like a regular guy," she marveled.

"I do *not* cook like a regular guy," Danny objected. "I cook like a star."

He took the "mmm-hmm" noises she made as she chewed to be agreement.

They stacked the dishwasher together. Buster hovered waiting for scraps, and Madison gave Danny a lecture on doggy etiquette—namely, he shouldn't give Buster the plate scrapings. He silenced her by pulling her close for another of those earth-shattering kisses.

If he was sensible, he thought as he made coffee, he'd send her home now. But he couldn't bring himself to end their time together. Besides, this afternoon's errand would look more natural if he had company. He handed Madison her coffee. "How about we take Buster for his first proper walk?"

"Great idea."

He loved that tender look she got in her eye. Too bad it only appeared when he did something nice to the dog.

"Maybe we could do some Christmas shopping, too," she suggested. "I'm running out of time to get it all done."

"No problem, as long as we can give Buster a spell in the park."

She raised her eyebrows, obviously impressed at his concern for the dog's welfare.

They took both their cars into Kannapolis, where they strolled hand in hand past stores decorated to the hilt for Christmas. Madison made several purchases, which they loaded into her car before they walked to the park.

Buster was ecstatic to be running around, foraging in damp leaves that had turned to mush. His pleasure made Danny feel a little better about not being honest with Madison.

They'd been there twenty minutes when a man carrying a camera approached them.

"Fred Elliott from the *North Carolina Chronicle*," he introduced himself. "I'd like to get a shot of you and the dog."

"Sure." Danny called Buster over, and Fred Elliott took photos of him and Buster playing tug-of-war with a stick, then jogging side by side along the cobbled path.

Madison watched the whole thing with no evident suspicion that the photo shoot was prearranged.

"How did he find you here?" she asked afterward.

Now was the time to come clean…but Danny didn't want to ruin the day's cozy intimacy. "A lot of people know my truck. Maybe he was just passing."

"Those guys should give you some privacy."

"I guess there's not a lot else going on." He made a strategic change of subject. "Are you looking forward to Christmas?"

Fortunately, Madison was easily distracted. "I was, but Roger, my boss, has asked me to work Christmas Day—we're open for emergency treatment. Trouble is, Mom needs me at home—my dad's coming, and he always ends up upsetting Mom."

She'd told Danny before that her mom had been pretty

cut up over the divorce. "Tell Roger you can't work," Danny said. "If he wants to stay open, he can do it himself."

"Roger never works holidays," she said wryly. "He'll make things unpleasant if I refuse. Besides, I don't want to jeopardize that clinic management course."

Danny didn't like the thought of her boss bullying her— nor of her having to act as a buffer between her parents. "If you're serious about starting your own practice, you can't wait around for your boss's goodwill," he said. "And quit worrying about your mom—she's old enough to deal with her own problems. If you're ever going to get what you want, you need to be tougher—with your boss, with your family. With yourself."

The words came out rougher than he intended, and Madison's chin went up in the air in a way that told him she didn't want the advice of a one-dimensional NASCAR driver.

That didn't bother him. What bothered him was the almost irresistible compulsion to go out there and fight Madison's battles for her, no matter that he didn't have time for anything other than winning the NASCAR NEXTEL Cup Series title.

MADISON SAT BACK in her padded leather seat on Danny's private jet early on Tuesday morning. "Not dating" a NASCAR driver had its perks.

Being whisked off to Kentucky at a moment's notice was one of them.

Danny sat next to her, and Buster lay at their feet. In theory, she was here to look after Buster, but this was the fourth time Danny had called with a request for her dog-sitting services that had turned into a thinly veiled date. Madison sipped at her soda. "Tell me what'll happen today."

Danny looked up from the car specifications he was reading. "I'll be testing our new cup car. We'll try different setups, see what impact they have on performance. In January we'll do some of our NASCAR-allotted testing at Daytona, but because Kentucky isn't a NASCAR track we can be more flexible and a little less pressured."

"So you're not racing anyone." She'd been looking forward to seeing Danny in action.

"It's still important. There'll be a potential sponsor watching. An extra couple of million dollars from an associate sponsor would mean we can run the season without having to compromise on spares or personnel—that can make all the difference." He had that look in his eyes that told her he was thinking ahead to the moment he won the NASCAR NEXTEL Cup Series championship.

"How can a sponsor see how good you are if you're the only driver on the track?"

He shrugged. "Sponsoring a car is a business decision, but you can't ignore the emotional side. I've seen a guy who wasn't sure he wanted to spend five million dollars write a check for eight million after he spent a day at testing." He scratched Buster's head. "All I have to do is drive like a star."

CHAPTER SEVEN

DANNY COULDN'T hit his stride in the new car. No matter that he and his crew chief been over every aspect of his performance, everything he'd liked and disliked about last season's car. No matter that, on paper, this car was perfect.

In reality, it felt way too tight, the front tires losing traction through the turns. At one stage, the damned thing almost hit the wall. But Danny was experienced enough to know he couldn't blame it all on the car. Maybe he was communicating badly with the crew—he'd been in and out of the pits several times, but it never seemed to get better. Or maybe he was driving like an amateur.

Right now, he wanted nothing more than to get out of the car, leave it to the experts to fix while he went to find Madison. Dammit, if this was how next season was shaping up, he was in trouble.

At lunchtime, Danny joined Madison in the media room.

"That didn't look like much fun out there," Madison sympathized.

"Couldn't get much worse," Danny agreed. A moment later, he revised that opinion when Trent Matheson breezed in, along with his fiancée, Kelly Greenwood. Danny knew Matheson Racing would be testing tomorrow; he'd seen the crew in the garage. But he hadn't realized Trent was here already—had his rival seen his abysmal performance?

Trent greeted journalists and guests with a charming smile and easy manner. He'd always been great with people, unlike Danny, who didn't have the patience to charm others.

Danny shook hands with Trent. "Trent, Kelly, this is Madison Beale."

Kelly greeted Madison with a friendly comment. Trent gave her that killer smile that had made him NASCAR's most popular bachelor and said warmly, "Great to meet you, Madison. How'd a jerk like Danny find someone as cute as you?"

Her reply was unusually subdued, and Danny wondered if Trent's presence had overwhelmed her. It hadn't bothered him before that Trent was Madison's favorite driver, but right now it did. He and Trent had a history of playing mind games with each other in their NASCAR NEXTEL Cup Series rivalry—he didn't want to start feeling jealous of the guy over a woman.

Trent said, "Hey, Cruise, you've had some good press recently—enjoy it while it lasts." The implication being that once racing started, it would be Trent garnering all the attention.

"No sweat," Danny said easily. "Some of us don't have to resort to a marriage proposal to score good headlines."

Trent took it with good humor. "Oh, yeah," he joked, "that was such a bummer." He tightened his grip on Kelly's shoulder. "I'm suffering, sugar, aren't I?"

He dipped his head and kissed his fiancée on the mouth. And kept on kissing her. So thoroughly that Kelly blushed, and made an effort to free herself, but soon she gave up the struggle and wrapped her arms around Trent's neck.

When Trent surfaced, he looked dazed. "Uh, what were we talking about?"

If Trent could get that distracted by a kiss, he'd be a pushover next year, Danny thought. Then he remembered Trent must have been making out with Kelly, a sport psychologist who'd been hired to coach him last season, for some time before he won the series. Maybe Trent didn't easily get hit by distractions…except his distractibility was what Danny had judged to be his rival's weakness through most of last season.

Danny's refusal to be distracted had been his greatest strength.

After a couple of minutes, Madison excused herself to check on Buster. Trent was dragged away by his team's publicity manager, leaving Danny alone with Kelly.

"I'm sorry you had that trouble after you didn't show up at our engagement party," Kelly said. "Neither Trent nor I thought you were a bad sport."

"Thanks," he said. "Uh, how are the wedding plans going?"

"Trent's dad wants us to wait until he's fully recovered from his heart attack." She grinned. "Let's talk about something much more interesting—how was your car today?"

"We had a few problems." Then—maybe because she projected that you-can-tell-me-anything shrink persona—he added, "But it wasn't all the car's fault."

"Hmm." She nodded sympathetically.

A classic shrink response, Danny assumed. Funny how it made him want to talk. "I was pretty burned up about coming second in the Cup again this season," he said. "It's hit my confidence harder than I like to think. The new season hasn't started yet, but already it's like I've lost that feeling that I can win."

"I see." She sounded interested.

"You realize that's not true," he deadpanned. "I'm saying this so you'll pass it on to Trent and he'll be lulled into a false sense of security."

Her frank blue gaze met his. "Sure. And because I don't want Trent to be fooled by your little act, I won't tell him."

Danny nodded, gave her a faint smile. "I find myself thinking, what if I can't get out there and win again? Last season was my best ever—what if that's as good as I get?" An attitude like that could become a self-fulfilling prophecy.

Kelly frowned. "First up, if there's anything you've let slide—your diet, your race preparation, fitness…make sure you have plans in place to fix it."

"Uh-huh." He had all that in hand—he'd hoped for something a little more inspiring.

"What I'm going to say now sounds a bit airy-fairy, but it works. You need to surround yourself with cues that remind you you're a race driver and a winner."

"Cues," he repeated doubtfully.

"Where do you keep your race trophies?" she asked.

"In the cupboard under the stairs. A few in the basement."

She chuckled. "Dust those suckers off and put them all around the house. Every room, even the bathroom." She grinned at his expression. "And the photos, ribbons, banners, everything. Put it all on display. Every time you look around, you'll see you're a winner."

"You think that'll work?"

"I think it'll help." Someone brushed past her and Kelly stumbled; Danny helped right her. "The same goes for the people you're with. Get rid of everything and everyone that reminds you of failure. Surround yourself with people who can attest you're a winner, who think of you that way."

"Does Trent do all this stuff?" he asked, curious.

"Trent's problem," she said drily, "has never been one of too little confidence."

Danny laughed, and realized he felt better. "Thanks, Kelly."

"We've only scratched the surface," she said, "Too bad you're the competition, because I could do you a lot of good."

Trent called her over to him, and she left Danny to mull over her advice. Getting his trophies out of the cupboard would be easy. It might feel dumb, but he could do it. Then he had to surround himself with people who thought he was a winner....

Hugh and Marj did, or they wouldn't have given him a ride in the NASCAR NEXTEL Cup Series. The team was fine, too, barring their understandable frustration today.

Madison came back into the room, drawing his attention the way she always did. Danny found himself thinking about her all the time—that couldn't be good.

Did Madison think of him as a winner? She did, Danny realized, but that wasn't what she wanted to see. She liked to dig deep to find the "regular guy," the part of himself he'd put under wraps for the duration of his career in the NASCAR NEXTEL Cup Series.

For the first time, he understood she was right to say they shouldn't date, not even for a few weeks. Maybe his other relationships had lacked depth, but those women dated him because he was a winner and they knew that was the most important thing.

Madison would probably say something else was most important. Like taking time to play with the dog. Like cozy Sunday lunches. Like Christmas.

He couldn't go on seeing her.

Danny was shocked to realize he might not have the willpower to give her up. This had gone way too far.

He'd have to rely on her willpower instead.

"TRENT MATHESON IS A JERK," Madison declared as their flight took off back to Charlotte.

Danny's driving had improved in the latter part of the day, but ever since he'd got out of the car he'd been quiet and distant, and Madison wondered if he was still worried about his performance. Her announcement got his attention.

"Trent's okay," he said, surprised.

"The guy's engaged to be married, and he was all but hitting on me."

Danny smiled, and the crease that had furrowed his brow the last hour smoothed out. "Trent's like that with every woman—except Kelly. That surface charm deflects anyone from getting any deeper with him."

"I wouldn't want a fiancé who told other women they're cute," Madison said.

Danny gave her a brooding look. "You want a regular guy."

"That's right." She wondered if a NASCAR driver could be a regular guy. At least, this particular NASCAR driver. Because the more time she spent with Danny, the more she wanted to date him. And not just for a few weeks. Out of duty to her emotional safety, she kept telling herself that was stupid—but she'd stopped listening.

She laced her fingers between Danny's on the armrest between their seats. His fingers tightened around hers; his strength coursed into her. With Danny, she felt as if anything was possible.

Then he pulled his hand out, looked down at his fingers as he straightened them. "The potential sponsor didn't rate my driving today."

No wonder Danny wasn't himself. "I'm sorry," she said. "If he got to know you he'd soon see—"

"Before you start taking on my problems as well as those of every stray dog or cat," he said abruptly, "I should tell you who the sponsor is."

The atmosphere in the airplane was suddenly charged with static tension.

"Who is it?" Madison said warily.

His eyes met hers, defiant in a way she didn't understand. "Poochy Packs."

"The dog cookie people?" She'd seen their distinctive purple packaging in pet stores and specialist pet bakeries.

"Uh-huh. Can you believe people are crazy enough to buy cookies for their dogs?"

She ignored that. "Did Poochy Packs get interested because you own a dog?"

"They got interested," he said deliberately, "*before* I owned a dog. Right after that photo shoot at your clinic."

The cabin felt suddenly airless; Madison half expected to see an oxygen mask drop down in front of her. "That's— that's why you adopted Buster."

He nodded. "I knew I'd have a better chance of convincing Poochy Packs to come on board."

She thought about how he'd convinced her to let him have Buster. "Not because you were lonely…or hurting."

"Loneliness isn't a big deal for me—I'm best when I'm on my own."

Madison felt hollow inside at the thought that Danny's kindness to Buster had been purely so he could attract money to his NASCAR NEXTEL Cup Series campaign. Other things started to add up. "That photographer in the park... You knew he'd be there."

"Yep. Sandra, my PR rep, tipped him off."

"Why did you take me with you that day?"

He hesitated. "I thought it would look more natural than me being there on my own."

"And you brought Buster to Kentucky to impress the Poochy Packs guy."

He nodded.

"And me?"

For a moment she thought he was going to reveal some other awful advantage her presence had afforded him. But he said gruffly, "I wanted you with me."

"I don't believe you." The ache in Madison's chest spread right through her. "You're not fit to own a dog, you're not fit to date me."

Danny didn't reply.

"Why are you telling me this now?"

His gaze slid away. "I don't want you getting the wrong idea about me. I want you to know what matters most to me."

The rest of the flight passed in a silence that had Buster confused, anxiously licking first Danny's hand, then Madison's.

Danny must have guessed the direction of her thoughts, her hopes about him, Madison realized. As they passed through thick clouds that buffeted the little aircraft, her pain receded, to be replaced by a pervasive numbness.

Right now it might feel as if Danny had run her over with his NASCAR NEXTEL Cup Series car, but in her mangled heart Madison knew he'd done her a favor.

CHAPTER EIGHT

THANKS TO the strong headwinds that slowed their flight, Madison was late for her evening shift at the clinic.

Danny, courteous as ever, escorted her inside, despite her assertion that he didn't have to. Roger had filled in for her until she arrived, and he was in a filthy mood, despite the fact she'd called to say she'd be late. When he started bandying about words like *carelessness* and *lack of commitment,* Madison snapped.

"Cut it out, Roger, you know I do more shifts than anyone. If it wasn't for me you might have to lift a finger around here more often." She sensed Danny's surprise, then his silent approval in the way he shifted closer to her. But she was mad at him, too; she didn't give a damn what he thought.

"And what's more," she told Roger, "I can't work Christmas Day. I've done it the last two years. It's someone else's turn."

Roger turned puce. "I need staff I can rely on. I'm surprised at your irresponsible attitude, given you think you should be attending the clinic management course in February."

Madison gulped. Was she willing to risk him pulling her off the course if she didn't work Christmas? Maybe she could work if she asked Mom to serve a late meal and—

Then Danny's arm landed around her shoulder, in a gesture that was supportive, protective, empowering. She wanted to throw it off; she didn't.

"It's my fault Madison can't work Christmas," he said. "I want to have Christmas with her and her mom."

Madison felt her jaw drop, and hauled it back into line. He was saying it to help her with Roger, because he felt guilty about using her and Buster.

Roger paused, but not for long. "That's all very well, but I have a business to run here. I can't have my people—"

"Then make sure you run it like a business," Danny said, his voice so hard that Madison was startled into looking at him. "A *businessman* wouldn't pull Madison off that management course, any more than he'd expect her to work Christmas three years running."

"It was never my intention to pull Madison off the course," Roger said stiffly. "I suppose I can find someone else to work Christmas Day."

"That's good news," Danny said calmly. He dropped a brief kiss on Madison's lips. It had none of the warmth or tenderness in it she'd come to expect, and she knew it was for Roger's benefit.

"I'll pick you up at six Friday night," he said. At her evident confusion, he added, "For the SouthMax Christmas party. You agreed to come with me."

"You've got to be—" She stopped, aware Roger was still there.

"Six o'clock." The hard purpose in Danny's eyes told her he meant it.

ON FRIDAY, Danny picked Madison up from her condo at six sharp. She opened the door to him wearing the new dress she'd bought over a week ago, right after he'd invited her to the party. She hadn't spoken to him since he'd left her at the clinic on Tuesday.

"Wow." As he presented her with a corsage, a beautiful white gardenia, his eyes traveled over the turquoise halterneck dress that molded to her curves and ended in a flirty swish above her knees. "I, uh, didn't expect you to be ready."

She suspected he'd thought he might have to forcibly drag her to the party after the way he'd behaved.

"Oh, I'm ready." She'd been doing a lot of thinking since she last saw him.

He took the purse she extended to him, held it while she pinned the corsage to her dress.

She waited until they were in the truck before she spoke again. "Those things you said on the flight back from Kentucky…that was to show me you can't be the kind of guy I want, right? You can't be a regular guy?"

"It was all true." He started the engine, pulled out into the traffic.

"Then why are you taking me to the party tonight, rather than some supermodel who thinks you're nothing more than a NASCAR star?"

For a moment, he said nothing. Then, reluctantly, he growled, "Because no matter that there's no future for us, we're not done yet." He glanced over his shoulder as he changed lanes. Their eyes clashed for a brief moment. "Why are you coming to the party when you're mad at me?"

"Because," she said, "no matter that you've been using me from the get-go, we're not done yet."

His mouth curved in a puzzled smile. "Why do I get the feeling you mean something different from what I mean?"

She opted for an oblique approach. "I went to see Mom yesterday and told her that if Dad comes home for Christmas, she can count me out."

"Whoa." Danny braked sharply for a red light. "What did she say to that?"

"She was surprised," Madison admitted. "But my sisters were there, and they jumped in on my side. Turns out Mom only lets Dad come home for Christmas because she thinks we need to see him. She knows he's bad for her. She said she'll call Dad and tell him to make his own arrangements. My sisters and I will catch up with him after Christmas."

"That's great," Danny said. "Well done."

"I have you to thank for making me so mad that I finally decided to stand up for what I want—with Roger and with Mom. And now, I'm going to stand up to you."

There was a pause while he passed a delivery van double-parked in the road. Then he cautiously asked, "What do you mean?"

"I've figured out why you decided to have Christmas with me."

He turned to look at her, his dark eyes intense. "Why is that?"

"Because you don't have anywhere else to go. You don't want to be alone, and you're relying on my feeling sorry for you, so you can use me again." Just the thought of Danny spending the holiday alone had her softening.

"Is that right?" His hands tightened on the steering wheel.

Madison swallowed, drew on every scrap of courage she possessed to make her stand. "I'm going to use your using me. I'm giving you until Christmas to figure out that in your heart you want a different kind of relationship."

"I don't," he said, alarmed.

"You don't *yet*," she corrected, praying this wouldn't backfire.

"You're overreacting to this whole Christmas thing. There's no way I'm going to change my mind."

"We'll see," she said with a stubbornness she didn't feel. "I really…like you, Danny. I don't want to fall in love with you unless I think you're going to feel the same. You have four days to figure out where this thing is going."

As tactics went, it felt dangerous—like trying to hold on to a wounded animal long enough to get a tranquilizing shot into it, without getting your hand bitten off.

Danny didn't say another word. After a couple of minutes he started to whistle. When Madison recognized the tune, her heart sank.

"Road to Nowhere."

MADISON LIKED Hugh and Marj Naylor the moment she met them. Hugh had a British reserve about him, but it didn't conceal his innate kindness. Marj was a North Carolina gal, her graciousness and warmth combining to give her an unassuming air, despite what Madison guessed must be considerable wealth.

Regardless of her trepidation about Danny, Madison had fun at the party. The team were such nice folks, the band played rock'n'roll versions of Christmas songs and there was plenty of dancing. Danny was obviously well liked by everyone, even if he wasn't as extroverted as some of the others.

He spent most of the evening at Madison's side, and she saw that as some kind of triumph, given the way she'd scared him on the journey here.

Around eleven, when Danny had been dragged away to meet the wife of one of the over-the-wall guys, a portly man introduced himself to Madison as Bob Haldane from Poochy Packs.

"You're thinking about sponsoring Danny," she said.

"Yes," he said doubtfully. "Though things didn't go so well in Kentucky the other day. There are a couple of other drivers I'm interested in."

Madison remembered Danny saying another associate sponsor would bring the extra money that might make the difference between him winning the NASCAR NEXTEL Cup Series title and being, once again, an also-ran. The extra money that might help him achieve his dream.

"Anyone can have a bad day, but if you talk to Danny you'll discover he's an amazing guy with a focus I don't believe any other driver can match," she said.

Haldane puffed out his cheeks and humphed.

"When Danny brought Buster into my clinic, it was obvious he knew nothing about dogs," Madison said. "But he did a wonderful job of calming Buster, and he's turned into a great dog owner—he's a natural."

It was a good choice of words. Haldane glanced at Danny, still chatting to his teammate's wife. "Hmm," he said.

Madison tried not to roll her eyes. This guy was a man of even fewer words than Danny—they were a perfect match. What she'd said about Danny as a dog owner was true, if she overlooked his motivation. But the real proof of how well he'd done could be seen in Buster's affection for Danny.

"Poochy Packs is the class act in dog cookies," she told Haldane. "Danny Cruise is a class act on the track and off."

He raised his eyebrows at her vehemence. More moderately, she said, "I'm sure Buster would love Poochy

Packs cookies." She realized that was the wrong tack. "I mean, I'm sure he already does love them."

Haldane laughed. "Danny's lucky to have you on his side." He reached into his jacket pocket, pulled out a small purple box wrapped with silver ribbon. "Here's one of our doggy stocking fillers. Give it to Buster with my regards."

AT ONE O'CLOCK, the band stopped playing and people began to leave. Madison went with Danny to say goodbye to the Naylors.

"Marj and I will expect you on Christmas Day, as usual," Hugh said to Danny.

Danny was supposed to have Christmas with his team owner? Madison looked at him. He didn't meet her eyes, and she saw a flush creeping up his neck. "Actually," he said, "I'm having Christmas with Madison. And Buster."

Hugh looked disappointed, but made an obvious effort to be pleased for Danny. Could Danny see how fond of him his team owner was, Madison wondered.

"Maybe we'll see you at New Year's, if you don't have plans," Hugh said.

"Sure." Danny glanced at Madison. "Then right after that, I'll be ready to put my all into my racing. I truly appreciate what you've done for me, Hugh. I'll do my best not to let you down next year."

Hugh frowned. "You had a good season, Danny. No matter who you were, I wouldn't keep you in my car if you didn't earn it…. But you know, however your racing goes, uh, we'll always, uh—" he cleared his throat "—there'll always be, uh, you'll, uh…"

"You'll always be part of the family," Marj said, patting Danny's cheek and rolling her eyes at her husband's inarticulacy. "You know that, don't you?" She pulled Danny into a hug.

"Sure," Danny said, just enough surprise in his voice for Madison to hear.

"Enjoy your Christmas, kids." Hugh kissed Madison's cheek. He moved on to Danny, hesitated, then punched him awkwardly on the shoulder. His fist lingered there for a moment.

Danny hesitated. Madison would bet money Danny wanted to hug the guy. Instead, Danny punched him back. "Happy Christmas to you, too, Hugh."

Marj Naylor's blue gaze met Madison's, and the older woman giggled, a surprisingly youthful sound. "What is it about these NASCAR guys that the only time they get emotional is on a race track? If you want a man who cares more about you than his car, my dear, you'd better look elsewhere."

It was a joke, yet her words struck a chill into Madison's heart.

The heart, she realized now, she'd bet on Danny's ability to be the man she wanted. So much for telling him she didn't want to fall in love without knowing he could feel the same. She'd already fallen in love with him—with his intelligence and sense of humor, with his unintentional kindness, with his sexiness, with that soul she saw deep inside him.

Everything she'd seen of Danny—his kindness to Buster, his affection for the Naylors, his tenderness toward her—told her this man was crying out to love and be loved.

But to Danny, none of that was more important than winning. If Marj was right, it never would be.

CHAPTER NINE

DECEMBER 23 FOUND Danny shopping for a Christmas present. For Buster. He couldn't believe he was doing this—he'd always thought people who bought gifts for their pets were pathetic.

But he couldn't concentrate on his fitness or his race tapes, or even on a conversation with his crew chief about car setup.

Ironic that, having made it crystal clear to Madison that they had no future, he was more distracted than ever.

He chose a ball with a rope tied around it for Buster—they'd have some good tugs-of-war. Now he had to find a gift for Madison. He would try Nordstrom—and he'd make it a combined Christmas and goodbye gift.

Danny's cell phone rang and he recognized the clinic's number. Forced himself not to pounce on it. "Cruise."

"Danny." Madison's voice wasn't much more than a whisper. "Buster's owner is here at the clinic."

"Huh?" It took Danny a second to click. *He* was Buster's owner. Then he remembered what he'd promised. If the dog's owner came back, he'd hand Buster over. He swallowed.

"He wants Buster home," Madison said, "for Christmas."

They agreed the guy should come to Danny's house at two that afternoon to collect Buster. Madison said she'd come over right away, and Danny didn't argue.

They spent the next couple of hours playing with Buster. Danny packed up the dog's stuff, in case the owner wanted it. He added Buster's wrapped Christmas gift to the large pile.

Then it was one-forty-five, everything was ready, and it was a matter of watching the clock tick over to two. Danny sprawled on the couch in the family room, Madison at his side.

The ringing of his cell phone—a call from Hugh—was a welcome distraction. Danny had called Marj earlier to cancel a lunch he had scheduled with the Naylors today.

"I hear the dog's owner turned up," Hugh said. "This could be just what we need."

"How's that?" Danny asked.

"Haldane from Poochy Packs has warmed up again on the sponsorship. Seems your Madison did a great job the other night of selling him on you as a dog owner and a driver."

"She did?" Danny caught Madison's gaze, raised an eyebrow. She gave him a puzzled smile.

"He's about ready to bite." Hugh laughed at his own wordplay. "One more push should do it, and that's where your dog comes in."

When Danny didn't say anything, Hugh continued, "You need to delay the handover of the dog so we can set up a photo shoot. It'll make a great Christmas Eve headline—Sandra said with the shortage of news, we might make the front pages. I'm certain Poochy Packs will sign when they see the story."

It was brilliant. Danny could see the headlines now, could envisage the heartwarming Christmas photos, the outpouring of sympathy he'd get from NASCAR fans and dog lovers.

"I guess," Hugh said, and Danny heard the frown in his voice, "we'll have to get you another dog."

Danny put his hand over the phone and said to Madison, "Sandra and Hugh think that if we can get a photo of me handing Buster over to his owner, the Christmas Eve headlines will swing the Poochy Packs sponsorship."

He waited for her to blow up, to tell him he was all kinds of jerk to consider using Buster like that again. Instead, she nodded, and said with quiet neutrality, "I see."

He knew what she saw. That he would do what he had to in order to secure the sponsorship funds to match his biggest rivals. The money that might make the difference in his NASCAR NEXTEL Cup Series challenge.

He tried to imagine handing Buster over to his owner in front of a bunch of journalists. He tried to imagine having any kind of relationship with Madison after he'd done that.

"Hugh," he said, "tell Sandra there's not going to be a story. I—I love that dog."

Beside him, Madison made a choked sound.

On the phone, there was a long silence before Hugh relayed the message. To Sandra's credit, she didn't argue. That was what Danny liked about her. She knew a good story, but she also knew how far was too far.

"Sorry, Danny," Hugh said gruffly. "I didn't realize."

He hadn't realized himself. Damn, it hurt.

He ended the call, slumped back into the cushions. Madison took his hand in hers, and even though it was only comfort, he felt the inevitable spark between them.

"I can't believe you turned down that story." Her voice came out shaky.

"At least some kid will have a happy Christmas," he said morosely.

"I—uh, what?" She seemed to be struggling to focus.

"Remember, the kid crying his eyes out because he's lost his dog?"

"Oh." Then, hesitantly, "Danny, I'm not certain there's a kid."

"Maybe the guy's blind," Danny suggested, "and Buster is his seeing-eye dog."

"A seeing-eye dog that ran out in front of cars wouldn't last very long," she pointed out gently.

"Oh, yeah." Danny let his mind wander to the implications of that and winced. Absently, he reached into the purple box on the coffee table and snagged a cookie. He bit into it. Hmm, not bad. Chocolaty, oaty, and something that might have been— He realized Madison had gone from tender concern to being convulsed with laughter.

"What?" he demanded around his mouthful.

"That's—that's—" she was laughing too hard to talk "—a Poochy Packs cookie."

The cookie assumed the texture of sawdust in his mouth. Danny sprayed it across the coffee table. "Ugh!"

The ring of the doorbell startled both of them, suspended Madison's hilarity. Buster, whatever else he was, had never been a guard dog. He lifted his head at the sound, then flopped back onto his paws.

Danny went to open the door. The man on the other side was about Danny's height, but fifty pounds heavier. Climbing the front steps had evidently exerted him, because there was a definite smell of sweat around him.

"Marty Bennett." He stuck out a hand. "I've come to pick up Monty."

Monty? "Oh, you mean Buster, uh, the dog." Danny stood aside. "Come on in."

The guy looked around him with unashamed interest. "Nice place."

"Thanks." Danny turned, saw Madison bringing Buster—Monty—on his leash. The dog gave a low woof and ran to his owner, jumped all over him. Marty Bennett threw his arms around his pet, laughing and crooning. Danny should have found the reunion touching. He found it irritating.

"Madison, this is Marty, Buster's owner," Danny said, when he figured the party had gone on long enough.

"Monty," the guy corrected.

"Hi, Monty." Madison stuck out a hand.

"No, I'm Marty, the dog is Monty. People often get us confused." The guy laughed uproariously.

Madison smiled politely. "So, how did you come to lose Bus—Monty?" she asked, with what Danny recognized and silently cheered as determination to check out whether or not the guy was a fit dog owner. Maybe they wouldn't have to give Buster back.

"I was on my way to the airport. I had Monty booked into the boarding kennels," Marty said. "I stopped to take a leak, and he got out of the car. He saw a rabbit and took off.

"I couldn't find him, but I figured he'd make his way home—it was only a couple of miles—he's done it before. I asked the kennels to call around to the house and get him. They came a few times but of course he wasn't there. Because someone ran him over." Marty directed a reproachful glance at Danny.

"He wasn't wearing a collar when Danny found him," Madison said severely.

"Yeah, he slips out of it sometimes." The guy knuckled Monty's head. "Don'cha, boy?" Buster licked the guy's less-than-clean hand with evident enjoyment.

Danny tried not to see it as a betrayal. But no matter how tacky it was to urinate at the side of the road, it didn't make a guy unfit to own a dog. Danny was going to have to let Buster go.

"I just about had a heart attack when I got back from Mexico and found Monty hadn't been seen since I left," Marty said. "I've been searching everywhere and in between times calling the shelters. Finally one of them mentioned the dog you'd found. I've never been so relieved—this big guy is my best friend in the world."

Danny could believe it.

Marty refused any of Buster's toys, saying he had "plenty of that crap around the place" at home.

"Thanks a lot for looking after him," he told Danny.

"No problem."

When Marty looked down and said pointedly, "Guess I'd better take my dog home," Danny realized he still had a hand on Buster's collar. Reluctantly, he uncurled his fingers.

He dropped down, took Buster's ugly face in his hands. "Bye, Buster, it's been great knowing you." Buster licked his face. Danny gave Buster a hug, mainly to hide the rapid blinking of his eyes. "Bye, buddy."

Madison hugged Buster, too. Danny heard her murmur, "Goodbye, gorgeous," into his coat. As Marty and the dog walked out to Marty's Ford Fusion she held Danny's hand. Probably to stop him making a fool of himself by running after them. He squeezed her fingers, felt an answering pressure.

After the car disappeared down the drive, he turned to Madison. Damn, she was beautiful. And smart and caring and passionate. What if Madison walked out of his life, the way Buster just had? A vise clamped around Danny's chest at the realization that losing her would be a thousand times worse than losing Buster.

Dammit, he'd fallen in love with her.

He only had to look at her, standing there in her cherry-red sweater, her long black skirt and her high-heeled boots, to know the way he felt about her was completely different from how he'd felt about any other woman. It always had been, only he'd been too blind, too stupid to recognize it.

Danny realized he had two choices. Finish with Madison, then throw himself into his racing with two hundred percent focus so that this year he might win the NASCAR NEXTEL Cup title. Or for the first time in fifteen years, open up his life to share it with someone he loved. A woman who would expect him to give as well as take.

Just as he'd given away the year's best photo opportunity—and possibly, the best associate sponsorship he'd find this year.

What if he decided she was worth it, and then he lost her anyway? It would just about kill him.

"Hell," he said.

"Danny?" Madison laid a hand on his arm.

He wanted to kiss her.

He took a step backward. If he gave in to this love, what would it do to his racing? Other drivers managed to win races while they juggled relationships, but he'd never thought he could be one of them. Yet without Madison, there would always be something missing.

"I just…remembered I need to do something." He grabbed her car keys from the console by the front door. "You'd better leave."

"Maybe I should hang out here. You're upset about Buster."

He was already halfway down the front steps. "I always knew I might have to give him back," he said over his shoulder as he unlocked her car. "Come on, time to go."

He needed to think about his future without the distraction of having her right in front of him.

She had no choice but to get into the car. "Are we still good for Christmas Day?" she asked in a small voice that told him his abruptness had hurt her.

"Sure." Even if he decided he couldn't have her, he still wanted Christmas with her. "I'll pick you up around ten."

He busied himself shutting her door, brushing a couple of leaves off her windshield, so that he didn't kiss her goodbye, didn't even look her in the eye.

MADISON WANDERED the mall with growing frustration. She didn't know for sure what had just happened back at Danny's place, but she could guess.

Danny had turned down the photo opportunity, risked losing the Poochy Packs sponsorship, and in his heart he blamed her for it.

"It's not good enough," she said sharply, attracting a surprised glance from a shopper laden down with Christmas parcels.

And it *wasn't* good enough. Danny loved Buster; he'd turned that deal down for his own sake, not hers. And he might not know it, but he felt something for Madison. Maybe he wasn't in love with her yet, but he had two more days to admit the possibility it might happen. What had Danny said? In this life you have to go after what you want and never stop.

She wasn't about to sit around hoping he'd realize what he'd lost. She couldn't make him love her, but she could make darned sure he knew exactly how she felt about him.

DANNY BUZZED Madison's doorbell just before ten on Christmas Day, more nervous than he'd been at the start of the race at Homestead last month. There was much more riding on today.

NASCAR was the last thing on his mind, thanks in part to yesterday's news that Poochy Packs had confirmed it would sponsor Danny in the NASCAR NEXTEL Cup Series. Danny's refusal to publicize the loss of Buster had impressed Bob Haldane more than any amount of great driving.

Madison opened the door. She looked soft, kissable in a wraparound red dress that showcased her delectable curves. She took one look at Danny and broke into laughter.

"Do you have any idea," he said in an injured tone, as he adjusted the Christmas stocking on his head to a more rakish angle, "how long it took me to find this thing?"

"If I looked anywhere near as dumb that night you came to the clinic as you do now," she said severely, "I'm not surprised you didn't trust me."

"You're going to eat those words when you see what I got you for Christmas," he growled.

She stood back and let him in. "I want to give you my gift first. It's in the kitchen, wait right here."

"How do you manage to wear your stocking for hours?" he demanded. "My head's already itchy as heck."

"Just naturally full of the Christmas spirit, I guess," she called over her shoulder, halfway to the kitchen.

"Just naturally full of something," he grumbled, and heard her chuckle.

She was gone just a few seconds. She came back cradling something in her arms...a puppy. With a dapper red bow around its neck.

"For me?" Danny took a half step forward.

She nodded, and he moved to take the animal from her. Even leaving aside that this little fellow only weighed about five pounds, he—a quick check confirmed it was indeed a he—looked nothing like Buster. This dog had shorter hair, black with a couple of brown patches on his head and one on his rump. He was as cute as all get-out.

"What breed is he?" Danny asked, trying not to choke up.

She shrugged. "I got him from the shelter yesterday. I'd say he's part Lab, part Jack Russell, part something else. Nothing fancy."

"He's great." Danny tickled the dog under his chin, and the little head burrowed into his hand, the tongue coming out to give a dry lick. "So, you think I'm the kind of guy who's fit to own a dog?"

Madison looked him in the eye. "I think you're perfect to own a dog."

For a long moment, their gazes locked. Then Madison blinked. "What are you going to call him?"

"I can't call him Buster," he mused. "So I guess it'll have to be Gorgeous."

She half laughed, half snorted her amazement.

"George for short," he elaborated.

Madison smiled, a happy smile that made Danny's heart flip over.

"There's a card." She nodded toward the ribbon around the dog's neck.

Danny opened the small gift tag. Just three words: *With love, Madison.*

He looked up at her. Her bottom lip was caught between her teeth. He knew those three words came from her heart.

"I got you a gift," he said, "but in a way it's more for me than it is for you."

She rolled her eyes. "That is such a guy thing to do."

Carefully, Danny placed the puppy on the floor. He reached into his pocket, pulled out the jeweler's box.

"Oh." Madison knew she must look like a goldfish, eyes and mouth wide-open, but all reason had fled at the sight of that black velvet box.

Danny opened it.

"Oh," she said again, displaying an embarrassing lack of imagination when faced with an enormous diamond in a gold setting.

"I'm hoping," he said, "for a yes."

Madison flew into his arms. "Yes. Yes, yes, yes."

He laughed, tossed the ring onto the couch, then squeezed her so hard she could scarcely breathe. "I love you, Madison," he said. "I know it's crazy, I know it's too soon, but I've felt happier the last few weeks than I have in my entire life. I don't know if I can win the Cup with you in my life, but I know I can't win without you."

He kissed her thoroughly. "I want you beside me, and I want to be the kind of guy you need. I want to be a regular husband, a regular dad to our kids—hey, did I say something wrong?"

Madison rubbed at the tears that streamed down her cheeks. "You said it all right. Just right. I love you so much." She kissed him until, if they didn't stop now, they wouldn't make it to Christmas dinner.

When Danny drew back, his dark eyes were serious. "Maybe you shouldn't rush into saying yes," he warned her. "I'm new to this regular-guy stuff. I've got a lot to learn about sharing, about loving you. Hell, what if I'm no good at it?"

Madison heard the thread of doubt in his voice. But she saw in his eyes his intention to do whatever it took to make this work. That two hundred percent focus of his would be channeled into their marriage, their family. With Danny, there was no other way.

She went up on tiptoe, planted a kiss on that firm mouth. "You're a natural," she breathed.

* * * * *

Coming in March 2008…
Watch for FULLY ENGAGED by Abby Gaines,
part of Harlequin's 2008
officially licensed NASCAR series.

REQUEST YOUR FREE BOOKS!
2 FREE NOVELS PLUS 2 FREE GIFTS!

♥ *Silhouette*®

SPECIAL EDITION®

Life, Love and Family!

YES! Please send me 2 FREE Silhouette Special Edition® novels and my 2 FREE gifts. After receiving them, if I don't wish to receive any more books, I can return the shipping statement marked "cancel." If I don't cancel, I will receive 6 brand-new novels every month and be billed just $4.24 per book in the U.S., or $4.99 per book in Canada, plus 25¢ shipping and handling per book and applicable taxes, if any*. That's a savings of at least 15% off the cover price! I understand that accepting the 2 free books and gifts places me under no obligation to buy anything. I can always return a shipment and cancel at any time. Even if I never buy another book from Silhouette, the two free books and gifts are mine to keep forever.

235 SDN EEYU 335 SDN EEY6

Name	(PLEASE PRINT)

Address		Apt.

City	State/Prov.	Zip/Postal Code

Signature (if under 18, a parent or guardian must sign)

Mail to the **Silhouette Reader Service**™:
IN U.S.A.: P.O. Box 1867, Buffalo, NY 14240-1867
IN CANADA: P.O. Box 609, Fort Erie, Ontario L2A 5X3

Not valid to current Silhouette Special Edition subscribers.

Want to try two free books from another line?
Call 1-800-873-8635 or visit www.morefreebooks.com.

* Terms and prices subject to change without notice. NY residents add applicable sales tax. Canadian residents will be charged applicable provincial taxes and GST. This offer is limited to one order per household. All orders subject to approval. Credit or debit balances in a customer's account(s) may be offset by any other outstanding balance owed by or to the customer. Please allow 4 to 6 weeks for delivery.

Your Privacy: Silhouette is committed to protecting your privacy. Our Privacy Policy is available online at www.eHarlequin.com or upon request from the Reader Service. From time to time we make our lists of customers available to reputable firms who may have a product or service of interest to you. If you would prefer we not share your name and address, please check here. ☐

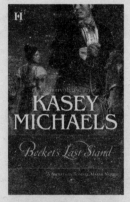